"Are you suggesti[ng...] baby...ourselves?"

Hope's cheeks turned bright pink.

"Exactly."

"Oh." She looked away. "I see. Well, that will take some getting used to. I'm not sure how to think about making lo—I mean having se— Well, doing it naturally. With you."

"It's not like I'm Quasimodo, is it?" Josh teased gently.

"Oh, no! Not at all! It's just that I don't want this to change anything between us. Our friendship, that is." Finally she met his eyes. "We'd have to be businesslike about it, right? We'd have to be very careful."

Careful not to enjoy it too much? he thought, but didn't dare say out loud.

"Right." He flashed her a smile he hoped looked reassuring. Why, if this was going to be a strictly friendly, strictly business kind of deal, did he feel so ready to make love to Hope that his nerve endings sizzled?

This was a question a bachelor like him didn't want to deal with.

Dear Reader:

Romance readers have been enthusiastic about the Silhouette Special Editions® for years. And that's not by accident: Special Editions were the first of their kind and continue to feature realistic stories with heightened romantic tension.

The longer stories, sophisticated style, greater sensual detail and variety that made Special Editions popular are the same elements that will make you want to read book after book.

We hope that you enjoy this Special Edition today, and will enjoy many more.

Please write to us:

Jane Nicholls
Silhouette Books
PO Box 236
Thornton Road
Croydon
Surrey
CR9 3RU

The Bachelor and the Baby Wish

KATE FREIMAN

SILHOUETTE™

SPECIAL EDITION ®

DID YOU PURCHASE THIS BOOK WITHOUT A COVER?
If you did, you should be aware it is **stolen property** as it was reported
unsold and destroyed by a retailer. Neither the author nor the publisher
has received any payment for this book.

*All the characters in this book have no existence outside the imagination
of the author, and have no relation whatsoever to anyone bearing the same
name or names. They are not even distantly inspired by any individual
known or unknown to the author, and all the incidents are pure invention.*

*All Rights Reserved including the right of reproduction in whole or in part
in any form. This edition is published by arrangement with Harlequin
Enterprises II B.V. The text of this publication or any part thereof may not
be reproduced or transmitted in any form or by any means, electronic or
mechanical, including photocopying, recording, storage in an
information retrieval system, or otherwise, without the written
permission of the publisher.*

*This book is sold subject to the condition that it shall not, by way of trade
or otherwise, be lent, resold, hired out or otherwise circulated without the
prior consent of the publisher in any form of binding or cover other than
that in which it is published and without a similar condition including this
condition being imposed on the subsequent purchaser.*

*Silhouette, Silhouette Special Edition and Colophon are
registered trademarks of Harlequin Books S.A., used under licence.*

*First published in Great Britain 1997
Silhouette Books, Eton House, 18-24 Paradise Road,
Richmond, Surrey TW9 1SR*

© Kate Freiman 1996

ISBN 0 373 24041 4

23-9701

*Printed and bound in Great Britain
by Mackays of Chatham PLC, Chatham*

With thanks to Doretta Thompson, my trusty critique partner, for laughing in the right places, and especially to Mark, my friend, lover and husband, for twenty-one years of reasons.

KATE FREIMAN

began creating stories with happy endings even before she could read or write, after the old movie *Frankenstein* gave her nightmares. She believes she holds the record for rereading Louisa May Alcott's *Little Women*, and, or course, grew up wanting to be Jo, the writer.

A casual meeting with one of Kate's graduate professors—to discuss a book, of course!—turned into true love, marriage and immigration from Conneticut to Toronto, Canada. Her husband, Mark, became a lawyer, and they have a teenage son, Ben, who can usually be found with an open book in one hand.

Other novels by Kate Freiman

Silhouette Special Edition®

Jake's Angel
Here To Stay

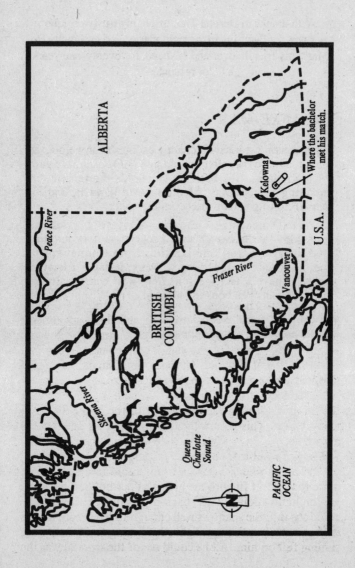

ALBERTA

BRITISH
COLUMBIA

Peace River

Skeena River

Fraser River

Kelowna

Vancouver

Where the bachelor
met his match.

U.S.A.

Queen
Charlotte
Sound

PACIFIC
OCEAN

N

Chapter One

"Hello? Anybody home? Okay if I use your phone?"

Josh opened the creaky screen door to the faded cabin and found himself peering through the shadows into the narrow stare of a shotgun. The way the muzzle of the gun wavered sent adrenaline through him like jagged lightning. He froze. So did his brain. The rest of him shook with a cold that had nothing to do with the chill breeze at his back.

"Tell me that thing isn't loaded," he croaked. This wasn't the kind of greeting he'd expected in the laid-back Kootenay Valley. This wasn't the kind of greeting he expected anywhere.

The gun wobbled. He started to pray.

"I'd hate to lie to you," a woman said in a rich, warm voice that didn't fit with the image of her holding the shotgun on him at point-blank, barn-door range. He wished he could see into the shadows well enough to tell whom he was dealing with, but the only light was coming from the porch, shining full on him. All he could see of the woman was the pale oval of her face. She must be dressed in clothes as dark as the shadows that hid her.

Might as well turn on the charm and see where it got him. He offered a grin. "I didn't mean to barge in like this, but I didn't hear you answer my knock."

"I didn't." The shotgun muzzle wavered.

"Oh." *Think fast,* he warned himself, but his brain stayed in neutral. "Well, uh, can I use your phone? My cellular was stolen from my van yesterday."

If he was expecting sympathy, he was in the wrong place. The woman didn't make a sound, didn't move. He added a few more silent curses at the punks who'd ripped off his phone, but that wasn't helping the immediate situation, which was getting on his nerves.

"I was expecting a camper, you know, an RV, waiting for me, but it's late and I don't see any sign of anyone from the RV place. I own the property next door. I'm planning to put up a cabin over the summer. I wanted to spend the long weekend out here just getting acquainted with the area, you know?"

He was blithering like an idiot, but getting not a word from the woman in the shadows. "I'll charge the call to my home number. It'll just take half a minute to—"

"Josh? Josh Kincaid?" the woman said.

He felt his jaw drop and leaned his raised hand against the door frame, trying to peer inside. The muzzle of that damn shotgun disappeared. A second later, the door opened. A tall, slender woman stood in the opening, backlit so he couldn't see her face.

"How do you know me? Do I know you?" he demanded, shuffling a step closer. Thank God she'd put the shotgun down. Curiosity wouldn't kill this cat, at least not right away. "Did I do some work for you?"

He heard a low, sexy chuckle that stirred something inside him, but not his memory. The sound made him grin anyway. Things could very well get better.

"No, but you were always trying to get me to do your work for you," the woman said.

"Huh?"

"Hope Delacorte. You were the bane of my last two years of high school."

In the time it took her to swing the door open the rest of the way, he remembered. Hope Delacorte, the string bean with the ninety-eight average and the stuck-up attitude. He'd teased her about doing his homework, about riding on his battered old motorcycle, about letting him teach her about the birds and the bees. And she'd look at him as if he were a pile of doggy doo, and turn away as though even talking to him was beneath her.

Hope stepped back, making room for him. Josh stepped inside, took a good, long look at the girl he hadn't seen in sixteen years and said the first thing that came into his mind. "You sure don't look like a nerdy bean pole any more."

"Careful, Kincaid. I've still got the shotgun," she answered, but he could hear the laughter behind her voice. Her turquoise eyes sparkled in a way they'd never done in high school. She wasn't wearing her reddish blond hair in tuggable, waist-long braids anymore, but had it piled on her head in a way that hinted it was still pretty long. And her lips parted in a way that made him wonder how they'd feel on his, which he'd never wondered before, since she'd had a mouth full of braces the last time he'd seen her.

"Yes, ma'am," he drawled. "I may be a hell-raiser, but I'm not a fool."

"The phone's in the kitchen. Come on. I can offer you a cold beer or a hot coffee if you'd like."

"Hot coffee sounds good," he answered. "It's colder out there than the weather guy said it would be."

Fishing the RV dealership's card from his shirt pocket, he dialed the numbers, then held the phone to his ear. Listening to ring after ring, he watched Hope moving around the kitchen. Those long, slim legs made tight, faded blue jeans look sexier than anything Frederick's of Hollywood could come up with. And the simple black top she wore clung just enough to show the trim lines of her torso.

Man, oh, man, he thought. Who would have believed Miss Priss would turn out to look so good? Just went to show how little a horny high school hotshot knew about the potential of a female bean pole.

The phone at the RV dealership kept ringing. Finally, someone answered.

"Nobody here," the gravelly voice barked when he asked for the salesman he'd dealt with. "Closed up early. Holiday weekend. Victoria Day, you know. 'Spect the government will change the name of this one, too, like they did Dominion Day. Canada Day! Pah!"

Josh felt his hopes sink as his anger rose. "My camper wasn't delivered. Can you find the salesman's home number for me? Or the manager's?"

"Not allowed. Musta been your RV that fell off the trailer."

"What?" His bellow echoed in his ear. "My RV *fell off the trailer?"* Hope's eyes went wide, then she turned quickly, probably hiding hysterical laughter.

He heard a wheezy chuckle. "One hell of a mess when that garbage truck nailed the tractor-trailer. Pow! Glass all over the road, right out front here. No, sir, you won't be getting your RV this weekend. You call back Tuesday. The salesmen fellas will be back to work." In the middle of another raspy chuckle, the phone clicked and went dead.

Josh stared at the receiver for a moment before hanging it up, then vented his frustration with a few well-chosen but ultimately useless curses. He was going to have to camp out or turn back. The thought of driving all the way home to Kelowna, tired, hungry and thoroughly ticked off, didn't turn him on. He'd stay, if only overnight. It was a territorial thing.

"Trouble?" Hope set a steaming cup of black coffee on the battered wooden kitchen table near him. She turned her back to rummage through a cabinet.

"You might say that," he snarled. "My damn RV got totaled by a garbage truck, and the dealership is closed for the weekend. Looks like I'll be spending the night in my work van."

His words met with silence, followed by a definite snicker.

"It's not funny," he barked, then turned on his heel and started for the door.

"Josh, wait!" He stopped and faced her. She held up a sugar bowl and creamer and smiled. "Have your coffee, then get whatever you need for the night. You can stay here. The sofa in the living room opens into a queen-size bed, so you probably won't even hang off the end of it."

Her offer made him forget how mad he was about the RV. "Are you sure? I mean, you really don't know if you can trust me."

Her smile widened. "That's all I need to know. If I couldn't trust you to, um, behave yourself, you wouldn't have hesitated."

Little did she know, he thought.

He lifted the hot coffee mug as if toasting her and grinned back. "Well, thanks."

Then he couldn't think of a thing to say, so he took a sip of the coffee. It was rich and hot, and warmed him all the way down, the way Hope's smile did. Sometimes, when things were going downhill, a guy lost track of reasons not to be cynical. Suddenly, things were beginning to look up. *Way* up. He was stranded with a beautiful woman, in a cozy cabin next to a river with some of the best trout fishing in the universe. It was enough to make a man count his blessings.

Hope carried her own cup of coffee to the wooden table and slipped into a heavy sweater before she sat in a rickety wooden chair. "I was thinking about lighting a fire before you knocked. It really is getting chilly. I hope it warms up enough to watch the fireworks Sunday night. The people at the little general store said there's quite a show every year.''

''Part of the fun used to be getting wrapped in a blanket with someone and drinking blackberry brandy. Remember?''

She sipped at her coffee, then shook her head. ''Can't say I ever did anything like that.'' She fixed those turquoise eyes on him. ''Too risqué for a nerdy bean pole.''

He winced, but her lips quirked up, letting him know she didn't hold a grudge. ''Hey, if I'd known you were interested, I would have offered you a corner of my blanket.''

''I probably would have fainted on the spot if you had,'' she told him. ''You scared me witless.''

''I did what?''

She lifted one shoulder. ''You were the kind of guy who made me very nervous back then. Brash, cool, good-looking.''

''You're not serious. *You* scared the pants off *me!*'' Her eyebrows rose. ''Well,'' he corrected, ''not exactly, but you were pretty intimidating. I don't think I ever heard you give a wrong answer in class. And you always looked at me like I was something that crawled out from under a rock.''

''I did not!''

Her eyes flashed. He must have hit a sore spot.

''You thought I was good-looking, huh?''

Her cheeks turned pink. ''In an adolescent way, I guess,'' she muttered. ''Not exceptional, of course.''

He grinned over the edge of his cup. She was lying. ''Of course.''

''You haven't changed in sixteen years,'' she said, lifting her cup to her lips. ''Still brash.''

''But still good-looking?''

She coughed and clamped one slender hand across her mouth, but he could see the laughter in her eyes.

"Sorry, but I owed you for laughing at my RV." He set his empty cup down on the table and looked at her. "You want to rethink that offer? I'll understand."

She smiled. "Go get your toothbrush. I've got some stew to reheat. Do you like dumplings or dinner rolls?"

He gave his standard answer whenever any of his lady friends started feeling domestic. "Whichever is easier."

"Frozen dinner rolls it is. Better hurry up before it gets really dark. If you break your leg in a marmot hole, I can't carry you."

"Yeah, but any attempts you made would sure take my mind off the pain."

She flicked her hand at him as if shooing away a fly, clearly not taking him seriously. "Go get your stuff before I regain my common sense."

He winked and went, whistling softly.

Hope waited a minute before following Josh out to the porch. Pretending not to be aware of his lanky, broad-shouldered body striding across the grass and wildflowers between the cabin and his gray van, she took a deep breath. The air was sweet but cool, unusually so for mid-May. The sun had already set behind the jagged-topped mountains, turning the sky pink and gold and purple. It was such a beautiful corner of the earth. She was grateful to her parents' friends, the Wilsons, for lending it to her for the weekend. It was the perfect place to sort herself out and re-order her priorities. She had some serious decisions to make, before her life spun out of control altogether.

She now also had a distraction who presented a very impressive rear view in his jeans, but that, she told herself firmly, had nothing to do with her. Besides, the back view of a man hit a sore spot, since that was the last angle at which she'd seen Kyle moments after she'd given him her good news—bad news speech.

Watching Josh yank open the rear doors of the van, Hope sank onto the creaky old porch swing and hugged herself to ward off the chill breeze. Maybe it was a blessing in disguise that Josh had turned up out of the blue. He could be a welcome distraction. She'd been in the cabin for just over a day, and boredom with navel gazing had already set in. Two more days of sitting alone in the middle of nature's splendor, dwelling on her problems, would probably send her running back to Kelowna too soon, without making a single useful decision.

With the toes of one foot, she gingerly set the swing in motion. As she rocked, she closed her eyes and wondered how she'd ever thought she could spend a long weekend in solitude. She was too accustomed to the bustle of other people, the chaos of work, the ticking of the clock, to know what to do with herself. And, she ruefully acknowledged, it was always easier to solve other people's problems than one's own.

Josh's problem, for example, had been a snap to solve. Hope was still torn between guilt and amusement. She shouldn't have laughed at his predicament, but he'd sounded like a wounded buffalo when he'd bellowed into the phone. The way he'd explained about the garbage truck and the camper had been pretty funny. Or maybe she just hadn't been laughing much lately.

The crunch of footsteps on the gravel in front of the cabin alerted her to Josh's return. She opened her eyes to find him just climbing the stairs, rising taller above her with each step. Okay, so she'd told a little white lie: he was *way* beyond unexceptionally good-looking. He was gorgeous, in a purely rugged, masculine and unselfconscious way. Totally different from the smooth, pampered handsomeness Kyle took so much pride in.

Not, she warned herself, that anything about Josh mattered to her.

* * *

The woman smiling up at him from the porch swing sure didn't remind him of the girl who used to stare at him as if he were a freak. This Hope looked soft, welcoming. He couldn't help wondering how welcoming. Not that he was into tomcatting, but it was a question any normal, healthy guy would mentally ask about a good-looking woman like Hope.

He balanced his gym bag on his bent knee and met her eyes. "I could use a shower before dinner, if that's okay."

"Absolutely," she told him, rising as gracefully as a dancer. "I'll show you where everything is."

She was moving ahead of him already. He followed her into the cabin. She led him down the short hallway, talking over her shoulder. "The soap I use is perfumed, but there's a bar of cedar soap in the cabinet under the sink. Towels are in the closet in the washroom. And I think there are some disposable razors in the drawer."

He walked close behind her. She stopped short and turned. He plowed into her, knocking her backward. Reflexively, he dropped his gym bag, reached out and caught her waist with both hands. His quickly indrawn breath brought him the mingled scents of her skin and perfume.

With a soft cry, she froze and stared up at him, her lips parted much too temptingly for a mere mortal to resist. He ground his back teeth, then forced a grin when his libido was bellowing at him to bend and taste her mouth while he still had surprise on his side.

"Sorry," he muttered. "You okay?"

She nodded, those startled eyes fixed on him. "I'll just... The stew... The oven for the rolls..."

He took his hands from her waist. A moment later, she was gone, shutting the door behind her. Slowly, he let out his breath. Trying to ignore the tingling in his palms, he searched for the cedar soap and towels Hope had offered. What he couldn't ignore was the way the room held her scent. He peeled off his shirt and jeans in a state of semi-arousal that got worse when he stepped under the hot shower and realized that, sometime earlier, Hope had stood there naked and wet.

With an impatient growl, he wrenched off the hot water and let the cold water pour over him until he was shivering. When he was dry, he climbed into his clean clothes, packed his gym bag and followed the aromas of stew and hot rolls toward the kitchen.

"Something smells good."

Josh's voice, coming without warning, startled Hope. Hastily, she shoved her notepad and pen into the nearest drawer and turned around. A quick glance showed her he hadn't put his boots back on, which was why she hadn't heard him walking along the wooden floor in the hall.

"Everything is almost ready," she told him, uncomfortable under the steady gaze of his bright blue eyes. She would bet he'd seen her hide her brainstorming lists. Embarrassment made her try to fill the moment with chatter. "Miracles of modern technology here in the boonies. The Wilsons even have a microwave oven."

"So does my RV," he said. "Or, it did."

She chuckled at his grimace. "It will again. Or one just like it."

"Yeah, well, I owe you for saving my worthless butt from a night on the floor of my van."

Thinking about how he looked in formfitting jeans, she was tempted to tell him his butt wasn't all that worthless, then thought better of it. A comment like that, definitely out of character to start with, would give him the wrong impression. She had to be straight with Josh and make sure he knew she was very much off-limits, to him or any other adult male.

"You can set the table while I throw a salad together," she told him. His brows rose, and she wondered if, like Kyle, he expected her to wait on him.

But Josh went to the cabinet without a word of protest. He whistled softly while he set the Wilsons' oddly assorted dishes and cutlery on the table. Hope wondered if that meant he was simply happy, or that he found her attractive but was too polite to try a wolf whistle or that he simply couldn't get that particular tune out of his mind.

By the time Hope had finished tossing the salad, Josh was opening the bottle of blush wine she'd had in the refrigerator. She set the hot pot of stew on the table while he took the rolls out of the oven. The way they worked together, in unspoken, unexpected domestic harmony, shook her a little. It felt cozy and natural, which was the precise opposite of the way Josh had affected her in high school. Well, everyone grew up, she mused, and she was no longer the shy nerd he remembered.

They met at the table and pulled out their chairs. Sitting, Hope looked into Josh's eyes and smiled. He smiled back, then took a roll and pulled it open. She watched the steam rise from its center as he tore off a small piece. His hands looked strong, his long fingers skillful. Unlike Kyle, his nails were neat but not professionally manicured. Silly as it was to dwell on, she decided she liked his hands.

"So," he said, giving her a quick look before moving his attention to the pot of stew, "what have you been doing with yourself for the past sixteen years? Do you still live in Kelowna?"

She nodded. "I got my business degree at Simon Fraser. My dad retired last year, so I'm the CEO of the family business."

Josh whistled. "I'm impressed."

"What about you?"

"I dabbled for a couple of years at the University of British Columbia, then decided to do something useful. I'm a lowly electrician. Got my own company, though. Kincaid Electrical, in Kelowna." The pride in his voice belied his self-described lowliness.

"Really? I'm impressed, but I didn't have a clue you were still in town."

"I guess we don't travel in the same circles."

She gave a little shrug. "Does that bother you? My being management while you're labor?"

"Nah. Why would that bother me? I'm not a snob." He grinned. "But I've gotta tell you, you don't look like any of the CEOs I've met. For one thing, you're a lot better looking. And softer."

Hope laughed, inordinately pleased by his flattery, although she knew they were empty words. "You should see me at work. The iron maiden. Power suits, imported shoes, not a hair out of place."

"Sounds pretty scary."

"Sometimes, I scare myself." Even to her own ears, her description sounded like one of those jokes that told the truth.

"What's your family business? I don't remember if I ever knew. Steel? Lumber? Something in aerospace?"

"None of the above. It's KidsCan Togs. We manufacture baby and children's clothes, and we're the largest Canadian catalog house for kids' things."

He let his gaze sweep over her, then back up to her face. "That doesn't exactly fit with the power-suit image. I'd have thought a kids'-clothes CEO would be, you know, more user friendly."

"The exporters and manufacturers and wholesalers I deal with aren't babies, Josh. If I were more, uh, user friendly, I'd get used. Tell me about your work."

Hope discovered that Josh could tell stories in a way that made even the most mundane events amusing. He related tales of everything from mishaps to abandoned pets and a house full of aging nudists who insisted on watching him and his men work.

When she was able to stop laughing, she asked, "Would you like more stew?"

"Nope. I'm stuffed. Wouldn't say no to a cup of coffee, though."

"You must keep your wife busy waiting on you," she said in a tighter, prissier tone than she'd intended. Give a man a meal, and he thinks he's entitled to special service. It was almost like having Kyle back in her life.

Josh didn't seem to notice her irritation. "No wife." He grinned. "You?"

She couldn't help smiling back. "No wife, either."

"Cute."

"You asked."

"What about a husband? Or a significant other?"

"No other, significant or otherwise."

To cover her abrupt tone, Hope stood and moved toward the sink carrying their dishes. Then she filled the coffeepot with water and measured coffee grounds from a can in the freezer. She certainly wasn't going to ask him if he had any woman or women in his life. It was none of her business.

"I don't have anyone special, either," he announced. "And no significant exes."

She glanced at him over her shoulder. "Ah! A Teflon man."

"A what?"

"A Teflon man. The opposite of a Velcro man."

"Okay." He leaned back in his chair until it rocked onto the back legs. "Enlighten me."

"A Velcro man sticks. Nothing sticks to a Teflon man. No commitments. No entanglements." She turned back to the sink. "No scratches."

He snorted. "Hey, I don't happen to have anyone special right now. Maybe it was the other way around. You know, maybe I got dumped. Maybe some cruel woman broke my heart.''

She turned around, a sponge in one hand. ''Sorry. I shouldn't make assumptions like that.''

He brought the chair legs down with a thump. ''Don't apologize. You were right. My last breakup was mutual. They're always mutual, when women realize I'm not the picket-fence kind of guy. Does that faucet always drip like that?''

''Pardon? Oh. Yes, I guess. I've been meaning to replace the washer, but I don't know where the owners keep spares. *If* they keeps spares. They're rather elderly, and they don't use the cabin much anymore.''

''I'll take care of it.''

She smiled, feeling unexpectedly playful. ''Is it safe for an electrician to fix the plumbing?''

He grinned. ''I'll practice safe plumbing. Promise. Anything else that needs fixing?''

''No,'' she lied. Something did need fixing, something terribly wrong with her, but Josh certainly wasn't the man to repair what was broken. ''Coffee's ready,'' she said abruptly.

''Thanks.'' Josh wondered what her sudden change of mood was all about. It wasn't as if an offer of help obligated her to anything more than a thanks and a smile. Not in *his* book, anyway. If he offered something, a favor or a night on the town, he didn't do it to get repaid, with sex or anything else. He did things because he wanted to. And he seldom did anything he *didn't* want to do. Hope might have forgotten that about him, but he intended to remind her before the weekend was over.

She carried two crockery mugs to the table, then filled them. The aroma of rich coffee floated into his head, soothing and jolting at the same time. Like Hope.

Pleased with that thought, he looked at her and caught her watching him. Immediately, she lowered her eyes and bit her bottom lip. Like the brush of a live wire, the desire to touch her lips with his own, to kiss away whatever was bothering her, zapped him.

But problem solving for distressed ladies wasn't exactly in his line of work as a Teflon kinda guy.

Chapter Two

The silence stretched between them while Hope sipped her coffee. The situation, she mused, could be awkward. She'd never been good at casual flirtations, hadn't even been good at casual dating, which this certainly was *not*. Her years with Kyle might seem wasted in some respects, especially in light of her current problems, but at least she'd known what to expect. Until, of course, Kyle's rather sudden departure. But dwelling on Kyle's behavior wasn't helping her figure out what to do for an evening with a man she hardly knew anymore, who was also staying the night.

She needed a distraction.

"I think I'd like to light a fire," Hope announced.

"I hope there's a fireplace."

She almost answered him seriously, before she saw the twinkle in his blue eyes. "Just for that, you can rub the sticks together."

"You aren't mistaking me for a Boy Scout, are you?"

Hope stood and smiled down at Josh. "Perish the thought. I keep remembering more about you, and Boy Scout is the last thing that comes to mind."

He rose, and suddenly, she found herself looking up into his face and losing her sense of equilibrium along with her smile. She noticed faint laugh lines in the tanned skin around his eyes, which she found appealing. He'd filled out from the bold, brash youth he'd been at eighteen, but he was still a tease. She hoped she could deal with it better than when she'd been an awkward teenage egghead.

"There's some brandy in the cabinet," she told Josh as she opened the glass doors to the fireplace. "The Wilsons explicitly said I should feel welcome to it, since they hardly ever come up here anymore. Would you like some?"

"If you'll join me."

The intimate timbre of his deep voice gave her chills even as she lit a long match to touch to the kindling. Without looking at him, she answered, "Sure."

The fire caught just as Josh squatted beside her and held out a snifter with an inch of amber liquid. The flaring light played on the planes and angles of his face and reflected in his eyes, warming his blue gaze. When she reached for the snifter, his fingers brushed hers. Deliberately, she forced herself not to react, even though her nerves thought she'd touched flame. She couldn't afford to be attracted to a man right now.

Josh tilted his own snifter toward hers. Holding her gaze with his, he smiled. "To chance," he murmured, then touched her glass with his so gently that she barely heard the clink.

"To making the best of a situation," she countered. "I don't like leaving things to chance."

"Sometimes, the best things just happen." He stood and held his hand out to her. Ignoring it, she stood on her own.

"A person can waste a lot of time waiting for good things to just happen." She knew that from firsthand experience.

He grinned over the rim of his glass. "A person can waste a lot of energy trying to make things go the way she wants."

She knew that, too, from experience. He must have a good memory, she mused, since he'd pegged her so quickly and accurately. Hope sipped at the brandy. The liquor danced on her tongue and spread a trail of fire down to her stomach. "I guess that depends on your point of view," she said stiffly, a little too defensively, turning toward the sofa. She sat in a corner, leaving him as much room as possible.

"Or in knowing the difference between what you can control and what you can't," he corrected a little too smugly.

Hope merely sniffed her disagreement. She wasn't about to indulge in petty bickering, not even for old times' sake. Josh settled beside her a moment after, his weight on the single long cushion causing her to tip toward him. Hastily, Hope braced herself before she ended up bumping into him. A quick glance at his face told her he was amused at her reluctance to get close. It was almost like being in high school all over again, hearing him wheedling her to go for a ride on his motorcycle while the other kids teased her for being a chicken.

"So," he said, giving her that knowing grin, "what brings you out here to the middle of nowhere? Somehow, I can't picture you in hip waders, casting for trout."

The mental picture made her smile. "Neither can I. I came out here to make some plans and decisions without the pressure and distractions of work and family."

"How much family?"

His question made her realize how little they'd known about each other back in high school. "My parents, my younger sister and her husband and their daughters, plus my baby brother and his fiancée."

"Your *baby* brother is engaged?"

Hope sighed. "No. I mean, yes, he's engaged, but I guess he's not a baby anymore. He's eight years younger than I am, and we all spoiled him because he was the only boy."

"I'm an only kid. I always wanted to have sisters and brothers, but my friends kept saying sibling rivalry is the pits, so I figured I'd count my blessings."

"They're right. Sibling rivalry is awful, especially when you don't want to be rivals."

He leaned against the sofa back and lifted an eyebrow. "So some are born to rivalry, and some have it thrust upon them?"

"In a manner of speaking." She forced a weak smile, then looked away. "The thing is, I love them both, but we don't always see things the same way." She rubbed her hands around the wide bottom of the brandy snifter and stared into the amber liquor to avoid Josh's eyes.

After a long moment, she felt Josh touch her shoulder, a brief, friendly touch that drew her gaze to his. All trace of his earlier amusement was gone from his eyes. "Sounds like you need to unload. I'm not going anywhere, if you feel like getting something off your chest."

Hope hesitated, unwilling to let down her usual defenses even a little. But she'd been bottling her feelings up for so long that his invitation to confide appealed strongly. Besides, she rationalized, they weren't quite strangers, but they weren't quite friends, either, so whatever she told him wasn't likely to come back to haunt her. Most important, she realized, Josh didn't seem to want anything from her. He was offering a sympathetic ear without asking her to protect his feelings or put his needs first. That alone made the opportunity feel safe. She decided to tell him some—but only some—of what weighed on her mind and heart. The heaviest of her problems she couldn't share with anyone.

Drawing in a deep breath, she began, "My father has always wanted his kids to take over the firm, to keep it in the family. I used to go to the office with him, even when I was little. He'd have his secretary put me to work stapling things, and later filing. I loved it when he'd take me to the factory floor, or when he asked my opinion about designs and styles. I got my degree in business so I'd be an asset, and worked part-time from the day I turned sixteen. I felt as if I was preparing to take care of this special treasure my father wanted to share with me.''

Josh nodded at her over the rim of his brandy snifter.

''On the other hand, my sister was never interested. She got married when she was twenty, dropped out of university and has three gorgeous daughters, from nine down to three. My mother, who did the same thing, doesn't understand why I can't be more like her and Gail. She's afraid if I keep working, I'll never get married and have babies, but I don't want to get married.''

Phrased like that, she thought, it wasn't exactly untrue. She *didn't* want to get married.

''I've heard that before,'' he muttered. The fire popped loudly.

She looked at him. ''What do you mean?''

''I mean, I've heard people tell me I should get married, and I've been saying I don't want to so often that I feel like I should get a tape recording made and save my breath.''

''I wish it was that simple for me. I was with someone for a long time, and everyone assumed we'd get married.'' His eyebrows rose. She shrugged. ''Everyone except Kyle. We broke up four months ago, and I haven't had the heart to tell my family yet.''

''Ouch.''

His reaction made her smile ruefully. ''My feelings exactly. My mother keeps hinting that Kyle and I will announce our engagement at Paul's wedding. I know she wants what she believes is the best for me, but I feel like I can't really deal with that rat dumping me when I have to protect her from bad news.'' And that, she thought glumly, didn't scratch the surface of what she had to tell her mother eventually.

He lounged back farther in the sofa and studied her. "Do you have to protect her?"

Hope nodded. "She's one of those people everyone feels they have to protect. When she's happy, she's so effusive that she makes everyone around her feel good. Giving her bad news, especially about one of us, is like kicking a puppy."

"She'll find out sooner or later."

"I know. Kyle is supposed to be in the wedding party."

Josh shook his head and sipped at his brandy, his eyes smiling at her over the rim.

Hope sighed. "I know. And I will tell her. I have to pick the right time."

As if, she mused, there would ever be a right time for some of her news.

Suddenly uncomfortable with how much she'd confided to Josh, Hope said brightly, "Okay, enough whining from me. Tell me about the cabin you plan to build."

Abruptly, he stood and, grabbing her free hand, tugged her to her feet. Hope was too startled to resist until he started leading her across the room. Then she tried, without success, to pull her hand from his warm, hard grasp.

"Josh, what are you doing?"

"Relax. Come to the window with me."

Still holding her hand, he halted in front of the big window that looked out toward the marked lot where his van stood. Then, releasing her hand, he shoved aside the coarsely woven curtain. With no lights behind them except for the fire, and the nearly full moon almost as bright as the sun, Hope could see clearly. The land was lush with grasses and wildflowers, looking like dark clouds lying across the ground. In the far distance, the mountains ringed the valley in dark shadows. Nearer, trees lined the rivers and streams that wound their way through the land. It was, she realized, the first time she'd actually looked outside the cabin after dark. She simply hadn't thought about looking last night.

"It's beautiful," she breathed, more than a little awed.

"I've been coveting a piece of this paradise for myself ever since I was a kid going fishing with my old man. We'd come out and pitch a tent, go fishing and hiking and just hang out. My dad kinda lost interest over the years, but I used to come up alone or with some buddies, and we'd camp out. Then, when business started to pick up, I got too busy to get out here for the last couple of summers. The last time I did, I decided I was getting old enough to appreciate indoor plumbing, electricity and a real bed. Not to mention a solid roof that didn't smell like mildew and let the rain and the wildlife in."

Hope started to turn to look up at Josh, but suddenly, she realized he was standing much closer than she'd thought. So close she could feel the heat of his big, lanky body at her back and smell the faint traces of cedar soap from his shower.

She swallowed hard and turned back to the view outside the window. "Wildlife?"

"Sure. Lions and tigers and bears."

"Oh, my!" she said, obligingly.

He chuckled, the low sound rumbling disturbingly close. "Well, no lions and tigers, but bears and raccoons and other varmints. I never liked packing a shotgun, so every time there was another bear sighting reported, I'd think more seriously about a cabin."

"Which reminds me, about that shotgun..."

"The one you were waving in my face?"

She nodded, feeling her cheeks tingle with heat at the memory. "It isn't loaded. The Wilsons don't have any ammunition. They just keep it here because there were some off-season break-ins in the past few years, and they figured a burglar wouldn't stop to ask if the gun was loaded."

"So that's how you knew I wasn't a burglar, right?"

Her answer caught in her throat when his hand dropped lightly on her shoulder. She couldn't remember the last time Kyle had touched her simply to share a moment. There was something very seductive about the gesture, even from a near-stranger. But she couldn't let Josh think she was available, even though she'd invited him to spend the night. Involuntarily, she half turned toward him, her body tensing.

"Hey, don't be so jumpy," he murmured, making her feel foolish. "I told you I wouldn't pounce on you. I keep my word."

She tried to smile. "Chivalry isn't dead?"

Beside her, Josh bowed deeply. "The Teflon Knight at your service, milady. Your wish is my command."

Hope's smile was so sad that Josh almost broke a cardinal rule and reached out to take her in his arms and offer her comfort. He'd already broken one rule and let her unload her personal problems on him. And he still wasn't sure how he felt about that.

"Are you sure you're okay?" he asked, part of him doubting she was even though he hoped she'd say she was fine.

Unless he had suddenly become a lousy judge of character, Hope was one of those people who thought they always had to take care of others and keep up a positive appearance. By her own admission, she'd come out here to the boonies to unwind, but she sure didn't seem to be doing a good job of it. She'd almost jumped out of her skin when he'd touched her. He couldn't remember a woman ever reacting like that around him. The women he wanted to touch usually welcomed the idea. Hope was quite a puzzle, he decided, one he couldn't decide if he wanted to solve or get the hell away from before he got into more trouble than he could handle. This was not how he'd expected his fishing weekend to turn out.

"You're a nice man, Josh Kincaid," she murmured, her voice sounding a little husky, as if she might cry. He hoped not. He didn't do well with crying women. They always made him feel guilty, even if they were crying over a dead goldfish. "But I can take care of myself. I don't need a knight to rescue me from my dragons."

That was exactly the answer he wanted to hear, so why did it make him feel dissatisfied? Damned if he knew! Just like back in high school, Hope seemed to be able to tie his brain in knots without trying. Heaven help him if she ever *wanted* to mess with his head.

"If it makes you feel any better, I don't usually look for damsels in distress," he told her. "That's one of the rules for the Knights of Teflon."

Her smile brightened a little. "Well, thanks for listening. I don't usually pour out my soul to a near-stranger."

He'd hardly call it pouring out her soul when he still didn't think she'd told him what was really bothering her. It was like chasing down a short in a complex circuit. He wanted to know what was wrong, and . . . and *do* something about it, damn it!

The first thing to do was make her laugh again. "Look at it this way." He crossed his eyes. "There are plenty of guys out there who are stranger than I am."

Her laugh warmed him like a swallow of brandy. He grinned at his success.

"Josh, I need to get some sleep," she said. "Let me get you some sheets and blankets so you can make up the bed."

He was a normal, healthy male. A beautiful woman said the magic word *bed,* and his body started to hum with interest. But this wasn't any beautiful woman. This one had him confused, because she didn't do any of the things other women did, like flirting and trying to take care of him. The reversal of what he was used to made him react without his usual caution. He wanted to take care of Hope, make her smile, get her to relax.

"Okay. I'll bank the fire and open the sofa." He didn't have to tell her *which* fire he was banking.

She took his empty glass and walked out of the room, giving him a chance to watch her long-legged body move like a dancer. The bean pole sure had grown up! He wondered how long her hair was and whether it was as silky as it looked. He'd pulled her braids a few times back in high school, startled each time by the indescribable softness. What a jerk he'd been! No wonder she'd turned up that straight little nose whenever he'd teased her.

He wondered if she'd believe him if he told her the real reason he'd been such a pushy kid back then. Probably not. No one would believe Josh Kincaid, the silver-tongued devil himself, had ever been shy and insecure. Why embarrass himself by trying to convince her now when it didn't matter? She apparently wasn't holding any grudges, even about him taunting her for being too chicken to ride on the back of his motorcycle. Good thing she'd refused. If she'd wrapped those long legs around him, he probably would have disgraced himself.

Josh lifted the cushion from the sofa and grabbed the handle of the frame. The instant his hand closed around the tubular steel, he was struck by a brilliant idea. He *needed* a motorcycle! Absolutely. Maybe one of those big, rumbling Honda Goldwings, with storage for a picnic lunch and a comfortable seat to cover the miles on. Big windscreen, radio, walkie-talkies, all the state-of-the-art bells and whistles. That kind of a motorcycle was so solid, it practically hollered respectability, but it went like a bat out of hell. Yeah, he'd been without a bike too long, and it would be a real kick to bring Hope on the inaugural ride.

With the tantalizing image of Hope's long legs clinging to his, her arms wrapped around his torso, her small, firm breasts pressed to his back, filling his mind, Josh dropped the frame of the sofa bed onto his bare foot.

"Here you go," Hope said from behind a pile of bedding. He stopped rubbing his smashed, throbbing instep before she could see him. "Give me a few minutes in the washroom, and then it's all yours." She lowered the stuff to the table next to the sofa and smiled. "Good night. Sleep well."

"You, too," he answered, suddenly realizing he felt pretty good for a guy who was about to sleep alone with a beautiful woman in the next room. Would wonders ever cease?

Hope knew she was dreaming, but she couldn't force herself to waken, nor could she make the dream stop. All she could do was watch it happening to herself, even as she felt it happening.

She stood before a hospital nursery window, with dozens of newborn babies nestled in their baskets, some in blue blankets, some in pink, some sleeping peacefully, some red-faced from squalling. Beside her stood a person; she couldn't tell if it was a man or a woman, but she felt the person's power. Power over her.

"Aren't they beautiful? Don't you wish you could pick all of them up and cuddle them close?" the person's voice taunted. "Don't you want one of them?"

In her dream, she turned to stare into the blankness of a nonface, an impersonal person, the controller of her fate.

"Yes, you know I do," she answered, her entire body clenched with tension. "More than anything else in the world, I do."

"But you can't have one, Hope."

Suddenly, the person next to her wore the face of her own doctor, Susan Donovan, but there was something twisted, something sinister in Susan's smile.

"Please, Susan! Don't say I can't!"

"You can't, Hope. I must say you can't. Unless..."

"Unless?" Hope repeated eagerly.

"Unless Kyle will help you."

The nursery began to spin slowly around Hope, *trapping her behind the Plexiglas wall,* as if she were in the center of a giant baby carousel. She reached out, trying to stop it. A man in a business suit dodged between the Plexiglas bassinets, pushing each one he passed farther from Hope's outstretched arms. Then he turned and faced her. It was Kyle.

"Sorry, babe. No can do. Not my style. Thought you knew. I'm outta here. You're on your own, Hope."

"Hopeless unless you hurry," Susan added beside her.

"Hopeless," another voice echoed, and another, and another as the babies spun away from her, into the waiting arms of their mothers. "Hurry! Hurry! Hopeless, hopeless, hopeless!"

Then the spinning slowed. A nurse with a blank white face drifted through the nursery, stopping at one of the Plexiglas baskets where a tiny bundle lay sleeping, its rosebud mouth making tiny sucking movements. The nurse lifted the baby. Hope couldn't see what color the swaddling blanket was, but she didn't care.

The glass wall separating Hope from the nursery dissolved. She held her arms out to receive the child. The nurse wafted toward her, closer, closer with the tiny, perfect infant held so Hope could see its peaceful face. Her heart melted. The nurse lifted the baby as if to put it into Hope's outstretched arms. Then the nurse turned, and even though she had no face, Hope knew she was smiling. But not at Hope. The nurse was smiling at a woman who had appeared beside her, holding out her arms, an eager, expectant expression on her face. The nurse gave the baby to the other woman, who clutched it to her breast and disappeared from Hope's side.

And suddenly, Hope was awake, sitting up in bed, tears sliding down her face. Oh, God, not again! Ever since her doctor had warned her that if she didn't start a family almost immediately, she might not be able to get pregnant in the future, that dream had tormented her. The more time passed, the more vivid the dream became, the more desperate it left her feeling when she struggled awake.

"Not 'hopeless,'" she muttered as if the sound of her own voice gave her strength to believe. "Damn Kyle! Damn, damn, damn!" She wiped at her tears with the edge of her quilt. "I won't let it be hopeless."

She sat a while longer, her head in her hands, willing her mind to erase the awful dream that had been haunting her for months. Then, with a deep sigh, she looked at the clock beside the bed. Half-past six, the time she always got up for work. Might as well get up now, even though she was supposed to be on a vacation. She doubted she could fall asleep again, and anyway, if she did, she might slip into that dream—no, that nightmare.

Hope dressed quietly in jeans and a sweatshirt, then washed in the cabin's only bathroom. There was no sign of Josh yet, so she tiptoed into the kitchen and shrieked in alarm at the sight of the lower half of a man under the sink. She heard a thud, a clank and a muffled curse, and then the rest of Josh emerged, bare chested.

For a moment, all Hope could do was stare. She'd never seen a torso like that on a real, actual live male. On models in underwear ads, sure. Or guys on TV demonstrating home-gym equipment. But not on someone she knew, who was almost close enough to touch. Thank goodness *almost* didn't count. Josh had the most amazing chest. And shoulders. And arms. Hard-muscled like a marble statue. Tan, smooth skin, with a soft-looking patch of fine, dark hairs across his chest, tapering down to a thin double line right into his jeans. And his belly muscles actually rippled when he moved.

He set a wicked-looking wrench down on the floor beside his hip. "If my head wasn't so hard, that would have done brain damage," he muttered, then flashed her a lopsided grin. "I fixed the faucet, and tightened the coupling underneath, where it was leaking, too."

"Oh. I, uh, thanks," she stammered, wishing he had used a better word than *coupling*. "I thought you were going to practice safe plumbing," she blurted, then wanted to bite her tongue.

His grin widened as he got to his feet. "Not before my morning coffee." He wiped one large hand across his shoulder, where several drops of water had glistened, and left behind a faint smudge.

"You, um, your hands need washing," she told him.

He followed her gaze to his shoulder, then looked into her eyes. "Yes, ma'am. Right away. And if you'll brew the coffee, I'll whip up a batch of pancakes."

He walked out of the kitchen, his incredible torso passing within touching distance. Hope clenched her hands at her sides until he was gone, then filled the coffeepot and poured two glasses of orange juice. When Josh came back, wearing a black T-shirt partially tucked into his jeans, he rummaged through the Wilsons' cabinets until he found a mixing bowl and frying pan. With a proficiency that surprised her, he prepared the pancake batter from a box he took out of a carton perched on the counter.

"I came prepared," he commented, following her gaze toward the carton. "All the comforts of home, except the mobile home."

"Good thing," Hope told him. "I was planning to make toast for breakfast. Do you have syrup?"

He turned from the counter where he was stirring the batter, which made his T-shirt cling in interesting ways to his torso. "Hey," he said sharply, "do I look like an amateur?"

"No, sir, you don't. You look pretty professional to me."

"Damn straight. Nobody does heart-attack breakfasts like yours truly. Syrup, bacon, eggs, it's all here or in the cooler."

"I'm impressed."

While the coffee perked, Hope set the table and tried not to watch Josh as he poured pancake batter and nudged the cooking bacon. She didn't like the way being with Josh made her feel. He distracted her from the very real issues she had to decide. She needed to plan her future, not fritter her time comparing him with Kyle. Even if she were interested in another relationship right now—which she wasn't, but which might solve *some* of her problems if she were—Josh had made it clear that *he* wasn't interested in anything serious. Hadn't he warned her that he wanted to make a tape recording of himself saying he didn't want to get married? She'd read enough magazine articles to understand he was setting the ground rules right up front. If she threw herself at him, he might accept a casual fling—at least she didn't think he found her unattractive—but he wasn't the kind of man she'd once believed Kyle was: committed, loyal, dependable.

And she certainly wasn't the kind of woman who indulged in casual flings.

So why couldn't she control the impulse to wonder how his large, strong, slightly rough-looking hands would feel on her bare skin?

Somehow, she managed to sit across the table from him and eat her pancakes as if she hadn't a care in the world and had never considered following the line of hairs down his belly and into his jeans. But when the phone rang, startlingly loud, she couldn't swallow fast enough and started to cough.

"Want me to get that?" Josh asked. She tried to say no, but he was already out of his chair and across the kitchen.

Lifting the receiver from the wall phone, he barked, "Yeah?"

Hope heard the faint, agitated voice over the wires and cringed. Josh's eyebrows rose under his tousled dark hair. "Yes, ma'am," he said politely, "she's right here." Then he cupped his hand over the receiver and grinned wickedly. "It's your mother. I think you're in trouble."

Chapter Three

With his ears still ringing from Hope's mother's agitated voice, Josh stuffed the last of his breakfast into his mouth, washed it down with coffee, tossed Hope a wink and went into the other room to put on his boots. The firewood supply was getting low, so he figured he'd spend some time working on the woodpile out back. Besides, he had no interest in eavesdropping, and it wasn't hard to see that his presence made Hope as tense as a deer pinned by headlights. Still, as he shoved his arms into a red plaid flannel shirt, he couldn't help hearing her say his name.

"Josh and I went to high school together, Mom. He's hardly a stranger." Pause. "No, I doubt Kyle would mind. Josh is just a friend."

He winced and shut the door behind him. Hope was asking for trouble by not telling her mother about this Kyle jerk dumping her. The more she put it off, the harder it was going to be.

Outside the cabin, Josh paused to draw in a deep breath. The air was so clean, so sweet and pure that his lungs seemed to expand more than usual. The sun was shining, just starting to warm up the morning. He contemplated his options, primarily the woodpile and the trout. What he should do is get his fishing gear from his van, hike over to the river for a couple of hours of fishing, then come back to tackle the firewood. Maybe he could persuade Hope to come for a walk later. That woman could use some fresh air and some time with no pressure—only his charming company to help her unwind.

Unloading his fishing gear, Josh shoved aside the nagging question of *why* he wanted Hope to unwind and feel better. It was easiest to tell himself that she was one very attractive woman who presented a challenge to his male ego and his male hormones. And that was all. He wasn't the kind of guy who tried to heal every wounded heart that drifted through his life. He had a buddy like that who was always attracting troubled women. Gray would get them over their crisis, and his thanks would be an invitation to yet another wedding, because they always fell in love with someone else.

Not that he wanted anyone to fall in love with him, he hastened to assure himself as he hiked toward the sound of gurgling water. Nope, that was one complication he always tried to avoid. He loved getting invitations to ex-girlfriends' weddings, 'cause that meant he was off the hook yet again. He had nothing against falling in "like," but falling in love, getting serious, just wasn't worth the loss of freedom.

The sound of the cabin door shutting gave Hope the signal that she could talk freely with her mother. It was on the tip of her tongue to gently lead into breaking the news of Kyle's desertion, but her mother didn't give her a chance.

"Sweetheart, I've been talking to Paul, and I feel I have to speak to you for him. I hate doing it over the phone, but you took off for the wilderness before I could catch you."

"What about Paul, Mom?" Hope asked even though she knew.

"He's ready for a promotion, Hope, but he says he can't talk to you about it. I hate to see my children squabble."

"We aren't squabbling, Mom. When Paul is ready for more responsibility, I'll give it to him. But he can't be ready if he won't try to talk to me. It's not like I'm an ogre."

"I know, darling. But you're so competent that it can be intimidating. Sometimes, you even scare me," her mother added with a little laugh.

Hope couldn't even manage a smile at her mother's small jest. It hurt. "I didn't realize... I'm sorry. I'm trying to do the best I can to fill Dad's shoes. He worked so hard to build the firm, and I want him to feel secure about retiring with me in his place."

"But you don't have to do everything yourself, do you? Isn't there something Paul can do on his own? It would help you, too, sweetheart, if you didn't have to run the whole show, wouldn't it?"

"I suppose," Hope grudgingly conceded, "but Paul hasn't worked there very long. If I give him more responsibility, I'll still have to supervise him. It's usually easier for me to do things myself while he learns the ropes the way I did."

"My darling control freak, you sound exactly like your father! Studies show that women who work as obsessively as men are just as prone to heart attacks. Don't you want to live long enough to retire?" Without giving Hope a second to defend herself, her mother went on, "Besides, you owe it to Kyle, and to the children you'll have together, to learn to make work your second priority."

The emotional pain her mother's words caused felt so real that Hope's knees buckled. She clutched the wall behind her for support. Josh was right. The longer she waited to tell her mother the truth—*all* the truth—the worse it was going to be for her and her mother. But she couldn't bring herself to blurt her bad news. Not over the phone. She knew her mother would want to hug her, would *need* to hug her, and Hope would probably need her mother's comforting touch, too. As soon as she returned to Kelowna, she promised herself. Tuesday, right after work, she'd go over to her parents' house and tell them...everything.

"Speaking of children," her mother gushed, "Gail gave us such wonderful news last night at dinner. She's expecting again! Can you believe it? She'd due the end of October."

Thoroughly shaken, Hope slid to the floor. She drew her knees in to her chest and pressed the phone so tightly to her ear that her mother's voice became muffled.

"Isn't that wonderful, Hope? The girls are so excited. Tom and your father are hoping for a boy this time, but I don't care, as long as it's another healthy grandchild. Gail is just glowing!"

Somehow, Hope forced herself to say, "That's wonderful, Mom. Gail is such a good mother, she makes it look easy."

Her mother chuckled. "Well, *making* the babies is easy. Mothering them is another question altogether."

How, Hope wondered, could she tell her mother about Kyle, about her, and ruin this euphoria? Maybe she could prevail on Kyle to pretend, only for the wedding. And the rehearsal dinner. And the stag Paul's friends were giving him. If she could bring herself to swallow her pride and ask, would that be so difficult for him? As for the rest of her bad news, that could certainly wait until after Paul's wedding.

"Oh! Here's your father, sweetheart. We're going to spend the day with Tom's parents to celebrate Gail's news. Tomorrow, we're taking the girls to watch fireworks, so we don't have to worry about crazy drivers on Monday night. Will there be fireworks where you are?''

''Yes, Sunday night. Give my love to everyone. I'll be coming home late Monday, so I'll see you Tuesday, after work, okay?''

''Come to dinner with Kyle. We don't see enough of you. With Paul moving out to his new apartment, I'm not looking forward to my empty nest.''

''Okay, Mom. Dinner on Tuesday,'' Hope managed to choke out almost cheerfully. ''Bye.''

Somehow, she reached up to hang up the phone before sinking back down to the floor. She stayed there, unmoving, for a long time, not really thinking, too much in pain to feel. When she finally forced herself to stand and go through the motions of cleaning the breakfast dishes, images from her nightmare and bits of her mother's conversation swirled in her mind. Wasn't it ironic, Hope concluded, that Gail once confided that she and Paul envied their older sister because everything came easy to her. But not the one thing she wanted most.

After rinsing the last dish, Hope went into the cabin's sole bedroom, a small room haphazardly stuffed with old furniture that would never, even with the passage of a long time, become antiques. Sitting on the rather lumpy double bed, she opened the briefcase she'd brought from home and placed her notepad in front of her. Then she spread out all the books and articles about artificial insemination, in vitro fertilization and single motherhood that she'd been able to carry.

Josh left his fishing gear in the van, peeled out of his flannel shirt and trudged back to the cabin with two big, beautiful trout dangling from his hand. He felt very pleased with his morning's work. Of course, the ones that got away were all the size of Moby Dick, but these two would make a very nice dinner for him and Hope. And he had a couple of bottles of good Okanagan Valley wine clutched in his other hand to add to the flavor of a quiet evening in the middle of paradise. Who knew what could happen when a man and a woman were attracted and had no distractions? He wouldn't pressure her, but he sure wouldn't push her away if she let him know she was interested.

He pulled open the screen door, then pushed open the inner door and stepped inside. With a frown, he noticed he hadn't made up the sofa bed before he'd left. Well, as soon as he divested himself of his fish and his wine, he'd fix that. He didn't want her to think he was a slob.

Calling her name, he went into the kitchen to place the fish in the sink with ice, and the wine in the fridge. Then he scrubbed his hands in the side of the double sink that didn't contain his prize catches. Less than a minute later, Hope appeared in the doorway. Her hair had come loose from the twist she'd put it up in, and her expression was odd, as if she were a million miles away.

"How about some lunch?" he asked, still holding the fridge door open.

"Lunch?"

"Yeah. Sandwiches?"

"Sandwiches." She spoke as if she'd never heard the word before. Definitely in another world, he decided.

"Yeah. Two slices of bread with meat and mustard or ketchup in between."

"Oh. Sandwiches," she said, making it sound as though *he* was the one who was, figuratively speaking, out to lunch.

"Is there a parrot in here?" he asked, looking around the kitchen. When he realized he'd gone off and left her with dirty dishes, he winced.

"Parrot?" she echoed, then laughed.

He grinned. "You should do that more often," he told her. "You have a nice laugh."

And to his complete surprise, the woman blushed.

He turned back to the refrigerator to cover his reaction. With his hands full of the sandwich meats he'd brought from his cooler, he stepped past her. Hope went behind him and took out a tomato and a container of what looked like coleslaw, then followed him to the counter. When she reached over the sink to wash the tomato, she yelped and jumped back.

"Dinner," he told her. Indulging his pride a little, he added, "I caught two of them," even though that was obvious. Jeez, he sounded like a little kid trying to impress his favorite teacher! *Get a life,* he told himself sternly.

"So I see," Hope said neutrally, apparently able to restrain herself from gushing over his expertise with rod and reel. Well, maybe she didn't understand enough of the finer points of trout fishing to appreciate his success. Not many women did, which is why he didn't bring women fishing.

"I'll clean them," he assured her.

She glanced at him, then ran a lethal-looking knife through the tomato. "I hadn't expected otherwise." The halves of the tomato fell to the cutting board.

"Are you okay?"

"Of course." A few quick flicks of her wrist, and she'd sliced the tomato halves into thin slices. "Beer or diet cola?"

"Beer. I'm on vacation."

"I'm not."

She slid the cutting board toward him, then turned back to the fridge, taking out a can of beer and a can of diet cola. He finished assembling three sandwiches, two for himself, while she set the table. Then they sat across from each other, and the silence made him want to do something outrageous just to break the ice and make her laugh again. That in itself was odd, because moody women usually made him break out in hives and leave.

"Music," he blurted.

"There's a box of CDs and a portable player in the living room. Help yourself."

He found the CDs and player under the shirt he'd taken off last night. Hastily, he flipped through the CD cases and pulled out a Suzanne Cianni CD. It wasn't his kind of music most of the time, but women seemed to like it. Maybe it would help Hope mellow out from whatever was bugging her now.

For the first couple of minutes of the music, he tackled his clutter, stuffing his clothes and things into his gym bag. Then he folded up the sofa bed and piled the quilt and pillow on a chair. Not perfect, but better.

Back in the kitchen, Hope sat like a statue, a half sandwich held in one raised hand, her eyes fixed on a spot on the wall. His first thought, as would be any normal male's, was that there was a spider there. A quick glance negated that theory. He sat down across from her, but she didn't seem to notice. This woman was going to destroy his ego without trying, he decided.

"Hey," he said softly, wanting to break into her trance without startling the daylights out of her. "What's the matter? You don't like New Age music?"

As he watched, the glazed look in her eyes cleared, but her sad expression didn't. She blinked, then met his eyes. He saw tears on her lashes and hoped they were simply the result of her staring contest with the blank wall. The half-hearted little smile she gave him wasn't very convincing.

"I'm sorry, Josh. I forgot to take that CD out of the pile, but that's okay. It used to be a favorite until Kyle decided to use it for mood music to walk out by." She blinked again, and her smile struggled to get a little brighter, but he wasn't buying it.

He shoved his chair back, stomped out of the room and pressed the Stop button on the CD player. Sifting through the CDs again, he found something as far from New Age as he could. By the time he'd turned around, the opening riffs of the Eagles' "Get over It" were blasting out of the speakers. When he dropped into his chair and looked at Hope, she smiled, and this time, there was a sparkle in those turquoise eyes that didn't come from tears.

"Touché," she said, then laughed lightly.

He grinned. "Eat your lunch before I do."

She took a bite, chewed, then swallowed. "Josh? Thanks."

"Hey, don't get serious on me again. I can't stand to be around long faces. After lunch, I'm going for a walk, and you're coming with me."

She tipped her head, and smiled. "Is that an order?" she asked softly. For one crazy second, he thought she was flirting. Then he thought better of that idea. Hope was still the least-likely-to-flirt woman he'd ever met.

"Whatever it takes."

"Sounds grim."

He grinned. "No, ma'am, no grim allowed."

She raised her sandwich to her lips, then lowered it again. "You know, Josh, you're a very nice guy. I guess I underestimated you back in high school."

He shrugged, uncomfortable with her compliment. "Nah. You were right. In high school, I was a jerk."

"Well, if I remember correctly, so were most of the other guys."

Her quick defense made him even more critical of his former self. "But I took jerkdom to new heights." Her chuckle made him feel a little better. "Finish your lunch. We're wasting sunshine."

"Yes, sir."

After their walk, Josh stopped at the woodpile. "Why don't you take the first shower," he suggested. "I'm going to chop some wood for later. There isn't much left inside."

She gave him one of those heart-stopping smiles that made him feel like a clumsy oaf. "Okay. If you don't mind."

"If I minded, I wouldn't offer," he told her. "I don't do things I don't like, if I can help it."

"Ah! So you do believe in exercising some control after all," she retorted, but softly.

In fact everything about her seemed softer now. Her voice, the expression in her incredible eyes, her touch. It hadn't done his equilibrium a whole hell of a lot of good to have her mellow out like that and still be out of reach.

"Yeah, you'd be amazed at the things I try to control," he muttered. More directly, he said, "Hurry up, woman. I'm gonna be hot and sweaty when I'm done."

Once she'd walked out of sight around to the front of the cabin, Josh grabbed the ax hanging from the back wall and went to face the woodpile. The way he was feeling at the moment—frustrated—he would probably be able to single-handedly clear-cut the entire province of British Columbia.

He selected a thick chunk of wood from the pile and set it upright on the battered stump obviously used as a chopping block. He swung the ax hard into the wood, burying the edge, then swung the whole thing down on the stump until the wood split. Setting the pieces aside, he repeated the process over and over, all the while thinking about Hope.

She was one very complicated lady, he decided. Much too much trouble to get involved with a woman like that, as tempting as she was. She was bright and fun and sexy, although in a subtle way, but she had obligations and problems and dilemmas, and she was so uptight she practically vibrated. Not his type at all, even if she had his libido racing even in neutral. He liked his women bold and easygoing, willing to meet him halfway and accept his limits. He was too much of a good-time-Charlie. A Teflon Knight.

If he had half a brain, which was all some of his teachers had given him credit for anyway, he'd avoid Hope like he'd avoid someone with the flu. Every time he turned around, she did something that made him want to take care of her, to fix whatever was broken in her life, to make her happy. Fortunately for him, she seemed to reject his impulsive and misguided attempts.

On the other hand, *un*fortunately for him, every time he looked into those unusual turquoise eyes or stole a glance at that willowy body, he felt a spark that short-circuited his common sense. Also unfortunately for him, it was a spark Hope didn't seem to feel whenever she checked out his eyes or whatever else of his she might check out. The lady was pretty cool for someone who claimed he would have made her faint if he'd offered her a ride on his motorcycle back in high school.

Well, he told himself as he gathered a load of wood to take into the cabin, this wasn't high school. Hope had apparently lost any inclination to faint in his presence, and if he was smart, he'd encourage her to stay upright.

Chapter Four

Humming softly, Hope gathered clean clothes and headed to the bathroom for a shower. All things considered, she felt pretty optimistic after communing with nature for a couple of hours. Josh had been right about it doing her good. Funny, she mused as she went down the hall, but he was a lot more sensitive and kind than he seemed to want her to think. Usually, guys tended to work the other way around, trying to convince a woman he was tender and generous until she needed him to be.

Like Kyle, the creep. At least he had a lot of others fooled about his character, like her family and friends, not only her. It was small consolation, but she felt a little better about not being his sole dupe. Still, all those years she'd invested, down the drain like the water pouring over her.

Tired from trudging through the fields with Josh, she stood under the spray and let herself lose track of time. The pounding on the bathroom window startled a scream out of her. Hastily, she turned off the water and grabbed her towel. Heart racing, she waited, hardly daring to move.

"Hope? Hey! Hope!" Josh bellowed through the closed window.

She sagged in relief and fastened the towel around her. "Is something wrong?" she hollered back, unable to unlock the window.

"Yeah. You locked the cabin door. I can't get in."

The absurdity of the situation made her laugh. "Sorry," she called. "Give me a sec."

Wrapping her hair and body in towels, Hope hurried to the cabin door. The air outside the bathroom chilled her wet skin, making her acutely conscious of the fact that she was close to naked. She heard Josh's steps on the wooden porch and felt her pulse speed up. Gripping the towel around her body tightly to keep it closed and as high over her chest as possible, she flipped the lock open. The door opened inward quickly, forcing her to step back. The towel around her wet hair came loose just as Josh walked in, the load of wood in his arms piled high in front of his face. Her hair spilled down like wayward seaweed, draping wetly over her shoulders. It was, she decided, a good thing she wasn't interested in seducing Josh. He'd probably take one good look at her impersonation of a mermaid and run the other way.

"I need a shower in the worst way," he announced, moving past her toward the fireplace.

"I'm almost done," she told him. "I just have to get dressed."

The load of wood crashed onto the hearth. Josh straightened and slowly turned around. Hope watched him look at her from head to toe and felt her cheeks flame. Judging by his stunned expression, he didn't find her water-nymph costume at all attractive. Too embarrassed even to excuse herself, she simply clutched her remaining towel and sprinted back to the bathroom.

* * *

Oh, Lord, it was going to be another one of those nights, Josh thought as he watched Hope run away. He could smell her, that suggestive scent of freshly cleaned skin and hair. Even though he watched her retreating back, with the towel outlining her slender hips and small bottom, in his mind he could still see her bare shoulders, her neck and throat, the hint of small breasts much too close to being exposed. There were still droplets of water on her skin, tempting him to sip at them. It wouldn't have taken much effort or strength for him to tug away the towel she clutched. Her hair was like wet silk, inviting his fingers to touch. But judging by the way she'd blushed and run, she must have read his mind, not particularly keen to be the star of his fantasies.

Crouching in jeans that suddenly fit much too snugly, he stacked the firewood he'd dropped. Then he went into the kitchen and opened a beer. The frosty brew went a long way toward cooling his throat, but did nothing for the heat caused by the sight of Hope in a towel. Even cleaning the trout, never his favorite thing to do, couldn't distract his libido from its fantasies.

"The shower's all yours," he heard her call. In the distance, a door shut hard, long before he was close enough to sneak another glimpse of her.

This time, the bathroom still held the humidity of her shower, the scents of her soap and shampoo sending suggestions in the close confines of the room. It was easy to imagine she was there with him, soapy and slippery as a mermaid, twisting and teasing in his arms. But would the real Hope make love playfully, or would she take it seriously, like a project, something to control? If he had a shred of common sense, a shred of decency, he wouldn't try to find out.

Hope turned from the counter, where she'd been chopping carrots and celery to mix into the wild rice, to the table, where she'd left the olive oil, and found Josh standing in the doorway watching her. He wore jeans and a chambray work shirt, the same clothes hundreds of men wore every day, but on Josh, they looked especially masculine, especially attractive. And that wasn't, she decided, a good line of thought for her to pursue.

"You're always sneaking up on me," she accused, immediately contrite about her shrewish tone.

But Josh simply grinned. "It's so much fun to see you lose your cool. Just like the good old days."

She sniffed her disagreement and grabbed the bottle of oil. Then she glanced at the now-cleaned trout lying in their ice bed. "How do you propose to cook those poor things?"

"On the barbecue outside. There's a grill thing for fish under the sink. I saw it when I was fixing the pipes. It might need a little cleaning up. I'll take care of it while the barbecue heats up."

Josh dug the grilling contraption out from under the sink and disappeared outside to play caveman with the Wilsons' aging gas barbecue. She puttered around the kitchen, putting together the rest of their dinner and setting the table. Shortly after he'd left the kitchen, the phone rang, startling her. Even though the phone was a fact of her life at home, not many people had the cabin number, so she'd stopped expecting calls. It was, no doubt, her mother, having worked herself into a stew that Josh had turned into a mad rapist or sadistic murderer.

"Hope, it's me," her best friend, Chantelle La Porte, practically shouted when Hope answered. "I've been trying to reach you all weekend, and finally called your mother. She gave me this number. I hope that's okay."

"Sure. What's up?"

"Me! I'm high as a kite! I wanted to tell you in person, but I can't wait!"

Chantelle's excitement made Hope smile. She could picture her dark-haired, gray-eyed friend bouncing in her chair over whatever had made her so happy. Probably her promotion at the bank had come through. Chantelle had been on pins and needles for months, waiting for news.

"So tell me," Hope prompted. "You got the promotion?"

"What? Oh, no. Not yet, anyway. No, this is a million times better. I'm pregnant! I'm finally, finally pregnant! Rob is so excited, I thought we'd have to peel him off the ceiling. Oh, Hope, I'm so happy! You know how much we wanted this, and I was so scared to jinx it by telling anyone, even you, too soon. But we just got the amnio results, and the doctor says everything is fine. It's a boy, Hope! I'm going to be a mother!"

Numbly, Hope clung to the receiver and listened, as if through cotton, while Chantelle shared her news. She knew how dearly her friend wanted to have children. She'd been holding Chantelle's hand through five years of negative results and discouraging words, never suspecting that she'd be facing the same situation herself...alone.

"That's wonderful, Chantelle," Hope forced herself to say warmly. "I'm so happy for you. You'll be a great mother. How are you feeling?"

"Fantastic! I'm over the morning sickness and heading into the nesting phase. We're designing the baby's room, and I can't wait to shop for furniture. And I'll probably be your best customer." Chantelle's voice grew husky, as if she were trying not to cry. "All those sweet little outfits. Oh, Hope! I'm almost afraid I'm dreaming and I'll wake up and not be pregnant."

At Chantelle's reference to the family firm's baby clothes, tears filled Hope's eyes. After swallowing hard, she said, "I can come over and pinch you, if you'd like."

Chantelle's laughter landed like tiny punches to Hope's heart. She was genuinely happy for her friend, and genuinely jealous. And her jealousy made her feel guilty, because Chantelle had cried so many tears and deserved this joy, and because she had a wonderful husband to share parenthood with her. Thanks to Kyle and Fate, Hope didn't have either.

After a few more minutes of exuberant chattering, Chantelle extracted Hope's promise of a visit soon after the holiday weekend, then said goodbye. Feeling drained, Hope hung up the phone. When Josh came back with the perfectly cooked fish, Hope could barely manage a weak smile at his pride. Numbly, she sat and watched him reverently lay a trout across each of their plates. He filled their wineglasses, raised his in her direction and said, *"Bon appétit."* Then he picked up his knife and fork and sliced into the steaming fish. Hope simply stared at him, the thought of eating making her stomach clench.

Josh swallowed his first bite, then looked at her. "Hey, dig in," he ordered. "It's too good to waste, and it's gonna cool off fast. If you want cold fish, might as well have sushi."

Moving as if through deep water, Hope felt for her fork. She poked at the fish on her plate, taking the tiniest of flakes into her mouth. The tender meat might as well have been sawdust for all she could tell. Guiltily meeting Josh's eyes, she tried another, larger bite, and managed to choke it down.

"If you don't like fish, you should have said something." Dimly, she recognized his strained tone reflected hurt feelings.

"It's delicious. I'm just not very hungry," she told him lamely, feeling a blush stain her cheeks as she lowered her gaze. Not knowing what else to do, she sipped her wine.

"This sudden change of mood have anything to do with the phone call a while ago? You sure seemed ready for dinner before then."

Her face grew even warmer. Not trusting her voice, she shrugged.

"Come on, Hope. Talk to me. Did you get bad news?" She shook her head. "Good news?"

Briefly, she met his eyes, then looked away as her own eyes filled with tears. With a sigh, she nodded.

"Must have been terrific news to make you cry."

His sarcasm jolted her out of her lethargy. "I'm not crying."

"Sure. Those tears about to spill over are from the rare beauty of the fish on your plate. That's why you can't bring yourself to eat, right?"

"I'm sorry," she murmured. "Let's drop it, okay? The fish really is delicious. If you promise not to nag, I'll eat it."

"Nag?" He snorted. "I don't nag! My mother nags. All I'm trying to do is see that you don't waste that fish."

His indignation almost made her smile. Somehow, she managed to eat about half of the tender fish. Josh kindly offered to finish what she left. Talking over a meal of fresh fish didn't seem to be a good idea, so they ate in silence, with only the sound of Clapton *Unplugged* on the CD player accompanying them. When Josh rose to clear his plate, Hope nearly leapt to her feet in relief. She'd had enough wine on an almost empty stomach to feel lethargic. All she wanted to do was be alone with her grief.

Hope ran water into the dishpan, filling it with soapy water while Josh cleared the table. Then they stood side by side at the sink, Hope washing, Josh drying. A spoon she hadn't noticed fell out of the rice pot, splashing soapy water into her eyes. With a cry, she shut her eyes, but she couldn't do anything more while she was still holding the pot in her soapy hands.

"What's the matter?" Josh said, closer than she'd expected.

Eyes stinging and tearing, Hope stood blindly. "Soap in my eyes," she choked out.

"Here, turn your head. I've got a clean cloth."

She felt his big hand on her shoulder, felt the lightly scratchy touch of a wet dish towel on her eyes. His touch was so gentle, his nearness so comforting, that she wanted to cry with the bittersweetness of the moment. Helpless as long as she stood there holding the pot over the sink full of water, Hope let Josh bathe her eyes with cool water.

"How's that?" he asked.

Hope blinked her eyes open. They were hazy with tears, but the sting of soap had been washed away. Meeting his anxious gaze, she gave him a tremulous smile. He didn't smile in answer. He looked at her intently, drawing closer as she stared up at him. Finally, he was so close that she had to shut her eyes. She felt his breath kiss her cheek, felt his warmth reaching out to embrace her.

Needing more than just that light contact, Hope reached for his arms, releasing her grip on the heavy rice pot. It fell into the sink, splashing her heavy cotton sweater with hot dishwater. With a shriek of outraged surprise, Hope leapt back away from Josh. He released her shoulders equally quickly.

"What the . . . ?" he bellowed.

They gaped at each other. Josh looked down at the water still dripping onto the floor, then back at Hope's sodden sweater. He tugged at a lock of his dark hair, then met her eyes, and a snort of laughter burst from him. A moment later, Hope was laughing helplessly with him.

"Go put on something dry," Josh told her, trying to hide how shaken he was by that near-kiss, and biting back the impulse to offer her help with her wet sweater. "I'll finish the dishes and meet you in the other room."

She gave him one of those sweet smiles that did something funny to his insides. "You really are a knight to the rescue."

If she only knew. "Let's hope I don't rust." Tarnish was more likely, he thought ruefully.

With a laugh, she walked out of the kitchen, leaving him to watch her hips sway just enough under a long, soft skirt to fuel his fantasies. He turned back to the dishes, thinking that being up to his elbows in hot water wasn't what he needed. What he needed was a cold shower. *Another* cold shower.

After he'd put the last pot into the drainer and dried his hands, he went into the living room. Hope was already there, standing beside a shelf of homemade videotapes, running one slim finger along the titles on the cases. She held her head tipped to one side, and her hair hung like lace, backlit by the lamp in the corner. She wore an oversize sweatshirt the same turquoise as her eyes. The shapeless shirt and long skirt seemed sexier, hinting at what was within, than anything skintight and low cut would be.

She glanced at him and smiled. "The Wilsons' tastes are a little old-fashioned. None of these would be my first choice under normal circumstances," she told him. "Lots of Doris Day movies, a couple of Gidget ones and about six episodes of 'Lassie, Come Home.'"

"You're kidding." She shook her head. When he stopped beside her and looked for himself, he saw she was right. "Jeez, the only tape here from the last decade is *Look Who's Talking.*"

She pulled the tape off the shelf. "Well, lucky me! I never saw it." Those incredible eyes sparkled with mischief.

He grinned. "Neither did I." Her playful mood was contagious. And a good sign that she'd gotten over whatever had put her into such a funk over dinner.

"Shall we?"

"You load the VCR. I'll get the fire going again."

When they were ready for the movie, Hope pressed the Play button on the VCR, which apparently had become separated from its remote control. Then she sat on the sofa, within touching distance but far enough away to make it clear that she didn't have snuggling on her mind.

A few minutes into the movie, Josh noticed that the lamp in the corner was shining directly onto the TV screen. He got up and switched it off, leaving the room dimly lit from two small wall sconces. He looked at Hope, but she didn't even glance away from the small screen, so he figured she either hadn't noticed he'd turned out the light or didn't think anything of sitting in a darkened room with him. Neither alternative was particularly flattering to his ego, but then, Hope was out of his league and out of his reach, so his ego shouldn't care that she wasn't interested.

The next time Josh glanced at Hope, he did a double take. She was wiping her cheeks as if she were trying to mop up a flood. "Hope? Are you all right?"

She sniffed. "I'm fine. Why shouldn't I be?" she answered, not looking at him.

"Because nobody in the history of Western civilization has ever cried over this movie, unless they were film critics."

"I'm not crying over the movie," she snapped, her voice thick with tears.

All his self-preservation instincts bellowed at him to drop the matter, but some perverse devil in his head had to pursue it. "Then what are you crying over?"

She angled stiffly away from him. "Nothing."

Another cue to back off and stay uninvolved. So what did he do? "C'mon, Hope. You're not the kind of woman to bust up over nothing. I should know. I used to tease you like a cat with a mouse, and you never gave me any satisfaction. This is about that phone call, isn't it? Your so-called good news?"

"Josh, please, forget it."

Strike three, and he was going to go down swinging. "Hope, I owe you. I may never see you again, unless you need an electrician, so you can unload on me and not have to worry about it coming back to haunt you. I'm a totally disinterested party. We Teflon Knights never get involved, so anything you say will just roll off me. But it might do you some good to blab it all out."

"I hate self-pity," she muttered. "Whining never does any good."

"So don't whine. But self-pity is just as ugly if you keep it inside as it is if you let it out. Maybe uglier."

She stood up so fast, she nearly fell over the coffee table. Josh leapt and grabbed her arm, keeping her upright. To his surprise and dismay, she struggled and whimpered as if he were attacking her.

"Hey, take it easy," he murmured, trying to calm her, hold her up and fend her off all at the same time. "You're going to fall on your face if you're not careful. And it would be a shame to dent that beautiful coffee table, circa 1960."

Hope gave a smothered laugh that turned into a sob, and collapsed against him. He held her hard, all thoughts of sex and its possibilities giving way to a protective urge he'd never felt before. Her arms went around him as if she were clinging to a life raft. She was trembling so hard he could feel the vibrations running through his own body. What the hell kind of bomb had someone dropped over the phone? Good news didn't do this to a strong, self-contained woman like Hope.

"Easy, baby," he crooned, finding the offer of comfort coming naturally. "Talk to me, Hope. Tell Uncle Josh what's wrong." She shook her head against his chest. Make that strong, self-contained and *stubborn,* he amended.

After a moment of silent clinging, Hope shifted enough to look up into his eyes. Her lips parted. Before he could think better of it, he bent and caught her mouth with his. She made a soft little sound and moved against his chest. When he realized she wasn't wearing a bra, a tremor ran through him. He started to break the kiss, but one of her hands slid up his shoulder to cup his head, telling him clearly that she wanted him to continue.

This was definitely a mistake, he thought even as he was touching the tip of his tongue to her lips. He stroked her slender back through the thick sweatshirt and felt her hair trailing over his hands like silken threads. A wonderful mistake, he thought as her lips softened under his and opened for his tongue. The fire popped loudly, echoing the explosion in his senses.

So sweet. Unbelievably sweet. It was more than he expected, even though he couldn't recall consciously expecting anything. He breathed in her scent and felt as dizzy as if he'd drunk the entire bottle of wine on his own. He probed the hot sweetness she offered and felt the blood surge to his loins. Suddenly, he was so hard with wanting her, he thought his legs would buckle. He rocked his hips against her. She made that soft sound again and rocked with him, her mouth clinging to his.

In the back of his mind, he marveled that he could turn her on so quickly when she'd seemed so cool and controlled.

The instant Josh's lips touched hers, Hope felt her soul crying out for comforting. His body was so hard, his mouth so soft. She grasped at him, clung to him, needing his unreserved strength, risking her own vulnerability to let him touch her. Oh, how she needed to be *touched!* It didn't matter that he was a virtual stranger. Instinctively, she trusted him.

He brushed his lips over hers. She gasped at the fleeting contact, suddenly desperate for more.

"Oh, Josh," she whispered, "I need..." Words failed her as his hands tightened on her shoulders and heat engulfed her from deep inside.

"What, baby? What do you need?" His ragged question came out no louder than her shaky whisper.

I need to be held, to be loved, she thought, *even if it's an illusion.* But she couldn't tell him that. She couldn't tell anyone. She was the strong one, the one people turned to for comfort, for love, for support. She was the giver, not the taker, and she didn't know how to reverse her role, didn't know how to ask for what she needed.

His mouth hovered over hers, teasing, offering, inviting. With a soft cry, Hope leaned up into his kiss. His lips touched hers, warm, soft and tempting.

She stopped thinking and met him kiss for kiss, letting the heat build as his hips ground against hers. He was already so aroused. A corner of her brain marveled that he had reacted so quickly to her. It had always taken Kyle a while to warm up. The rest of her mind was slipping beyond rational thought. Josh was offering her passion and escape. Her soul craved both.

He broke the kiss, leaving her dizzy and disoriented. She reached up to bring his head down to hers, but he refused to yield. He moved back enough to break the contact between their bodies. Without his body warmth, she felt cold. Breathless, wary of one more defeat, she turned her face into his chest. With tears burning her eyes, she absorbed the pounding of his heart.

She felt him draw a shaky breath. "I'm sorry, Hope," he said in a low, gravelly voice. "I can't lie about wanting you, but not like this. Give my ego a break, eh? I'd like to think sex with me is worth more than a diversion from your problems."

The ugly truth of his words hit her like a slap. Her knees buckled. Josh caught her, held her from falling, but there was no passion, no desire in his touch. His reserve, after his fierce embrace, brought an ache to her heart. She'd hurt him.

"Josh, I'm sorry," she muttered into his soft shirt. "I'm so, so sorry."

"Forget that," he said gruffly. "No harm done."

When he cupped her chin in his big, warm hand, she let him lift her face toward him. It amazed her that he looked concerned, not angry, even though he had every right to be. She *had* been trying to use him. She sighed. "I feel like a complete fool, going ballistic like that. And I didn't mean to... to..." She couldn't get the word *tease* past the lump in her throat.

"Hey, lighten up, will you? I'm not exactly a choirboy. I seem to recall making the first move. It was one of those things that can get out of control but didn't. Okay?"

Gratefully, she nodded. Hope sank onto the worn old couch to watch him. What a beautiful man he was. Beautifully built, lean and muscular, but more importantly, beautiful inside. Knowing she hadn't treated him very well, she let her guilt gnaw at her while he set another log on the fire.

When he turned toward her, backlit by the flames, she felt suddenly exposed to the big man towering over her, more than if she'd been naked. He'd seen her lose her composure in a way no one else had ever witnessed. He'd held her and kissed her and felt the desperation she'd never revealed to any other person. Worse by far, he'd caught her trying to use him, and had shamed her with his dignity. Could she face him now?

Josh stood in front of the couch, silently watching her, the candles casting a soft light on his rugged face. A frown creased his forehead. Was he worried that she'd fall apart again? She smiled to reassure him, feeling far from sure of herself even in the warmth of his answering smile.

His weight on the couch tipped her toward him. Would he think she was trying to throw herself at him again? She reached out to brace herself. Josh caught her hands in his and held them firmly. She met his eyes, then looked away as a new wave of shame washed over her when she recalled the way she'd kissed him. Thank God he'd had the presence of mind to stop her from making fools of both of them.

"Relax," he said softly. "Talk to me."

"You don't have to play father confessor for me, Josh. I'm used to keeping my own secrets."

"What sorts of secrets? Business problems? Hell, everyone's having business problems. Crawling out of this recession has taken everyone years longer than anyone expected. You can't blame yourself for that."

His attempt to reassure her almost brought her to tears again. "The business is fine. Thriving, in fact. People always seem to be having babies...." Her voice broke. She turned her head.

"Is that it? You're pregnant?" She couldn't hold back the short, bitter laugh. "Okay, you're not pregnant. Were you?"

It took her a moment to understand his question. She swung her head toward him, glaring. "No!"

"Hope, you'll have to help me out here. I seem to be asking the wrong questions."

Hope drew in a shaky breath. "I feel buried under all these secrets and I can't say anything to anyone, because I'm the one everyone else in the family unloads their problems on."

Josh swore under his breath, then gently stroked the backs of her hands with his thumbs. She smiled at him, trying to cover her discomfort, and tugged her hands free. Immediately, she regretted her action, but she knew putting some distance between them was the only sensible thing to do.

Josh let her pull away. At that moment, he didn't trust himself not to try to seduce her after all. He might be allergic to commitment, but he wasn't immune to beauty. He was still half-aroused, and Hope had seemed more than a little turned on herself, even if she hadn't intended to get that way.

She looked at him with those magical eyes, and he had the weird sensation that she was seeing right into his soul. "I trust you more than I trust myself. You could have taken me just now. You stopped us when I would have dragged you into bed just for the comfort of your touch. I'm sorry."

Her honesty and her sad little smile wrenched at something inside him. His shrunken conscience, probably. "Hey, don't make me into a hero. If my ego hadn't been doing the talking, we'd be in bed right now."

Hope sighed. "You know, I really need a friend, not a lover," she murmured. "Would you be my friend, Josh Kincaid?"

"I can try." To his surprise, he realized he meant it.

Chapter Five

Sunday morning, Hope tiptoed into the living room, past Josh's sprawled form on the sofa bed, to retrieve the book she'd been reading Saturday. She didn't want him to find it—especially after she'd made such a fool of herself crying over a silly movie. Just because it was about a single mother who finds a man who loves her and her tough-thinking infant! It was a miracle Josh hadn't picked up and left right then or called for the men in white coats to take her away. In fact, he'd been very sweet about it, even after she'd further humiliated herself by climbing all over him when he'd only been offering a sympathetic shoulder.

Pausing to reach for her book, Hope stole a glance at Josh. He lay on his back, one bare arm across his broad, also bare chest, the other flung out to his side. One foot poked out from the untucked end of the quilt. His dark, wavy hair was tousled around his head like a small child's, and there was a little frown line between his brows, making his handsome face look more serious in sleep than awake.

The shadow of a beard lent him an almost dangerous aura that surprised, and fascinated, her.

His frown deepened, reminding Hope that she was invading the privacy of a man who was still essentially a stranger. She moved quietly toward the kitchen to brew a pot of coffee and read until Josh woke up.

"Was I snoring?" His gravelly voice stopped her in her tracks.

Hope turned to meet his amused eyes. "Like a grizzly bear," she lied with a straight face.

Josh merely chuckled, a warm, sleepy sound. Then he sat up and stretched, which bared the rest of his chest and made the quilt pool in his lap. How could a mortal have muscles like those? Kyle spent hours in the gym and didn't look like that!

Hope felt her cheeks heat up, whether from her fascination with Josh's physique or her pathetic tendency to keep thinking about Kyle as if he set some kind of standard for masculinity, she couldn't have said. In self-defense, she turned away, speaking over her shoulder, "Coffee will be ready soon. Do you have any plans for today?"

Irrationally, because they really had no connection with each other, aside from a few shared meals and some conversation, she hoped some of his plans might include her.

"There's a place not too far where we can rent horses for a couple of hours, if you're up for that. And there's a Victoria Day carnival in one of those little towns a few miles past there. I thought that might be a good way to spend the afternoon. They'll probably have fireworks tonight, too. Interested? Or do you have a briefcase full of work stashed in the other room?"

The reminder of the nature of the material that stuffed her briefcase brought more heat to her cheeks. "No, I'm supposed to be relaxing all weekend," she told him. "I haven't been on a horse in ages. Do you think they have one that only has first gear?"

"More likely, they don't have any that have high gear. Those trail horses learn pretty quickly that they don't have to work too hard with tourists."

"You sound like you know horses."

"Yeah. I spent a few summers during college wrangling at guest ranches and outfits like the one near here that do short rides."

"I spent my summers working at the family firm. I was indoors from nine till about seven, but I usually played some tennis a few evenings a week and went swimming on weekends. It must have been fun to be outside, riding, most of the day."

Josh stretched again, then vigorously rubbed his scalp, tumbling his hair even more. "Mostly, it was damn hard work, with a lot of having to be polite to stupid tourists who didn't think about tipping the help. The horses could be jerks, too. But sometimes, a lady tourist would take a shine to me. Then the perks were pretty damn good." He flashed a wicked grin that told her exactly what kind of perks he meant.

At a loss for words, Hope shook her head in disapproval. Josh's grin widened. Then he started to throw his covers off. Face flaming at her reflexive curiosity about how much more of him was as bare as his upper body, Hope turned away quickly, retreating into the kitchen.

When Josh reappeared a little while later, he was dressed in faded jeans and a plain navy T-shirt, clean shaved, and his dark hair curled damply and wildly. He went to the refrigerator and took out eggs, milk and bacon, then began mixing batter for French toast. Once everything was ready, Hope stood beside him, placing the slices of batter-soaked bread on the hot frying pan and occasionally poking at the bacon to see how it was doing.

"I don't think I've had this much cholesterol in the entire past year," she told him as they took their seats at the kitchen table.

He shrugged. "I only eat like this on weekends when I'm not working. The rest of the week, I wolf down a couple of muffins or cold pizza, whatever's around."

"Cold pizza?" She shuddered at the thought.

He grinned. "Hey, it's got bread, vegetables, protein, and it's fast. What more could you ask for?"

"Good taste?"

"Most mornings, I'll settle for 'tastes good.' "

She smiled and sipped her coffee. "I guess you must be pretty busy. Kelowna is growing so fast."

"Yeah." He filched the last slice of bacon off the edge of her plate. "I started out with just me and an apprentice, and now I've got three crews working for me on different jobs. It's just about all I can handle. An old buddy of mine keeps trying to get me into a partnership with him—he's a general contractor—which would take some of the administrative hassles off my shoulders. But I don't like the idea of getting tied down to something." He shrugged. "Hell, what if I decide I want to move, or I want to do something else for a living? I'd be stuck with a partner. This way, I only have to answer to myself." He bit off a piece of bacon with straight, white teeth.

"And the men on those three crews."

"Well, yeah," Josh admitted after he'd swallowed. "I'm not saying I'd pick up without warning and leave everyone in the lurch. I just like knowing that I can."

Like Kyle, Hope thought bitterly, then scolded herself to get him off her mind.

"Do you do residential work or commercial?"

"Both ."

Crossing the floor to bring the coffeepot to the table, Hope spoke, "Do you know anything about computers?"

"You mean, besides the fact that they always eat your ATM card before a hot date on a Saturday night?"

She refilled his coffee mug. "You're incorrigible. I mean, is special wiring necessary for them?"

"Depends." He lifted his mug. "Thanks. Why do you ask?"

Hope sat across from him again. "Well, we've got a bunch of new computers on order for the offices, and Paul—my little brother—says we need to upgrade the wiring and do something to protect the system from power failures. But I don't know. We've had computers in the offices for years and never had a problem."

"Depends on what kind of drain you're going to put on your existing circuits. What sort of computers are you getting?"

"Beige ones." At the expression on Josh's face, Hope nearly choked on her coffee. "Seriously, that's all I know. Paul and some consultant are looking after all the details. Personally, I don't think we need new computers yet, but Paul was desperate to put his stamp on something on the firm, so Dad convinced me to let him take this on. Paul swears I'm going to love it, but I don't have any complaints about the system we have."

Josh stood and stacked their empty plates. "Tell you what. Next time I'm in your neighborhood, I'll stop by and look at what you've got. If I think you need to upgrade, I'll be happy to submit a bid. Fair enough?"

She smiled. "More than fair."

"Good. Now, let's stop talking shop and rent us a couple of trail horses. We're wasting daylight."

Josh shook hands with the wrangler who had saddled their horses, slipping him a generous tip at the same time. The other man had agreed to let them ride out unaccompanied, and had given them lively but sensible mounts. They'd followed well-worn trails, letting the horses set the pace. Now, he waited for Hope to finish hugging her horse and crooning over it as it munched the apple she'd fed it. The wrangler grinned at him in a way that said it all: *women!*

This particular woman, Josh thought as Hope finally joined him at her car, was definitely one of a kind. He'd bet anything she didn't have a clue how sexy she was. Not if she could ask him to be her friend, and *mean* it, after setting him on fire with her kisses last night. And she sure did mean *friend,* as in buddy, not as in bedmate. This was going to be a novel experience for him.

Still, he liked her enough to try. Hell, she could be fun once she stopped being so serious. Her sense of humor had surprised him more than once. And she listened as though she cared about what he was saying. He'd have talked her ear off on their trail ride if he hadn't gotten sick of the sound of his own voice.

"Where are we going?" she asked.

"There's a carnival not far from here. I can drive." He held out his hand for her keys. She moved past him as if he were invisible and opened the driver's door. "Hope?"

She slid behind the wheel and smiled sweetly. "You can navigate. I like to drive."

"Right. Because then you're in control."

"Exactly. Hurry up and get in."

Chuckling, Josh rounded the car and opened the door. "Turn right at the end of the lane."

He caught her sidelong glance as he buckled his seat belt, which he would have done after their drive over, even if it hadn't been required by law. Hope drove as if she were on a mission to save the planet and life as we know it, not as if she was going out to have fun on a Sunday.

"Does it bother you that I'm driving?" she asked, flicking another sidelong look his way.

"Nope. I'm not the control freak. Can't say I'm crazy about taking corners on two wheels, though, unless it's on a motorcycle."

Hope wrinkled her nose at him, which made him grin. She was still fun to bait.

With the windows open, they heard the carnival before they saw it. Hope slowed to a legal speed and drove into the field that was being used as a parking lot. Across the field were the usual carnival sights: the Ferris wheel and other rides, the flapping triangular banners, the lost balloons floating away. And the smells: hot dogs, popcorn, the burned sugar of cotton candy. He could hear the screams of kids being whirled and spun and dipped, and couldn't wait to join them.

Grabbing Hope's hand, he hustled toward the main gate of the carnival. By the time they reached the ticket booth, Hope was out of breath but laughing. It was, he decided, a very nice sound. And she looked pretty damn nice with her eyes sparkling and her cheeks pink. Man, he needed some heavy-duty distractions. Being friends with this woman was going to keep his libido in a constant state of attention.

"Tilt-a-Whirl or Ferris wheel?" he asked as he folded the economy-plan strip of tickets to fit into his pocket.

"Oh, God! Can't I just stick with the carousel?"

"Chicken?"

Her chin went up and her eyes narrowed. "Cautious."

That got a snort of laughter from him. "Yeah, the way you drive, you don't have a nodding acquaintance with cautious. C'mon, choose, or I'll choose for you."

"You're a bully."

"Yep. Choose." He grabbed her elbow and turned her toward the Ferris wheel, which wasn't his first choice.

"Okay, okay! The Tilt-a-Whirl."

Now, why wasn't he surprised that she'd chosen the opposite of what she thought he wanted?

A few minutes later, his smug grin had turned into a stoic grimace. The whirling ride kept plastering her all over him, making her laugh helplessly, and it felt too damn good for his peace of mind. And trying not to think about it was like trying not to think about elephants after being advised not to.

"That was fun!" she said as they staggered down the ramp when the ride was over. "Now what?"

Josh stifled a groan. "How about the Ferris wheel?"

"Sure. But if you make the car swing when we're at the top, you'll live to regret it."

"Yes, ma'am."

This time, Hope tugged him along by the hand, only letting go when they'd gotten to the end of the line. She was practically bouncing beside him, full of excited energy that surprised him. In high school, she'd barely cracked a smile, let alone gut-hugging laughter. And even though he could see she'd found a sense of humor somewhere along the way in the past sixteen years, he hadn't expected this kind of animation. It was, unfortunately, kind of appealing to see her loosen up like this.

The sound of a kid blubbering broke into his thoughts. Then something grabbed at one knee of his jeans. Josh looked down into the tear-streaked face of a dirty little cherub of indeterminate gender. The kid blinked, then screwed up its face and began to howl, still clutching a handful of jeans. Josh felt bad. He didn't normally think of himself as someone who scared little kids. Even on Halloween, they never took his Dracula act seriously.

"Oh, dear," Hope murmured. "Looks like someone got lost." She crouched beside the kid, who clutched Josh's jeans harder and howled louder.

Josh dislodged the sticky little hand and knelt so he was almost eye to eye with the kid. "Hey," he said gently, "what's up, sport? You lookin' for Mom and Dad?"

The toddler's eyes and mouth went round, but the howling stopped in midbellow. It was, Josh suspected, a boy. A grubby thumb popped into the open mouth, and the tousled head nodded. Josh grimaced at the thought of putting that much dirt into the digestive system of anything more highly evolved than an earthworm. But something about the kid got to him. He met Hope's eyes and saw she was smiling as if the kid was something very special.

Josh cupped the kid's dirty little elbow in his palm. "Want me to pick you up so you can look for them from way up?" Hope's expression told him he'd said the right thing.

Again, the kid nodded, his mouth firmly corked by that thumb. Josh grasped the little body under the arms and stood, amazed at how light the kid was. With his free hand clutching Josh's hair, the kid held on like a little monkey. Josh held him high, breathing in the scent of dirt, ketchup, laundry detergent and little boy, and hoping the kid spotted his parents before he had another panic attack. Hope, standing again, was patting the kid's back and murmuring encouragement for him to look for his mommy.

"Josh! Oh, Josh!" a woman's frantic voice called. Josh swung toward the sound, wondering who could know him out here. "Oh, my baby, where did you go? I was so worried!"

Mystery solved. Here was Mom. The toddler squirmed and kicked his feet, thumping Josh in the chest with his little red running shoes. The woman who appeared breathlessly at his side looked so much like the kid that there was no question who she was. Gratefully, Josh lowered the boy into her reaching arms. The toddler clutched his mother around the neck and buried his face in her hair.

"Hey, sport," Josh said. The boy didn't turn around. Josh patted his little back the way Hope had done, but awkwardly. "My name's Josh, too. Isn't that funny?"

The mother gave him a megawatt smile. "He's too young to appreciate that, but I'm very grateful." She hugged her son tighter. "Joshie, say bye to Big Josh."

They settled for a wave and a goofy smile that brought a lump to Josh's throat. He turned back to Hope and shrugged at her smug expression. Then it was their turn to get into one of the swinging baskets of the Ferris wheel.

Suddenly, Josh was stepping back in time. Where to put his arm? Over the back of the seat, where it could fortuitously fall onto Hope's shoulders? Or at his side, which was cramped and no fun at all. He opted for over the back of the seat, which had always been a good move for a guy with a pretty girl on the Ferris wheel.

The basket jerked backward as the next one reached the landing. ''Big Josh, huh?'' Hope murmured.

''Say that again, and all bets are off about rocking this boat,'' he warned.

Her laughter warmed him in places he didn't know he had. Somehow, he survived the ride, even with Hope's scent wafting to him on the breeze, even with the press of her hip and thigh against his. And he survived the ride on the carousel, and the sight of her eating her hot dog reminding him of the way her mouth felt under his and the way she grabbed his arm in excitement when he won the biggest damn stuffed polar bear he'd ever seen in his carnival-game career. It hardly fit into the back seat of her car.

And then the sun was going down and it was time to find a good vantage point for watching the fireworks in honor of Queen Victoria. He carried the blanket they'd brought, following Hope through the crush of people. She led him to a spot in the middle of hundreds of other blankets. He shook his head.

''C'mon over this way. It's less crowded.''

He led her to a small knoll, then spread out the blanket. She sat on one side. He sank down onto the other. In the darkening sky, he could see the evening star. It wouldn't be long before it was dark enough for fireworks. Not for the first time, he wished he hadn't given his word so quickly to be Hope's friend. After spending the day with her like this, he sure as hell wouldn't mind ending it with some fireworks of their own. But, he reminded himself, that wasn't the way the script went. Well, what the hell? He knew plenty of other women who didn't want to be his pal.

"You were very good with little Josh," Hope said.

He shrugged. "Poor kid was lost and scared. It was no big deal."

"It was to him. And to his mother."

"Yeah, well, like I said, it was no big deal." He lay back and propped his head up in his cupped hands, emptying his thoughts of anything more taxing than memories of the morning's trail ride. It might take a while to get his cabin built, but he sure was going to enjoy having his own little piece of this place.

Hope turned to look down at him, the movement catching his attention. The little frown line between her eyes warned him that she had something on her mind. "Have you ever thought about having kids?"

He snorted a sharp laugh, mainly at himself for not seeing that one coming. "Good thing we agreed to be friends. That kind of question usually gets me looking for the exit ASAP."

"I'm familiar with that reaction," she muttered, sounding surprisingly bitter.

"Well, hell, Hope, not every guy wants to be a father."

"Apparently." Now she sounded as if she'd been sucking on a lemon.

"Not every guy is cut out to be a father."

"True. But I couldn't help wondering, since you seemed to have a rapport with little Josh."

He angled himself up on one elbow but he still couldn't see into her face. "I don't dislike kids," he told her. "In fact, I really like other people's kids, 'cause I can give 'em back."

"Oh," she said softly, and didn't say another word until the first fireworks display drew the obligatory "Oooh!" out of her. After that, they both lay back on the blanket, not quite touching, and watched until the last explosion of light had faded to a trail of smoke and the smell of cordite.

It would have been easy, he thought in between fireworks, to get into the mood. Easy, lying near Hope, knowing that her kisses could set off fireworks in his libido, to fool himself into thinking he could have anything more than friendship with her. She made him ache physically, which was something he didn't mind as long as there was something he could do to relieve the ache. Lust was safe enough, when practiced with the proper precautions.

But Hope touched him emotionally in places he didn't want to be touched, and that wasn't safe. Not for either of them. He knew himself well enough by now to know he'd want to take off as soon as he felt the net tightening, and that would hurt Hope the way that jerk Kyle had hurt her. He didn't want to hurt her. He wanted to protect her and make her laugh.

That impulse alone, he realized, was enough to make him want to cut and run. That wasn't like him. Not the way he saw himself. Being around Hope for only a couple of days could be changing him, changing the way he thought and felt. He didn't like that idea one little bit. He'd seen too many guys changed—and not for the better—by women they thought they loved. Next thing a guy knows, he's trapped into a life-style, an identity, that isn't really his. Look at his father, he reminded himself. A classic case. A visionary turned into a drudge by a demanding wife who'd forced him to settle down. No way he was going to stick with a woman who tied him down and tried to change him the way his father had stuck with his mother, making the three of them miserable out of a misplaced sense of loyalty and responsibility.

Still, when Hope turned to him in the darkness, after the fireworks were over and the crowd was starting to rise and leave, he felt the tiniest, scary temptation to pull her into his arms and take his chances.

Fortunately for both of them, he was a Teflon kinda guy, so that urge slid off him even before he'd stood up to haul Hope to her feet and fold the blanket.

Monday morning, after Hope had washed and dressed, she came into the living room to find the sofa bed made up and the bedding Josh had been using piled neatly on it. There were no lights on in the kitchen, and no sign of Josh or his belongings anywhere in the small cabin. With her heart sinking, she stepped out onto the front porch, into a shimmeringly bright morning, and looked across the field to the property where he planned to build his own cabin. His van was gone.

"Doesn't that figure," she muttered, tamping down her hurt feelings. "As soon as you tell a guy you only want to be friends, he gets carried off by aliens." To be fair, she thought, he had said he'd be leaving fairly early that day to get a head start on returning holiday traffic. But she'd assumed that *early* meant before dinner, not before breakfast.

Back inside the kitchen, she made a pot of coffee, then started to clean out the refrigerator in preparation for the trip back to Kelowna. There wasn't much food left, since she and Josh had been sharing supplies, although he'd left his beer and one bottle of wine. Perhaps he'd left them behind as a consolation for deserting her without a goodbye, or, if she were being more generous minded, as a thanks for her hospitality.

When the coffee was ready, she filled a mug, then shook dry cereal into a bowl and poured on the little bit of milk that was left. With a book on the joys of single motherhood propped open in front of her, Hope absently ate cereal and sipped coffee while she read. As if her thoughts were a sound track playing over the words on the page, she kept thinking about her own situation. And the more she thought about it, the more certain she became that she could—and would—have a baby on her own.

A noise at the door startled a yelp out of her. "Coffee smells good," Josh called from the front room. "Got some homemade pie to go with it."

Even as his booted footsteps were coming closer, Hope was frantically searching for a place to hide her book. Her instincts told her that Josh would tease her mercilessly if he had a hint of what was on her mind. Just before he came into the kitchen, she stuffed the book under the groceries she'd been packing into a small carton. Standing, she smiled and reached for plates.

"What a great idea," she said much too brightly. "Where did you find homemade pie?"

"I saw a sign yesterday when you were imitating a low-flying aircraft. so I figured we'd end the weekend with something special." He filled a mug with coffee for himself, then looked at the now-empty pot. "You only made two cups?" She met his questioning eyes, then looked away as a blush warmed her cheeks. "You thought I'd taken off, huh? O, ye of little faith."

Hope shrugged and started to make more coffee, since she could use a second cup herself. "Your van was gone. Your stuff was gone. Even the dirty socks were gone. How was I supposed to know what you were up to?"

"Faith."

She shot him a look that she hoped expressed the exasperation she felt. "I hardly know you, for pity's sake! Why should I have faith that you'd be back with a pie?"

He slid the pie onto a large plate. "I didn't say goodbye, did I?"

"That in itself doesn't indicate that you didn't *mean* goodbye."

He sighed. "Okay. You're right. I should have woke you at dawn to tell you I was going to be back, so you could keep sleeping."

Hope sliced into the still-warm apple pie with a large knife. "You could admit you were wrong not to even leave a note."

He sat in what she had come to think of as "his" chair and grinned crookedly. "Honey, when you're holding a knife that sharp, I'll admit to anything."

Realizing that he had, in fact, conceded the point while trying to save face, Hope served him a huge slice of pie and sat opposite him to eat her much smaller portion. After they'd eaten, Josh helped her tidy the cabin and pack up the perishables. Reluctant to leave immediately, Hope suggested they take a walk. She matched her pace to Josh's easy stroll, and found herself breathing in the sweet air, listening to the birds and trying to store the sights in her memory. Back at work, back in her real life, with everything closing in on her, she had a feeling she'd want to conjure up these pastoral images and relive the soothing sense of peace that this place gave her.

All too soon, however, Josh was heading them back toward the cabin. "Time to hit the road." He paused and turned in a slow circle, scanning the sky, the horizon and, finally, smiling down at Hope. "This was a good weekend, in spite of my RV's belly flop. Think you'll be coming out here again any time this summer? I'll be starting work on my cabin soon, so I'll be here most weekends as long as the weather is good." He shrugged. "Hell, even if it isn't, the fishing will be good."

Hope smiled, but she felt a sense of loss. "I doubt it. This is going to be a very busy summer. Paul's wedding, and all the things that lead up to it. But I'll know where to find you if I can get away." They started walking back toward the cabin. "And maybe I'll see you in Kelowna. It's not exactly a huge place."

"Sure. I promised to stop by and check out your wiring, remember?"

"Right. Whenever you're in my neighborhood." It was, she knew, a variation on that classic male line, *I'll call you.* And it shouldn't, she told herself sternly, mean a thing to her whether he would or wouldn't.

And sure enough, when Josh was ready to leave, he cupped Hope's chin in his big hand and tipped her face up toward his. Then, very softly, he brushed his lips over hers, and murmured, "I'll call you."

And if she believed that, Hope thought with a twinge of sadness as his van drove out of sight, there was a bridge in Brooklyn for sale at a bargain price.

Chapter Six

Josh hit the Rewind button on his answering machine and shrugged back into his jacket. The other messages could wait. His mother's call about her fridge not working couldn't. He drove the twenty minutes to their modest house, trying to think of any woman he'd dated who could distract him from his fantasies about Hope. By the time he was letting himself into the house, he still couldn't think of one who made the memory of her kisses fade. Oh, well, he thought. He'd never been one to shrink from a challenge. There had to be a woman in Kelowna who was Hope's equal, one with no strings attached.

"Hi, Mom," he called into the house. His mother hurried out of the kitchen smiling. She hugged him as if she hadn't seen him in years instead of days. "What's the problem?"

After a firm kiss on his cheek, she released him. "The refrigerator is turned as high as it can go, but it doesn't feel as cool as it's supposed to. And the freezer seems to be defrosting. The ice cream is like soup."

He followed her into the kitchen. She went to the sink, which was full of steaming suds, and scrubbed at a pot. His father was sitting at the table, a cup of coffee beside a notepad, pencil poised, a faraway expression on his face. Odd pieces of paper lay scattered across the table. It was a familiar scene.

"Hello, son. Coffee?"

"Sure."

"Ruth, get the boy some coffee. I could use a refill myself," his father said. "I would have had a look at the thing, but you know how I am about motors. Don't understand them one little bit. Good thing you take after your mother's side there."

Josh grinned. His father had a million investment ideas, but when it came to mechanics, he didn't understand even a hammer. "No problem. I'll do what I can."

As usual, he started with the simplest, most obvious possible causes of mechanical failures. Opening the refrigerator, he listened to the hum of the motor, which didn't sound right. His mother handed him a mug of steaming coffee, then crossed the room to replace his father's mug. Then she came back to stand beside him, her face deeply creased in a frown.

"I hope it isn't anything serious," she said. "Repairs are so expensive."

Josh opened the freezer. "Let's take this stuff out first," he suggested. "I have an idea."

His mother began pulling containers of her homemade sauces and casseroles off the freezer shelves. She piled some of them on the kitchen table. His father looked up and frowned. With a sigh, she moved the containers to the counter. "The man hates distractions," she muttered under her breath. "For the life of me, I don't know what this is distracting him from."

It was the same old refrain, Josh thought as he took several soft cans of orange juice from the top shelf. His mother never understood that his father needed peace to think. She was always complaining, always nagging the poor man to be more practical. Hell, she'd forced Josh to learn to cook and do his own laundry when he was a kid, going on and on about how she wouldn't have her son turn into a carbon copy of her husband. Not that he wasn't glad he could take care of himself now that he was on his own. But he hated the way she put the old man down. Maybe if she'd believed in him more, Henry Kincaid would have seen some of his dreams and schemes come true.

The protective cover over the freezer fan shifted, then fell off. Immediately, the fan began to spin. The motor stopped moaning and began to hum. Josh grinned at his mother.

"There's your problem. You had something wedged too tight against this plastic, so the fan couldn't turn."

His mother set the container she was carrying down on the table a little heavily. "You see, Henry? If you paid more attention to the way you crammed things into the freezer instead of thinking about pie in the sky, we wouldn't have had to drag Josh out in the middle of the night."

His father looked up, his expression surprised. "Well, Ruth, I guess if I can't do a thing right, I shouldn't do it at all," he said mildly.

Josh tuned out their voices and turned his attention to fitting the fan cover correctly. His mother then restocked the freezer with the containers she'd removed, her lips drawn into a tight, thin line the whole time she worked. When the freezer was full again, she looked at Josh, and her face relaxed a little.

"Thanks, honey. I always know I can count on you." She put her hand on his arm and smiled. "So, are you seeing anyone special these days?"

He shoved aside the thought of Hope's sparkling eyes, her honeyed kisses, and gave a little snort of a laugh instead. "Nothing's changed since you asked last week," he lied.

Her smile gone, she shook her head. "One of these days you're going to wake up a lonely old man."

"Better than waking up a disappointed old man," his father muttered. "Leave the boy alone, Ruth. He's got his choice of pretty girls, and he's got his freedom. Plenty of time for him to get himself tied up in obligations and responsibilities. Let him enjoy his youth."

"He's thirty-four, Henry! Not fourteen."

"Or twenty-two," his father countered. That was, Josh knew, the age his father had been when his parents had married.

His mother's face went tight again.

"Hey, I have to get up early tomorrow," he said before they could start another round of bickering with him in the middle. He drove home yawning, but instead of thinking of ways to—as his father put it—enjoy his youth, he found himself thinking of excuses to see Hope again. Well, hell, he finally asked himself, what's wrong with a man wanting to spend time with a friend?

Tuesday noon, Hope's secretary, Milly, stuck her head in the doorway of Hope's office. "Have you stopped to breathe this morning?"

Hope blew a stray wisp of hair off her forehead and leaned back in her chair. "No. Was I supposed to?" she replied with a grin.

Milly, having been secretary to Hope's father for twenty years, was like a second mother, which was both a blessing and a curse. She knew where everything was, who everyone was, and kept Hope on top of the business. But she also fussed and nagged about Hope's incessant work schedule, her haphazard mealtimes and her single status.

Milly shook her head. "For you, it's an option. Are you going to get out of this place for lunch, or shall I order you a nice, healthy salad plate? It's a gorgeous day, you know." The older woman made a wry face. "Or you would know, if you'd turn around and look out your windows."

"I looked." Hope smiled. "Looking out the window was pencilled in on my agenda. Now it's ticked off, so I can go back to work. Don't bother with a salad. I've got some yogurt—" Milly raised her hand, her set expression reminding her that arguing was a waste of breath. "Okay. I give up. A crab salad, hold the onions, and a diet cola."

Hope nearly laughed at the satisfied look on Milly's face. "I'm going to check to see that you finish," Milly warned. "Honestly, Hope, you were only out of the office Friday. We were closed yesterday. It doesn't look to me as if we're that far behind. Besides, Paul was in on Friday, taking care of the routine matters. You work harder than your father, which I never thought humanly possible."

"I don't want to let him down," she declared. "Paul hasn't been working here long enough to know what he needs to know."

"He'll learn faster if you give him real work to do, dear. Your father doesn't expect you to be what he spent thirty years working himself up to."

Hope shrugged. "Chalk it up to the overachieving-first-child syndrome. I've got some calls to return now, so reception can answer any incoming calls while you have your lunch."

"Okay, dear. And I'll order your lunch now." Milly started to duck back out of Hope's office, half turned, then said, "Oh! Oh, my! May I help you?"

Hope couldn't help being curious. She'd never heard Milly use that tone, almost fluttery, as if Gregory Peck had materialized in the outer office. She heard the rumble of a low male voice, then watched Milly smooth her perfectly coiffed short silver hairstyle.

"Yes, of course, go right in," Milly said, still fluttery, opening Hope's door wider and stepping aside.

To Hope's astonishment, Josh filled the doorway, his cocky grin lighting his eyes. He wore a chest-and-shoulder-hugging black T-shirt, faded jeans that molded to his body and one of those tan leather tool holsters that defined his narrow hips and drew attention to the front of those explicit jeans. Hope felt her jaw drop and snapped it shut. Then she felt her cheeks grow warm.

"I was in the neighborhood," he announced, his grin growing even wider. "Figured I'd check out your circuits."

Overheating, Hope thought. Her circuits were definitely trying to carry too much electricity at once, because her brain seemed to have shorted out. How else could she explain forgetting how appealing Josh was after not seeing him for only sixteen hours? How else could she explain this ridiculous reaction to the sight of him, when they'd already agreed, at her insistence, that they would only be friends? She knew very well that there could be no other sensible course of action for her, not at this point in time. But looking at Josh made her wish she could eat her cake and have it, too.

He used to pride himself on his memory, Josh thought while grinning stupidly at Hope, but somehow, he'd managed to forget in less than a day how beautiful she was. Good thing he'd decided to show up as soon as possible. With surprise on his side, he might have a chance to convince her to drop the whole idea of being "just friends." Friends didn't rob friends of much-needed sleep by starring in X-rated fantasies.

"Oh," Hope answered with a funny little gasp that made him wonder if his fantasies were more mutual than he'd first suspected. That would be nice. He had lots of women friends, some of them even former lovers now attached to men friends. But he'd never had a friend knock his socks off the way Hope did. Maybe he'd find some way to be her friend *and* her lover.

He had a feeling that would take being far more devious than he liked to be. He was always up front with women he dated: his intentions were strictly dishonorable. He was there for a good time, not a long time. Sometimes, however, they forgot. Sometimes, they heard what they wanted to hear instead of what he was saying. But he never misled them, and he always let them down gently when they tried to take more than he was willing to give. A real knight in shining Teflon. So why did it bother him that Hope didn't want to start something he didn't intend to finish?

"If you can find out what kind of computers your brother ordered, how many and where he plans to install them, I can give you an idea of—"

"Hope?" A woman's voice from the outer office cut off his words. Hope winced and whispered a mild curse. "Hope, darling, what on earth has happened?"

A shorter, rounder, older version of Hope burst through the doorway, nearly plowing into him. "Excuse me, young man," she said, barely looking at him. "Hope, darling, why didn't you tell me about Kyle? I feel awful."

Hope's expression looked like equal parts embarrassment and desperation, Josh thought. He turned away, not wanting to make the situation worse for her. Assuming it could get worse.

"I'm sorry, Mother," Hope murmured. "I didn't want to trouble you."

"Trouble me? Hope, honey, it's *you* I'm worried about! The formal-rental store just called to tell me Kyle canceled his tuxedo order, so I phoned him at his office. He said the two of you broke up and he's no longer planning on taking part in Paul's wedding. To think we were ready to welcome that . . . that *rat* into the family!"

While Hope's mother was speaking, Josh crossed the office and crouched at the electrical junction box mounted on the wall. He stole a peek at Hope. Her white face made him feel guilty for eavesdropping, but he couldn't push past her mother without calling more attention to himself.

"Kyle, um, we, ah," Hope stammered. She took a breath and started again. "I know I should have told you sooner. We're going to be an usher short, which puts Paul on the spot if he has to ask someone at the last minute. I was thinking of calling Kyle and asking him to come to the wedding anyway."

Josh bit back a curse and stood. Both women turned to stare at him. He forced himself not to glare at Hope for being so stupid. How could she even consider begging that slime ball to go to the wedding with her? Didn't the woman have any self-respect? Or did she care too much for other people's feelings? Either way, he knew exactly what to do to save the situation.

"Forget Kyle, Hope. I'll take his place." He grinned. "I clean up pretty good, and I've had a lot of experience at weddings."

Hope's expression was priceless. He was tempted to warn her that she'd catch flies if she kept her mouth open like that.

"Who are you?" Mrs. Delacorte demanded.

"Oh! Sorry, Mother." Hope's cheeks turned bright pink. "This is Josh Kincaid, the electrician I told you about. We went to high school together, and he bought the lot next to the Wilsons' cabin, so we just met this weekend for the first time in, what was it?" She looked at him for help.

"Sixteen years," Josh told her mother.

"I don't recall Hope ever mentioning you back then," Mrs. Delacorte told him, her eyes checking him out the way he'd examine a faulty connection.

He winked in Hope's direction. "We weren't exactly friends, ma'am. Hope was too smart for me, and I was too wild for her."

Hope's mother shook her head. "Well, it looks like Hope has become less smart and you've grown less wild."

"Mother!"

"Hope, darling, Paul's wedding is two weeks away, and, as you say, we're now an usher short, which means we're short an escort for you. If this young man cleans up as well as he claims, and Paul doesn't mind, I think we should accept his offer. He is, after all, an old friend, isn't he?" Mrs. Delacorte beckoned him toward her with a graceful crook of her finger. As he approached, she tipped her head back to look into his face. "Do I have your word that you're reliable?"

"Yes, ma'am." He was beginning to feel like a fly who had buzzed too close to a spider. Mrs. Delacorte was a hell of a lot less in need of protection than her daughter thought.

"Thank you, young man. Hope, introduce him to Paul. Josh, you'll have to phone the formal-rental store and tell them you'll be in today before closing for a fitting. Now, if Paul is agreeable, do you have a good suit? You'll need one for the rehearsal and dinner after."

"Yes, ma'am. Navy pinstripe."

She patted his cheek with cool fingers. "You'll do nicely." Mrs. Delacorte turned to face Hope. "All right, darling. I'm leaving. We'll see you for dinner. Seven sharp." She smiled at him. "Bring Josh, if possible. Your father will need time to get used to the substitution." A second later, she breezed out of the office.

That went pretty well, Josh thought, then glanced at Hope and wondered if he should run for cover. Apparently, she wasn't nearly as pleased as he was. Sparks lit her eyes as she leapt to her feet. As long as he was out of range of actual bodily damage, he could admire the way her anger turned up the wattage. She definitely had fire under that cool surface. It made her a lot more exciting, he decided, than the women he'd known who wanted to please so badly that they erased all evidence of their own passion.

* * *

"Are you out of your mind?"

He had the nerve to look puzzled. "Why? I just saved your bacon. Does that make me crazy?"

"You stepped into something that didn't have anything to do with you. Kyle and my parents are *my* problem, and I don't recall asking you to solve my problems for me."

He shook his head and grinned. "You're just ticked off because something happened that you didn't have any control over. Hell, Hope, your mother's happy with my offer, and she was going ballistic before I offered. And this way, you don't have to go crawling back to Kyle to ask him to play a role he doesn't want."

That stung. She hadn't expected Josh to be cruel. "What a rotten thing to say! I have no intentions of *crawling* back to Kyle to beg a favor. I plan to approach him with dignity and appeal to whatever decency he has left. He must feel some sense of obligation to my family, to me, even if he doesn't want to make our relationship permanent. After all, we lived together for four years."

Was it her imagination, or did Josh wince at her last words? Well, he'd do more than wince when she finished giving him a piece of her mind. How dare he? And her *mother?* How could she be so thoughtless about Paul and Elaine, asking a total stranger to be an usher at their wedding? And how could either of them have assumed it would be a fait accompli without even asking her? Didn't she have any say in the matter of whom she went to her own brother's wedding with, whom she spent the evening with? To be fair, Josh didn't know her at all, but her mother certainly knew how she hated to have people making plans for her as if she were a piece of furniture to be rearranged.

"Don't do it, Hope," Josh said earnestly. "Don't lower yourself. I'll go talk to Paul." He paused, studying her. "Unless you want to try to patch things up with that creep."

Hope glared at Josh. "Don't you have work to do?"

He grinned with maddening smugness. "Yes, ma'am." He turned toward her office door, then looked back over his shoulder. "You have very old wiring here. Introduce me to Paul and tell him what's happening. Once we've settled the wedding stuff, I'll find out what computers Paul ordered, then submit a bid."

Before she could tell him not to bother about bids, because she never wanted to see him again, Josh was grasping her hand and towing her out of the office.

"Well, m' dear," Hope's father said, pushing his chair back from the dining room table, "that was a wonderful dinner, as usual, and I'm delighted that Hope could find the time to join us. But Seattle is playing Toronto, and I hear the remote control calling me." He kissed his wife's cheek and winked at Hope.

Hope met her mother's eyes and smiled. "We'll call you for coffee," she told her father, who had already started clearing the table. Hope took a handful of cutlery from him and shooed him out of the kitchen.

"That man and his baseball," Hope's mother sighed. "You'd think he owned the Seattle team."

Hope chuckled. "Don't give him any ideas."

She and her mother finished tidying the kitchen, then sat at the breakfast counter of the granite-topped cooking island to wait for the coffee to brew.

"I know it's early yet, but I'm sure you'll want to plan a baby shower for Chantelle," her mother said. Somehow, Hope kept her expression neutral. "I wonder if it would be inappropriate to have a shower for Gail."

"I think it would," Hope answered. "This is her fourth, after all."

Her mother sighed, a happy smile on her still-pretty face. "Yes, it is. And I've no doubt that Elaine will want to start a family soon, too." She patted Hope's hand. "That only leaves you. I had hoped you and Kyle... I don't suppose there's any chance..."

Hope shook her head vehemently.

"Oh, honey, isn't it possible to reconcile? I know he wasn't happy about the hours you were spending at work. If you turned over some of the responsibility of the firm to Paul, do you think he'd—?"

Hope shook her head vehemently. "Take me back?" she interrupted, ignoring her mother's mildly chiding expression. "I wouldn't take *him* back." She was on the verge of saying something about the real reasons for their breakup, then caught herself. Her mother had enough worries just with the wedding. "Besides, he's already seeing someone else."

"So soon?"

"It wasn't that soon, really. We broke up in February." The coffee was ready. Hope stood and went to the cabinet for cups and saucers. She started pouring the coffee into the first cup, grateful for the excuse not to have to meet her mother's eyes.

"Oh! I thought it was more recent than that."

Hope's hand jerked, spilling coffee onto the counter. She bit her lip to keep from speaking the mild curse that sprang to her mind. "Mother, I'm sorry. I just couldn't figure out how to tell you without upsetting you."

"Well, I certainly was upset, and I still am. I don't like to think of anyone hurting my children. Now, I hope this Josh person is a decent human being. He's a handsome young man. And he has very nice manners." Her mother paused, drew a breath, then shook her head. "I'm sure the boys will work things out, as long as Elaine and her family aren't put out." Her mother sighed. "I hope they aren't. After all, no one but the family needs to know the truth. It's no one else's business."

Hope winced. "I'm certainly not going to offer any explanations. Everyone should focus on Paul and Elaine. As far as I'm concerned, the rest of us are decorations."

Her mother smiled. "I'm grateful Josh volunteered. He is rather good-looking, in a rugged sort of way. Not as polished as Kyle, mind you, but I don't think we'll have cause to complain, as long as he doesn't belch out loud or eat with his fingers."

In spite of herself, Hope laughed out loud. *"Mother!* Honestly! Sometimes, you astonish me."

Her mother looked entirely too pleased with herself for Hope's peace of mind. "Getting back to Chantelle's shower, I know you'll plan something wonderful for her. Poor girl, she's wanted children for so long. We'll give her a nice gift certificate for whatever she wants from KidsCan Togs, of course. It's always special to have the ones you love dressing their babies in our clothes." Once again, her mother breathed a heavy sigh. "I suppose by the time you can give me grandchildren, we'll be making our products out of space-age fibers tested on moon walks."

Her mother's gentle teasing cut into Hope's heart, leaving pain, and surprise at how much pain. Hope longed to confide in her mother, needed to share her anguish, her frustration. Her mother would understand. She would fold Hope into her arms and comfort her as only a mother could. All it would take was the momentary courage to confess why Kyle had walked out on her to explain the decisions she'd made over the weekend, and to ask for her mother's support.

Hope watched her mother arrange creamer and sugar bowl on the tray with the coffee cups. "Mother?" she began hesitantly.

Her mother didn't look up. "Yes, darling?"

Hope's courage deserted her. "I'll carry that," she said instead. This wasn't the time, she rationalized, to dump her enormous problems on her mother, especially when she was so involved with Paul's wedding. There would be plenty of time to try again later. Or not. Wishing she could kick herself and walk at the same time, she carried the tray into the spacious family room, where her father sat mesmerized by the baseball game. He accepted his cup of coffee with hearty thanks, but his gaze never left the extralarge TV screen.

"Hello? Anybody home?" Paul's voice drifted in from the front of the house.

Hope's mother was out of her chair and hurrying down the hallway before Hope had a chance to set her own cup down. She heard their voices rising and falling, but there seemed to be an extra voice. Probably, she guessed, her brother-in-law, Tom, who occasionally escaped his wife and three girls to watch a game with her father. The crack of a well-hit baseball brought her attention back to the TV, where one of the Toronto players was trotting rather smugly around the bases. Just to rub it in for disgruntled Seattle Mariner fans like her father, the instant replay followed the Blue Jay runner's triumphant arrival at his own dugout, where everyone high-fived everyone else. She hid her smile at her father's heartfelt groan.

"Come meet Hope's father," her mother said as she breezed into the room.

Startled, Hope looked up, right into Josh Kincaid's amused blue eyes. For a moment, all she could do was stare, her thoughts scattered.

"Marcus, darling? I'd like you to meet someone." Her father tore his gaze from the screen. "Marcus, this young man is Josh Kincaid, an old friend of Hope's from high school. He's going to take Kyle's place as an usher for Paul's wedding. Josh, this is my husband, Marcus Delacorte."

Josh strode across the family room to shake hands with her father, who grinned, then stopped grinning, dropped Josh's hand and started sputtering. "Who? He's what? Kyle who? Kyle Lewis? Hope's Kyle? Why would this boy take Kyle's place? Emily, what's going on here?"

"I was waiting for the right time to tell you, dear. Kyle won't be in Paul's wedding party, so Josh volunteered to take his place as usher."

Hope's father actually switched off the TV. He glared at her. "And why the hell isn't Kyle going to be in Paul's wedding party?"

Hope froze. She couldn't force herself to say the words "He left me" one more time. She met Josh's eyes, feeling helpless until he winked.

"Well, sir," he said, "it seems this Kyle guy is too stupid to know a good thing when he had it, so he and Hope aren't together anymore. But since Hope and I know each other from 'way back, and it's okay with Paul and Elaine, I'm happy to step in."

Her father swung his glare away from her and aimed it at Josh. "You follow the Mariners?"

"Yes, sir, I do."

"Sit down, then." He picked up the remote control. "Paul, you, too. Won't have many chances to sit around watching a game with your old father after you get married." The TV flared to life as Josh and Paul took their seats.

Hope's mother gave her a look that bespoke affectionate amusement. "Can I get you fellows coffee?" she asked.

Josh swiveled around to smile at her and her mother. "Yes, ma'am. Thanks."

The look her mother gave her then suggested that Kyle was fast becoming a faded memory in the Delacorte family history.

Chapter Seven

Bemused, Hope stared after her mother's retreating back for a long moment. Finally, she moved into the kitchen to pour coffee for Paul and Josh. She added two heaping teaspoons of sugar and a fair amount of cream to Paul's coffee, then set the two mugs on the tray her mother had been piling with cookies.

"I see you know Josh well enough," her mother said dryly.

Hope glanced down at the black coffee intended for him and felt herself blush. No one else in the family took black coffee. "I know how Chantelle and Tom and my secretary take their coffee, too."

Her mother just laughed lightly. "Come back and sit with me for a while, dear. I can't bear listening to your father trying to coach the players."

Paul accepted his coffee with his eyes fixed on the TV. But when Hope set Josh's mug down beside him, he caught her wrist in his long fingers. Startled, she met his eyes. He winked, then released her wrist. Hope retreated into the kitchen without a clue as to the meaning of that wink but wanting to wring Paul's neck for bringing Josh home with him. Fortunately, their father had reacted well to the changes in wedding plans. But Hope felt she should have been the one to tell him, even if it meant having to explain about Kyle. The fact that Josh had done it with more grace and tact than she probably would have only increased her annoyance. She didn't like surprises. And she didn't like people taking over for her.

For the next hour, Hope chatted with her mother. Torn between happiness and jealousy for both her sister and her best friend, she talked about their pregnancies and tried to hide her feelings. Her mother was so blissful about being a grandmother again, and about Chantelle's success after so many failures, that Hope doubted she'd notice anything amiss in her oldest daughter's manner. When she was able to steer her mother onto the topic of their annual design-planning event, in which they invited mothers and children to come to the plant and offer suggestions, Hope felt a little less brittle. Even that subject made her restless, however, because she'd be spending a full morning surrounded by local moms and their kids.

Once again, she stifled the urge to confide in her mother. With all the excitement about Paul's wedding and Gail's and Chantelle's pregnancies, her problems would only cast a pall over the prevailing happiness. Besides, she couldn't imagine what her mother would think of the solution she'd settled on.

Actually, Hope thought, she *could* imagine her mother's reaction, not to mention her father's, and it wouldn't be pleasant. No, best not to spoil her mother's joy with bad news and a decision that was sure to be upsetting. So Hope steered the conversation toward neutral topics and kept her problems to herself.

Eventually, the game ended, with the Seattle Mariners losing by a margin that had the three men grumbling as they wandered into the kitchen.

"More coffee?" Hope's mother offered. "It's decaf."

Josh smiled. "No, thanks. I should be going."

"Hey, Hope, can you give Josh a ride back to his van?" Paul grabbed her loosely braided hair and tugged gently. He was wearing his most winsome expression, the one no one ever seemed able to resist. "He's parked at the lot, and I've gotta go in the opposite direction."

She glanced at Josh, who gave her a shrug. Hope sighed. "Yes, I suppose so. Ready?"

Josh nodded, then turned to her parents and told them how glad he was to meet them. Hope's father beamed. Her mother fluttered. Josh clapped Paul on the shoulder, nearly knocking him over. Then they shook hands, grinning widely, causing Hope to grit her teeth. She kissed her parents and thanked her mother for dinner. Paul trailed behind them as they walked toward the front door. Josh stepped outside first. Paul held Hope back with a touch on her arm.

"Hey, uh, thanks for taking care of things the way you did. Probably for the best, anyway. Kyle is a schmuck. He didn't deserve you. Josh is cool. He even said he'd come to the stag the guys are planning."

"I'm sure that won't be a hardship for him," she muttered.

"What?"

"Nothing. Sorry. I'm tired." She stepped down to the walk, then turned back to smile at Paul. "I'm glad you don't mind the way this worked out. I should have said something ages ago. It could have been very awkward."

"Nah." He gave her a touchingly sweet smile. "I understand. Anyway, you always manage to make things right, no matter who screws up."

His words brought tears to her eyes, which she knew would embarrass him. Blinking rapidly, she gave his arm a light poke. "Just doing my job," she told him brightly, hoping he wouldn't hear the sudden thickness in her throat caused by emotion. "I better go."

She made her way down the driveway to her car, where Josh already sat in the passenger seat. The sight of him reminded her that he'd somehow made it past her objections to take Kyle's place. And he'd wormed his way into her family's good graces, too. He'd probably even set the evening up so that she'd be forced to drive him back to his van. She couldn't imagine why, but he must be up to something. If she'd learned nothing else from Kyle, it was that people—male people in particular—tended to look out for their own interests first.

The way Hope turned the ignition key, Josh wondered if she was imagining it was his neck. Okay, so he'd barged into her family's life and manipulated events so that she'd drive him back, but that hardly made him a villain. Hell, he was doing her and her family a favor, and all he wanted was a little time alone with her, in what he'd hoped would be a receptive mood, to ask a favor in return. No wonder he was still a bachelor. Women were hazardous to a guy's health. His *mental* health.

"I suppose you think you're pretty clever," she said as she took the first corner on two wheels. At least, it felt that way to him.

He snorted. "C'mon, Hope. Why don't you admit what's really bugging you? You're ticked because someone did something that wasn't in your plans. You didn't get the final say. Poor baby."

To his astonishment, she braked hard and pulled the car to the shoulder of the road. "If you start walking now, you'll probably get to your van before tomorrow." But it wasn't anger in her voice. She sounded as if she was ready to cry. He didn't get it.

Hoping she wouldn't take it wrong, he put a hand on her shoulder. She was so tense, he could have bounced a brick off her. "Hey, take it easy. I was only teasing. Tell me what's wrong."

She wrenched her shoulder out of his grasp. "No, you weren't teasing, damn you! You meant it."

Aw, jeez. He was right; she was practically crying. Man, he hated that. Whatever he did or said was bound to make it worse.

Before he could say something to get his other foot wedged into his mouth, she turned in her seat and glared at him in the faint light from the streetlights. "You're right. I need to control things. And I'm trying to d-deal with s-s-something I have n-no control over, and it s-scares me!"

Hope lowered her head so he couldn't see her face anymore. He took one of her hands in his and stroked the silky skin until he felt her relax. He thought very carefully before speaking. "This isn't about the wedding, is it? Is it about Kyle?" She shook her head but didn't look up. "What, then? Just let it out, sweetheart. Cry on me if you want to. That's what friends are for."

For a moment, he thought an alien had taken over his brain. Was that the real Josh Kincaid, the one allergic to tears, offering his shoulder for a woman to cry on? It must have been, because the next thing he said was, "Whatever it is, I swear I'll never tell a soul. I hate to see you tearing yourself up like this."

Hope made a tiny choking sound, then moved toward him. With their seat belts fastened and the gearshift between them, all he could do was touch her forehead with his and massage her tense shoulders through her jacket. He felt her shaking, but he didn't hear her crying. Finally, she drew in a long, whispery breath and pulled back.

"This won't make any sense to you," she said softly. Her voice was husky. Somehow, he forced himself to concentrate on her words and not on his body's reaction to that sexy little rasp. "I know you don't want to get married, and you don't want to have kids, so I don't expect you to understand."

He waited. "Understand what?" he finally prompted.

"I . . . I can't . . ." Suddenly, she turned away and shoved the car into gear. "Not now. I can't believe I'm baring my soul on the shoulder of the road."

Hope aimed the car back onto the road, and they roared away, the sudden speed pushing him back in his seat.

He watched her tense profile. "Hey, in my younger days, I got the girls to bare more than their souls on the side of the road."

Her laugh sputtered, then came out freely. "Oh, Josh! You really are a good friend." She sighed. "Maybe I should unload this on someone who doesn't have any vested interests. Will you come up to my place? It's not far from the plant. Unless it's too late?"

"Nah. It's not even eleven. I'll follow you home if you promise not to drive like Mario Andretti."

She flashed him a quick smile, then went back to steering her car as if it were a torpedo. She screeched to a halt beside his van, then actually waited for him to warm up his engine and pull up behind her before she headed back to the road. The house she parked in front of was modest, with a fenced yard, probably four bedrooms upstairs and a barbecue on the patio. A perfect family home, nothing like his rented town house.

Hope unlocked her front door and waved him inside. As he'd expected, her house felt welcoming, but it was very, very neat. The living room she led him into had simple furniture, in soft colors, and lots of plants. The thick Oriental carpet on the polished hardwood floor made him want to take off his boots and dig his toes into it. Somehow, the room looked lived-in at the same time that it looked carefully arranged.

"Have a seat." She gestured toward the sofa and chairs, all three invitingly well stuffed. "Can I get you a decaf coffee or a beer or something?"

"What are you having?"

She made a face. "Either Scotch, neat, or white wine."

"Beer is fine for me."

"Coming up. Feel free to put some music on." She disappeared into the hallway as she spoke.

Hope's CDs and tapes ran an interesting gamut, from classical to zydeco, with everything from New Age to Celtic to rock in between. Drop the New Age stuff and add some new country, and he could be looking at his own music collection. After sorting through the possibilities, he decided on a collection of Mozart's serenades he figured would be soothing.

The smile she gave him when she came out of the kitchen with a cold beer for him and a glass of white wine for herself told him he'd made the right choice. He sat against the corner of the sofa, wondering if she'd sit in the opposite corner or take one of the chairs. To his surprise, she sat on the sofa, set her glass on the coffee table, then leaned back, eyes closed. Gazing at the way her slender neck was exposed, Josh kept his imagination on a short leash.

"What I was trying to tell you before, when we were in the car," she began, "was the reason Kyle left me. I'd just bought this house when we met, so a year later, when Kyle's lease was up, he moved in. We were together here four years. I thought things were fine. We weren't kissy-face, huggy-bear in love, but we got along well."

She looked over at him. He shrugged, then grinned. She turned away again, closing her eyes.

"This February, my doctor told me I should consider having a baby within the year, or else I might not be able to at all. I'd always assumed we'd get married when we decided to start a family. I'd always assumed Kyle wanted a family, too. So I told him what the doctor said. And he announced . . .''

Her voice broke. Josh waited through her pause as she swallowed and got her voice under control. He wanted to reach for her, comfort her, because he knew what was coming, and he knew she was still hurting.

''He announced that if I wanted a baby, I'd have to do it without him. He grabbed a suitcase and went to a hotel. I thought he was upset at the idea of being rushed. But the next day, he brought movers in to pack his things and take them away. The last thing he did was give me a check for his portion of the mortgage payment, minus the remainder of the month. I found out a few weeks later that he was already dating a woman from his firm. Apparently, he'd been seeing her even when we were still together.''

Josh reached out now. He took Hope's hand, ignoring her tiny gasp of surprise and her weak tug to free herself. Her hand was cool between his big paws, cool and soft and small.

''So the guy was a jerk,'' he murmured. ''You admitted you weren't in love with him. There are lots of other guys who want to marry and have families.'' Not that he was one of them, he thought, finding it unexpectedly uncomfortable to have so much in common with Kyle. Had he hurt any of the women he'd known over the years, the way Kyle had? Or had he been straight with them and bowed out, as promised, when they tried to change the rules?

Hope's head snapped upright. ''In case you haven't noticed, I'm not exactly a social butterfly. I work long hours, and I don't go to places where singles hang out. Not singles I'd care to meet, anyway. And I'm thirty-four. Not ancient, but no spring chicken, especially under the circumstances. I gave Kyle five years of my life, and now I'm left with nothing.''

"It's not the end of the world. Lots of women have babies later than thirty-four."

She shook her head. "I may never if I wait too long." He'd forgotten about that. "My doctor said the sooner, the better. Even a year could be too long."

He wanted to help her look on the bright side, but he was having trouble seeing one himself. Still, he tried. "Lots of women never have babies and go on to live useful lives."

"Fine. But I want to have a baby."

With each word, she tugged her hand a little farther out of his, until she freed herself. He resisted the impulse to grab her hand again. As if she suspected he might try, she reached for her wineglass.

"Why?"

Hope set her glass down without taking a sip. "Why? *Why?*" She stared at him for a long, uncomfortable moment. "You really don't understand, do you? I want to have a child so that when I die, I will have contributed something real to the world, not just worked a lot of hours and amused my friends."

Josh tried to digest that notion. He *almost* understood, but he sure didn't relate to it. "Don't you think you're contributing to the world now, even if you don't have your own kids?" She opened her mouth to speak, but he raised his hand to tell her to wait. "I mean, you make all those special things for kids to make their mothers' lives easier, you're a good daughter and a devoted aunt and a fair employer who treats her workers like family."

She narrowed those turquoise eyes. "How do you know any of that about me?"

"Paul started bragging about you and I couldn't find the Off button."

Now her gaze went wide. She had the most amazing eyes, he thought. The color was unusual, and they were huge and expressive, and he could still see them drifting shut when he kissed her back at the cabin. Which, he decided when his pulse promptly responded to that image, he really shouldn't think about. But hell, a guy should never give up hoping. Or was that a guy should never give up hope?

"Really? Paul talked about me like that? Bragging? I thought he was upset about not having more authority in the company."

Josh took a swallow of his beer. "He is, but he sorta sees your side of it. He's trying to prove himself. Maybe you need to start looking closer."

Hope caught her lower lip between her teeth and stared past him. Then she met his eyes and nodded. "You're right. I guess I might as well start with the computer installation, since he got the ball rolling. When you get ready to tender your bid, you can deal with him."

He grinned and didn't tell her he'd already arranged with Paul to do just that. She was making progress at relinquishing a little control. And it hadn't been as slow as Paul had predicted it would be. Just went to show that Hope could be reasonable when she put her mind to it and someone showed her the way.

She lifted her wineglass, then looked at him over the rim, her eyes suspicious. He had to wait for her to swallow before speaking to find out what new obstacle her brain had come up with now.

"How did we get from the subject of my wanting children to my relationship with Paul?" she asked.

He shrugged. "From the ridiculous to the sublime?"

There were sparks in her eyes when she leapt to her feet. "Wanting a child isn't ridiculous!"

"It is when you're single and when there are already enough kids no one wants."

"And if I weren't single?"

He set down his beer bottle, wondering why he found the notion of Hope permanently involved with someone else disturbing, when he had no inclination toward permanence himself. He shook his head. "Sometimes being married doesn't make it right to have kids, either. Some people aren't cut out for parenthood."

She perched on the arm of the chair near his end of the sofa, her expression clouded. "True. With all the abused, battered kids around, it makes me wonder why those people had them if they weren't going to love them."

"Sometimes love isn't enough, even if the kids aren't being battered."

"You never really told me about your family," she said in that gently probing tone women used when trying to torture a confession out of a guy. "Was that the way it was for you? That would certainly explain your attitudes toward marriage and children."

The speed at which her brain worked was frightening. So was the accuracy. He tried to shrug her off. "My parents were always great to me, but I don't think they've ever been happily married."

"Tell me about them."

"You don't want to hear about them."

To his astonishment, she dipped her fingers into her wine and flicked a couple of drops at him. "I wouldn't have asked if I didn't want to hear. They're both alive, right?" He nodded. "What does your father do?"

"Everything and nothing." At her puzzled frown, he added, "He's an entrepreneur, but he isn't much of a detail man, and he puts too much faith in the wrong partners. He has great ideas, but something always seems to scuttle them before he can strike it rich. That was one of the reasons we traveled so much when I was a kid. Dad was always on the lookout for something new."

"Ah. What about your mother? No, let me guess. She's the practical one who keeps the family going."

Once more, her perceptiveness caught him off guard. She was not a woman to underestimate, which, he realized, gave her a lot in common with his mother. He nodded. "She's a registered nurse. A very practical, down-to-earth person."

Revealing so much about himself made him feel as if he were parading around in his emotional altogether. This was what happened when a guy let a woman get too close. She started to understand him, decided he had some little quirks and problems and tried to "fix" him. Next thing he knew, he was losing little bits of himself. He'd seen it too many times to get caught himself.

He made a show of looking at his watch. "Hey, it's late. I better go. Need my beauty sleep." He flashed a grin as he stood. "Thanks for the ride back and the beer."

"I guess it is late. You're so easy to talk to, I lost track of time." She stood up, close enough that he could smell her sweet, enticing scent. He almost gave in to the impulse to touch her cheek, then thought better of it, but damned if he knew why. "Drop by when you come to the plant to see Paul."

"Will do," he promised. Try to keep him away. "I'll call you to talk about the wedding and the rehearsal dinner. Paul wants me to drive you. I'll borrow a car so you don't have to climb into the van."

She sniffed. "I can drive myself, for pity's sake. You don't have to go out of your way. It's enough that you've offered to do us a favor."

"No big deal. I get a couple of free meals."

They were walking toward her front door now. He wanted to take her into his arms and kiss her thoroughly, the way he had at the cabin. He wanted to remind her of what she was missing. The trouble was, he didn't want to go home alone to spend the rest of the night remembering what *he* was missing!

Hope leaned toward him. He realized she was going to kiss his cheek and debated the merits of turning so she got his lips instead. He opted for patience and suffered quietly when her soft, warm mouth touched his skin.

"I owe you a favor in return," she murmured. "Think about something I can do to repay you for helping me and my family. Okay?"

His mind rapidly sorted through the possibilities, but most of them would get his face slapped. "You don't owe me, but I'll think about it anyway. I like to keep in touch with my friends."

Her smile sent him to his van with a warm glow in his heart, a sinking sensation in the pit of his stomach and most of his blood supply flooding down to his loins.

"Here, hold this," her sister Gail ordered, then thrust a sleeping infant into Hope's arms. "Her mother's the one in blue trying to explain to her two-year-old that she can't eat the chalk."

Hope adjusted her hold around the infant so the bundle of baby and blanket fit better against her. With her free hand, she moved the edge of the blanket aside to peer at the tiny face. For a long moment, she breathed in the scent of the warm little one and imagined that this was her baby, that she wouldn't have to give her back to her mother in a few minutes. But there was no pleasure in the fantasy. She didn't want to borrow babies and pretend she was a real mother. She wanted her own child. Wanted a child so badly that it had become a physical ache, whether she held an infant like this or played with older children, either her nieces or the dozen or so who now tumbled around the playroom at KidsCan Togs.

"Velcro is beating snaps by about ten to one," Gail told her, holding up a small garment. "Much easier to use."

The annual design open house was the only time Gail involved herself in the company. Hope had always thought that was a waste, because her sister had a fair amount of design flair. Gail consistently denied she had any interest in working, except as a full-time mother and wife, but her active mind kept coming up with suggestions that Hope was more than happy to incorporate. Indeed, the open house had been Gail's idea, back when Roberta, her oldest, had been an infant. Some of Gail's friends had made casual comments about wishing mothers had more say in the design of baby and children's clothes. Hope, newly promoted to vice president, had managed to persuade their skeptical father, and now, they were celebrating their eighth annual event.

Hope fingered the leg fastening with her free hand. "It does work better, doesn't it? But I think the new way the romper opens makes a difference, too. And that was your idea. You really ought to think of coming on board part-time."

Gail shook her head, her short strawberry blond curls bouncing.

Hope sighed. "Okay, how about as a consultant? You wouldn't even have to come into the office." Gail started to speak, but Hope cut her off. "Think about it, okay? You've got the experience with using the garments that I don't have." Somehow, she managed not to choke on the words.

Gail smiled her serene smile. "You can consult me whenever you need to, Hope. We see each other all the time."

Hope smiled back. "I know. But if I'm going to make a profit on your ideas, you should be compensated for them. You don't give yourself enough credit for your talents."

Gail probably would have argued, except that two toddlers crashed into her knees, drawing her attention away from Hope. Smiling, Hope cradled the sleeping infant and began to circulate around the playroom. She paused at each table where mothers were making notes about the clothing they were testing. With a shock, she recognized one of the youngest mothers as a girl she used to baby-sit in high school. Now, Jessie had a baby boy who was objecting strenuously to trying on another outfit.

At some point, Hope became aware of the feeling she was being watched. When she searched the faces in the room, however, everyone was intent on her own children or talking to people nearby. Finally, she saw that the playroom door was ajar, and a shadowy form stood in the opening. Her first thought was that it was someone's husband coming to fetch his wife and child home. But why watch her?

The door opened a little more, and Josh stepped inside, a sheepish grin on his face. Near his work-booted feet, two youngsters had constructed a wobbly series of towers from wooden blocks. Josh looked down, then met her eyes and raised his brows. Smiling at his thoughtfulness, Hope made her way across the room until she was standing close enough to speak without waking the infant she held.

"Hi. What brings you here?"

"Paul said I could find you here. He didn't warn me what was going on, though."

Briefly, absentmindedly patting the infant, she explained what was happening. While she spoke, Josh's gaze roamed the room, to return to the baby she held. A strange look crossed his face, then disappeared into a smile.

"So this is the user-friendly part of the business," he said.

She nodded, snuggling the infant closer.

"Some of these kids look like pretty tough customers."

Hope chuckled. "Some of them are. That's why we reinforce all the knees and elbows. And the infant clothes come with several matching detachable bibs so the whole garment doesn't have to get washed when a baby upchucks." She chuckled again at the way his mouth twisted in disgust.

"Can we change the subject?"

"Sure. What's on your mind?"

"Dinner."

"It's barely half-past two."

He grinned roguishly. "Not now. Tomorrow."

Just then, the mother in blue came to claim her sleeping daughter. Hope tried to hide her reluctance to hand over the warm pink bundle. She took a few seconds to exchange pleasantries with the mother and give the little one a final pat. Then she turned back to Josh, her mind absolutely blank about what he'd been saying. All she could think of was how empty her arms felt without the warm weight of the baby in them.

She couldn't quite meet his eyes. He was the only person here who knew her secret. That made her feel very vulnerable and a little foolish that he'd caught her in midfantasy. "I'm sorry. I, um, I got distracted."

His smile stayed steady. "I'm calling in that favor you say you owe me. I want you to come to dinner with me tomorrow."

Oh, dear, had she mistaken him after all? What happened to his promise to be her friend? "But—"

He raised his hands, palms toward her, a gesture of surrender. "It's not a date. It's business. One of the general contractors I do a lot of work with has been trying to convince me to form a partnership with him. He and his wife invited me to dinner at their place. I know they're going to try to soften me up."

"So you want me there to keep you hard?"

His breath hissed out in a strangled whistle. "Jeez, woman, not in front of the kids!"

She felt her face flame and looked away from Josh, but not before she saw two red spots spring to his cheeks. "That's not... I mean... I don't... I just..." she sputtered. He snorted a quiet laugh. "Oh, forget it!" she snapped. Her face grew even hotter, which she hadn't thought possible until that moment. "What time and what should I wear?"

Chapter Eight

"Why don't you show Hope around the house, Dinah, and let Josh and me talk business over the barbecue. Then we won't be so boring at dinner." Bob Eberhardt winked at Hope. Past his shoulder, she could see Josh roll his eyes, then shake his head. She understood he didn't want Bob to be able to divide and conquer.

Hope smiled at Bob. "I don't mind at all if you talk business at dinner. It's my raison d'être, after all. I'm always interested in learning something new. But I'd love to see the house."

Dinah Eberhardt linked her arm through Josh's. "You come, too. You haven't seen little Bobby in weeks. We have a sitter for the evening. They're upstairs playing before his bedtime, but he'll be happy to see his Uncle Josh."

Hope's heart sank. It seemed that wherever she turned these days, there were babies. Of course, part of that was the nature of her business. She still hadn't recovered from her afternoon of wall-to-wall little ones yesterday, praying no one would see the naked longing in her heart.

"Upstaged again," Bob grumbled, grinning as he set down his barbecue chef's apron. "Of course, he gets his good looks and charm from me."

"And his brains from Dinah," Josh chimed in.

The Eberhardts led them through the spacious, modern house, pointing out various features Bob was particularly proud of. Hope had already learned from Josh that Bob had designed and built the house himself, and that Dinah, an interior decorator, had done the finishing. The house was too modern, too crisply rectangular, for Hope's taste, but she could certainly admire the workmanship and the care that had gone into every square inch. And she could also, secretly, guiltily, envy the Eberhardts their obvious happiness in each other.

Bobby sat in the lap of a grandmotherly woman who was reading *The Cat in the Hat* to him, even though the boy was barely a year old. Hope watched the child point to the pictures on the page and chortle with glee. She wanted to ask to take the sitter's place, to hold that happy little one close and share the silliness of the story. She wanted her own little one to snuggle and read Dr. Seuss stories to. The smile froze on her face as yearning settled into her heart with a familiar ache.

When Bobby saw Josh, he screeched happily and tried to climb out of the sitter's lap. Chuckling, Josh lifted him and spent a few minutes tossing the little fellow into the air and making airplane sounds with him. It took Dinah several minutes to console Bobby when Josh finally relinquished him to the waiting sitter. Hope smiled, but her face felt frozen.

"I'll be back for a good-night kiss," Dinah told the older woman, who nodded while settling Bobby back in her lap. "Okay, folks, how about putting a dent in those appetizers? We planned a very casual evening. It's been ages since

I really had a chance to talk to you, Josh, and I want to get to know you, Hope. C'mon downstairs.''

"Is there anything I can help you with?" Hope offered as they made their way down the stairs.

"Now that you mention it, I could use a hand bringing out some of the munchies. Bob, you and Josh are in charge of drinks and meat. We'll take care of the rest."

Hope took the tray of vegetables and dips outside to the cedar deck, where Josh and Bob were lounging. Josh handed Hope a frosty glass of white wine as she sat near him.

"Has this reprobate told you I've been trying to talk him into a partnership for the last year?" Bob growled good-naturedly. Hope smiled and nodded. "It'd be the best thing for both of us. We do most jobs together anyway, but a partnership would spare him the hassle of doing his own books. Doesn't mean we can't take separate jobs if something special comes up, but pooling our resources would give us more chances at bigger jobs. I can't think of a single negative. Do you think you can talk some sense into him?"

Hope caught Josh's subtle head shake. She smiled again at Bob. "Personally, I don't think it's possible to talk sense into Josh. That would be like trying to reason with a brick wall."

Bob's hearty laugh rang out. Dinah laughed also. Josh grinned. "Thanks a lot, babe. I owe you one," he told her, then winked, as if making sure she caught his real meaning.

After several more attempts to convince Josh that a partnership between them would be the best thing since peanut butter and jelly, Bob gave up, and the conversation turned to other topics. Hope discussed business trends and forecasts with Bob and fabrics and design with Dinah, all the while aware of Josh's attention fixed on her. She felt as if she were auditioning for some sort of role, but didn't have a script. By the time they were walking to her car, however, calling a last good-night over their shoulders, Hope felt she'd made new friends, and Josh still wasn't convinced he needed a partner.

"Want me to drive?" he offered.

"No, thanks." His low chuckle made her wrinkle her nose. "I *like* to drive," she said when they were inside. "I like my car. It doesn't mean I'm a control freak."

"You're right. I don't know where I got that idea." He flashed her a maddeningly smug grin when she turned to guide the car backward out of the driveway. "What did you think of Bob and Dinah?"

"I like them. And I think you should reconsider Bob's offer. He makes a lot of sense, and it's obvious that you two have a good rapport."

"You sound like a wife." His tone made it clear this was far from a compliment.

"How would you know?"

"Because almost every guy I know is married, and their wives all sound alike. Always talking about being sensible and practical and responsible, instead of being open to possibilities, ready for new chances."

"Ah." She thought about that for a moment as she drove. "Well, since women are the ones who bear the children, I guess it's part of our genetic job description to seek stability and safety."

He was silent awhile, apparently thinking, although his head was turned so that he was looking out the side window. Then, at a red light, he turned to face her. "I guess you have a point. But I'm not married, and I don't have kids, so I can afford to take chances. Right?"

She smiled. "Sounds to me as if you're a control freak yourself, in an anticontrol sort of way."

"Who, me? Mr. Play 'Em As They Fall?" He snorted. "Nah. I just don't want anyone else putting limits on my possibilities."

"Which, by definition, wives do?"

"You got it."

Hope thought about their conversation for the rest of the short drive to her house, where Josh's van stood. The contradictions didn't make sense. Everything about him, except his attitude toward partnerships of any kind, pointed to him being responsible, practical and grounded. She simply couldn't see him as the kind of man who drifted on the winds of chance, which is the way he seemed to think of himself. He was still living in the same town he'd moved to eighteen years ago, and he'd built a thriving business by his own hard work. From her conversation with Bob, she'd gleaned that Josh was involved in a number of community projects and gave a fair amount of his time and money to local charities. So what was his problem with personal relationships?

"I have to be honest," she blurted as he walked her to her front door. "I'm very glad I'm not interested in starting another relationship with a man. It's good we decided to be friends right up front." She looked up into his handsome face, searching for answers she didn't think he knew himself.

He straightened as if she'd hit him. "Oh, yeah? Why?"

"Because you're too darn charming otherwise."

Josh gave her a lopsided grin. "Likewise. But I guess you're an all-or-nothing kinda woman. No casual flings, huh?"

She smiled, remembering an article she'd read about men and women being friends. The general consensus was that men never gave up hoping their women pals would cross the line and become lovers. Women, of course, could keep the two roles separate, even if a man friend was as attractive as Josh. They had to. The consequences of crossing that line could be devastating. At best, the friendship would suffer irreparable damage. At worst, the woman would be left with a broken heart.

"No flings, casual or serious," she assured him. Nothing to complicate the plan that was taking hold of her mind.

"Okay, then I've got a proposition for you." She felt her brows rise as if on their own. "No, not that kind of proposition. Even I can take a hint if you give it often enough." He grinned. "Here's my idea. I've already volunteered to be your escort for Paul's wedding. There's a barbecue a bunch of my old friends and I do every year. It's a whole-day party. Just about all of them are married or engaged or living with someone, so it's a real family kind of thing. I don't want to take any of the women I've dated in the last little while, because whoever I bring every year ends up thinking it's a prelude to a proposal. Then I'm the bad guy because I let them down. So, how about you going with me, like you did tonight? Sorta like camouflage."

It was, she realized, a perfect plan, and a nice way for her to thank Josh for helping her and her family with Paul's wedding. "Sounds like fun. When is it?"

"The Sunday a week after the wedding."

"Fine." Was it her imagination, or had Josh leaned a little more toward her in the past few seconds? Was he thinking about kissing her? She hoped not . . . didn't she?

"Good enough. I'll talk to you soon. And thanks for tonight."

He lifted his hand, brushed her cheek with his fingertips, a touch as soft as a kiss. Then he turned and strode down the driveway whistling. As he drove away, Hope touched her tingling cheek with her own fingertips and wondered if she'd made a colossal mistake in judgment.

Somehow, time sped up after the dinner with Bob and Dinah. Josh spent his weekdays working overtime. After a replacement RV was delivered, he rushed to the site for the weekend to stake out the foundation for his cabin and catch a couple of trout for his freezer. He spoke to Hope several times on the phone, but she was also busy with whatever things women did before a wedding in the family. He wouldn't go as far as admitting that he *missed* her, but he did find himself thinking about being with her that coming weekend. First, there was the rehearsal and a dinner, then a stag for Paul and some kind of female party for Elaine, none of which really interested him. But images of dancing with Hope after the Saturday-evening wedding kept disturbing his normally sound sleep.

Their last face-to-face conversation played in his head at least once a day, grabbing his attention like a pebble in his shoe. Was she right about the partnership thing, that he was worried about losing control? Was it a real concern, or would the benefits of a partnership outweigh any drawbacks? How the hell was he supposed to know until he committed himself and it was too late to change? How did anyone know when it was time to join forces with someone else instead of muddling along alone, looking for the next opportunity that might be better than whatever was already there? Hell, put like that, a partnership sounded like marriage!

Impulsively parking his van in the KidsCan Togs lot shortly after noon on Thursday, Josh mulled over Hope's other comments about their relationship. How could she criticize him, he thought as he sauntered toward her office, for refusing to give up control of his life, when she was so set on keeping control of hers?

"Hi," he said to her secretary, who smiled warmly back at him. "Think Hope has a couple of minutes to see me?"

"Oh, dear. Hope wasn't feeling well. She went home about an hour ago."

Josh felt a little chill of alarm. Hope had struck him as the kind of person who wouldn't wimp out unless she was really sick.

The secretary must have read his mind. "You needn't worry. It's really nothing serious. She'll be phoning in later for messages, so I can tell her you stopped by. Is there anything you want me to tell her?"

"No, thanks."

Back in the van, he considered his options. Go back to work as if he didn't know Hope was sick, phone her to check on her—probably waking her—or drive the five minutes to her place to make sure she wasn't dying.

Put like that, what choice did he have? He phoned his assistant from the new cell phone in his van, then drove to Hope's house.

It took way too long until he heard the click of her dead bolt. The door opened slowly, just a few inches. "Do I have to sign for that?" a voice croaked.

"What the hell?" he muttered. "Hope? It's me. Josh. What's the matter?" He tried to ease the door open a little more, but it didn't budge. "You sound like you're dying."

"I feel like I'm dying," she said, her voice pinched. "I'm waiting for a prescription to be delivered."

"Do you want me to pick it up instead?"

"No, really. It can't be much longer. Why are you here?"

"Because your secretary said you went home sick. What's wrong?"

"Cramps." The word came out like a gasp.

"Was it something you ate?" He pushed at the door a little harder. It gave, but not more than a couple of inches. He still couldn't see inside. "Don't you need to go to the hospital?"

After a long silence, the door swung slowly inward until he could just see Hope's face in shadows. "Josh, I have cramps. Not food poisoning. You know, *cramps?* Haven't you ever lived with a woman?"

As her meaning sunk in, his face started to get warm, until his skin burned. What an idiot he was!

"No, actually, I never have," he managed to answer.

The door opened the rest of the way. "C'mon in. I can't stand here anymore."

He stepped inside and pushed the door shut behind him. Hope stood with one hand on the wall, looking as if her knees wouldn't support her. She wore that heavy white terry robe she'd had at the cabin, and her face was as white as the robe, making her eyes glow like jewels on satin.

"That bad, huh?"

She nodded, then made a funny little sound and pressed her hands to her middle. He caught her around her shoulders, then turned her very carefully so he could get his other arm under her knees to lift her. It was obvious that she was in agony. The last thing he wanted to do was cause her more pain by moving her too quickly or too roughly.

She shifted as if to try to escape, then wrapped her arms around his neck with a low moan. Hope wasn't exactly a feather, but he managed to carry her easily, although the trip up the stairs left him a little more winded than he'd like to admit. He didn't have to ask where her bedroom was. The rumpled king-size bed in the largest upstairs room, the one that was draped in lace and filmy stuff, with delicate anti-quey-looking furniture and shelves of frilly dolls, was a good bet. He set her down on the bed as if she were made of glass, then drew the lacy cover over her even as she was turning onto her side and curling into a fetal position.

"Is there anything that will make you feel better?"

Her answer came out on a sigh. "Time and my medicine, which I forgot I'd run out of."

"The stuff that hasn't been delivered yet?" She grunted something that sounded like agreement. "Anything else?"

"Doubt it."

But he had an idea. He'd remembered one of his friends saying that when his wife felt this rotten, he'd climb into bed with her and hold her with his hands on her stomach. It wasn't the kind of information he usually picked up from his pals, but this was during one of those poker-night conversations when the guys were kidding Nick that getting married was going to kill his sex life. And Bob Eberhardt had said something about sex not being the only way to get close. At the time, Josh had scoffed. Now, he was beginning to appreciate his friend's wisdom.

"What are you doing?" Hope mumbled when his first boot hit the floor.

"I'm taking off my boots." He dropped the other one, peeled off his work shirt, then moved around to the other side of the bed and climbed in on top of the cover. Hope gave a little yelp and tried to scoot away. "Relax." He got his arms around her and pulled her back against his body. Suddenly, he was surrounded by the scent of her, the feel of her, even muffled by all the layers of clothes and bedding. Despite his best intentions and silent prayers, his libido went into instant readiness.

"Tell me where it hurts," he asked, all too aware of where *he* hurt.

She didn't speak. Instead, she wrapped her fingers around one of his wrists and guided his hand against her belly. For a long while, she lay stiffly in his arms. Finally, he felt her sigh and go limp.

"Better?" he whispered into her neck, her hair tickling his face.

"Yes," she whispered.

He lost track of how long he held her. The doorbell chime sounded like a cathedral bell in the silence. Hope started and tried to pull away.

"Stay put. I'll take care of it."

He signed for Hope's prescription, then went upstairs with the bottle, reading the directions as he went. From her decadent bathroom, he brought her a glass of cold water. She gulped her pills, handed back the glass and curled down under the covers again. From inside, he heard her muffled thanks.

If she expected him to desert her now, she'd better think again. "How long do your cramps usually last?" he asked as he unbuckled his belt.

"Couple of hours. Medicine and sleep help. Honestly, I'll be all right as soon as the pills start working."

Josh unzipped his jeans and peeled them off, along with his socks. In his undershirt and briefs, he climbed onto the bed, trying not to jostle her. Then he pulled the covers up to his waist and eased closer to her, not quite touching. He slid his arms around her again. Hope made a soft sound somewhere between a moan and a purr, and wriggled backward until they were pressed together like spoons. With only her robe between them, he could feel the hard arch of her pelvic bone when he placed his hand on her belly. She made that little sound again and rested her hand over his. He started praying she wouldn't notice that he was totally, painfully aroused with her bottom nestled against him.

The sudden rigidity of her body told him she'd noticed. "Josh? I... You..."

To his disgust, he felt his face flame. "Ignore it," he muttered. "Happens every time I get this close to a beautiful woman. Doesn't mean I have to do anything about it."

"Oh, good," she said groggily. She gave another little wriggle against his loins, then went limp.

Josh bit the inside of his cheek and forced himself to breathe at regular intervals. Mentally, he replayed highlights from several of his favorite World Series games, a couple of Stanley Cup hockey play-offs and his weekend fishing trip. The next thing he knew, he was waking slowly, disoriented and still aroused, with Hope lying quietly in his arms. He couldn't see the clock radio on the nightstand, but the sun was setting, casting a pinkish gold light into the room.

"Mmm." Hope stirred and ran her fingers up his arm, sending tingles over every square inch of his skin. "Oh! Good grief! You're real," she gasped. "I thought I was dreaming."

"More like a nightmare," he teased, trying to keep the mood light. "How do you feel now?"

"Better. Much better. Thanks."

She eased away slightly. He took the hint and released her. Trying not to jostle her, he sat up and swung his legs off the bed, then stretched. He felt oddly enervated yet restless. When was the last time he'd napped in the middle of a workday? Never. No, once when he'd had a wicked case of flu. The ache in his loins made him think having the flu might be preferable.

Hope was slowly sitting up on her side of the bed. With her long, reddish gold hair loose and draped around her and her eyes huge and unfocused, she looked like a lost child.

Turning away, he reached for his jeans. "Does this happen every time?"

"Mmm-hmm. Sometimes it's worse, sometimes it's better."

He swore. "Can't you do anything about it?"

"I'm doing everything I can, short of drastic surgery. Everything except one thing," she answered, enunciating carefully as if she were drunk. Those painkillers must have been strong.

"And what's that?" Standing, he tucked his work-shirt tails into his jeans and zipped his fly. Then he turned to look at her again.

Hope looked up at him. Her eyes were sharp and clear now, and there was a sad little twist to her soft lips. "Have a baby," she said quietly.

"Having a baby would help this?" That didn't make sense to him. From what he'd heard from guys who'd been with their wives during labor and delivery, having a baby was only one step removed from a slow, painful death. And that was for the father. He couldn't begin to imagine what the mother felt, except that it would have to be worse than what Hope was going through now.

"That's what everyone I know who's had children says, including my doctor. At least, it's a good possibility. But as I said before, I might not be able to get pregnant if I wait much longer." She shrugged and suddenly, she looked very small and fragile. "Doesn't matter. I don't need Kyle, or anyone else, to have a baby. Or to try to."

Josh dropped the boot he was about to put on. "You want to run that by me again?"

"I've made up my mind to have a baby by myself."

He shoved his foot into his boot, then met her eyes. "Hope, honey, last I heard, the female of our species can't do that without help from a male."

She stood and faced him, hands on her hips. "I know that."

"Yeah. And we both know you aren't the type to nail some likely-looking guy for a one-night stand."

"Ever hear of sperm banks?"

"Aw, jeez! Hope, are you out of your mind?"

Her chin went up a notch, and her eyes blazed. "I'm perfectly sane, thank you! Just because you can't relate to my desire to have a baby doesn't mean I'm crazy. Maybe *you're* the crazy one. After all, most of the human race wants to reproduce."

"Do you have any idea what can go wrong? Hell, haven't you seen the movies or read the stories about sperm banks making mistakes? And what about that doctor who impregnated dozens of his patients himself, making all those half siblings who didn't know they were related? And the twins with different fathers?"

Hope tightened the belt of her robe and moved away from the bed. "Those things are the exceptions, not the rules. They make the headlines because they're so sensational. I've been doing research into this, and there are reputable, reliable clinics that have impeccable reputations." She walked toward the door.

"Sure," he snapped, following her into the hallway. "They probably settle out of court to avoid the bad press." Hope was already heading down the stairs. He went after her. "Do you have any idea what kind of nut-bars and weirdos donate sperm? Or sell the stuff? I know hundreds of perfectly normal guys, good-looking, intelligent, healthy guys. Not a single one has ever made a deposit to a sperm bank. So who does? Hell, Hope, we're talking about psychos and egomaniacs. Misfits and emotional defectives. Is that the kind of genetic material you want to recombine your DNA with?'' The thought made his stomach lurch.

"And medical students with high IQs. I don't know why you're so upset," she said a little too mildly. "It's my business and my decision." At the entrance to the kitchen, she paused and looked back at him. "I'm hungry. Would you like something to eat? I've got lasagna in the freezer."

"Sure. Anything. But listen, Hope, I want you to re-think this. You could still meet the right guy to be a husband and a father." He didn't stop to question why that idea made him uneasy. He was too concerned with talking her out of this lunacy. "You still have some time, don't you?" She shrugged, then nodded, but he could see the stubborn light in her eyes. "And hell, it's not the end of the world if you don't have a baby, is it?"

"No," she said in a husky murmur, as if there were tears she was trying to hold back. "It won't be the end of the world, but it will make my world that much smaller."

Josh folded his arms over his chest and watched her rummage in her freezer. Her movements were stiff and jerky. She didn't look at him as she crossed the kitchen to put a container into the microwave. Each beep of the control panel sounded like a voice prodding him to say something, do something, to prevent her from making a drastic mistake, but he couldn't think of a thing.

Hope set two plates on the glass kitchen table, then met his eyes and smiled. "Relax, Josh. You know I like to have everything organized and planned out. I won't do anything I can't control."

He shook his head. "You can't control nature."

Her smile widened. "Maybe not, but I can control a lot of the factors. And I promise, I'll be as careful as humanly possible. Now, would you like beer or diet cola?'' she added with a false-sounding cheeriness he didn't trust.

It was time, he realized, for a strategic retreat before he alienated her altogether. But he was going to have to do some serious thinking about how to save Hope from her own well-meant but misguided intentions. What else was a friend for?

Chapter Nine

"He's not coming," Hope muttered again under her breath.

Ignoring Gail's assurances, she pushed open the heavy church door and hurried down the stairs. After the cool dimness inside, the bright sunlight made her blink and squint as she gazed up and down the street. A tall man in a trim navy suit strode toward the church as if he owned the sidewalk. Dismissing him as no one she knew, she turned to gaze in the opposite direction. Behind her, footsteps drew closer, then stopped. Hope turned and felt her eyes widen in shocked recognition. It couldn't be, but it was! He'd promised her mother he cleaned up well, but Hope hadn't imagined he could transform himself quite so thoroughly.

Josh gave her a smile that told her he knew exactly the effect he'd had on her. Then he cupped her elbow in his warm hand and directed her toward the wide stone stairs. "Something wrong?" he asked as they climbed side by side.

"No. Far from it. I just didn't expect you to look . . . like you do."

"You didn't think I'd come in my work clothes, did you?"

"I didn't think you'd come at all." His fingers tensed on her arm. She paused, then glanced up to meet his eyes. To her dismay, he looked hurt. "No, sorry. I was afraid you wouldn't come."

"I gave my word. I don't make many promises, but when I do, I keep them." He urged her up the stairs again, toward the landing. "You look a lot better than you did yesterday. How do you feel?"

"Like yesterday never happened." Except for the memory of his strong, hard body holding her close, easing her pain.

Suddenly, they were surrounded by the rest of her family, plus the friends who would make up the wedding party. Her father drew Josh away to introduce him around. Her youngest niece, Carla, was crying because her next older sister, Erica, had teased her that she would drop the rings during the actual ceremony. While Gail took Erica aside to reprimand her quietly, Hope crouched down and dried Carla's tears.

"Oh, sweetie, you aren't going to drop the rings. They'll be tied onto the pillow with a little ribbon. You're going to be a wonderful ring girl." Carla sniffled, then gave Hope a wavery smile. Josh appeared again by her side. The girl's gaze slid to his knees, then traveled all the way up, until she was tipping her head way back to see his face. Hope smiled ruefully at her niece's suddenly adoring expression. Another conquest, and he hadn't been trying.

When Hope introduced them, Josh crouched down and took Carla's little hand in his big one. Hope fought back the ache in her throat at the sight of the child and the man, who could have been father and daughter if she didn't know who they really were. Josh spoke softly to Carla and quickly had her giggling. Moments later, Josh stood and shook hands all around as Hope's father introduced him to the rest of the group. To her relief, no one asked about Kyle's absence.

The rehearsal went quickly and smoothly, feeling neither real nor solemn without music. Before long, Hope's mother was shooing everyone out to a nearby restaurant. The crowd grew with the arrival of out-of-town guests who had been invited to dinner with the wedding party. Cousins, aunts and uncles caught her up in the general swirling activity of a family reunion, hugging, kissing, laughing and chatting. But no matter whom she was with or what she was doing, Hope was constantly aware of Josh. She told herself it was because she was responsible for seeing that he met the others and had a tolerably good time. But every time their eyes met across the room, she feared her interest wasn't so simply explained away. Somehow, she'd have to maintain her distance, her objectivity. She and Josh were friends, playing a role. To allow herself to imagine anything else was to flirt with disappointment. She didn't have the strength to go through two heartbreaks in less than six months.

When her mother rounded them up to find their assigned places at the tables, Hope discovered that she'd been seated next to Josh. He drew her chair out for her. As she settled her napkin in her lap, she caught sight of her brother giving Josh a quick thumbs-up.

"What was that about?" she asked quietly, hoping no one else had noticed.

He leaned toward her, his arm over the back of her chair, his lips brushing her ear. She felt engulfed by his warmth, by his solid presence, by his subtly spicy scent. His breath tickled as he whispered, "Nothing much. Paul thinks it's a good idea to give everyone the impression that we're a couple, so they won't bug you about Kyle."

"Oh." She was going to have to have a little talk with her baby brother about that. It was her role to look after him, not the other way around.

"That okay with you?"

"I hardly think it's necessary. No one's asked about him so far."

His fingers toyed with the loose hairs near her neck, giving her chills. "But they might, and Paul doesn't want you to be put on the spot." The way his lips teased the skin below her ear made it impossible for her to speak. However, Josh didn't seem to need an answer. He went on murmuring against her skin, "After all, it's Paul and Elaine's wedding. People should concentrate on that, not speculate about your love life. Right?"

And then, to her shock, he delicately flicked the tip of his tongue at the skin his breath had been tickling. Heat suffused her. She wanted to tip her head back in encouragement, but she fought the impulse. It would be unseemly here, in front of everyone, even if it weren't an act. Knowing it was *supposed* to be an act, she shouldn't react like this. Before she could pull away, however, his fingers traced the line of her jaw, sending tiny waves of sensation along her nerves. The memory of Josh's kisses at the cabin rushed back to her, stealing her breath in a little gasp.

She had to regain control of this outlandish situation. "If you keep overacting like that, my supposed love life will be the only thing people will be able to think about," she said tartly. "Behave yourself."

He moved away and winked. "Yes, ma'am."

For the rest of the meal, Josh did, in fact, behave himself. Hope couldn't help admiring his easygoing way of talking to the other guests. He charmed everyone at their table, breaking the ice with a somewhat censored retelling of the way he and Hope had met that had everyone laughing. And after dinner, he won Gail's obvious approval when he jollied the overtired Carla out of her pouting refusal to go home to bed.

"Ready, Kincaid?" Tom asked, clapping a hand on Josh's shoulder. Then he grinned at Hope. "Gail says we're supposed to make sure Paul's stag doesn't get out of control, since we're the old men of the group.''

Hope shook her head, unable to understand the attractions of a stag party. ''Just see that Paul gets home safely, and keep him away from the stripper his buddies have no doubt hired. He's getting married tomorrow.''

Josh winked. ''That's the point, babe.'' He leaned down and gave Hope a light kiss on her cheek. She resisted the urge to touch the tingling spot with her fingertips. ''I suppose you ladies are planning to go somewhere and swap casserole recipes, right?''

''As a matter of fact—'' Hope smiled sweetly ''—yes.'' He didn't have to know that Elaine's friends had booked tables at a ladies-only club.

With disbelieving snorts, Josh and Tom strode out to join the rest of the young men. Hope watched Josh's broad-shouldered, slim-hipped figure as he made his way toward the parking lot.

''What a hunk!'' her sister said from behind her. ''And a sweetie, besides. He has a nice way with the kids. Kyle definitely fades in comparison. I'm really happy for you, Hope.''

With a guilty start, Hope held up her car keys. ''I'll drive. That way we can both leave early. I don't think I'll have much patience for ogling seminaked men.''

Gail chuckled. ''Isn't it great to be spoiled by having our own good-looking men around to ogle?''

Annoyed that her explanation about Josh being a friend seemed to be universally misunderstood by her immediate family, Hope sighed. ''Nice talk from a pregnant mother of three.''

Gail linked her arm through Hope's. ''Hey, how do you think I got to be a pregnant mother of three?''

As they walked out into the balmy evening, Hope bit her lip to keep from blurting that she'd settle for just being a pregnant mother of one.

* * *

Josh smiled and offered his arm to an elderly woman who carried a cane. "Bride's side or groom?" he asked. After escorting the woman to a seat, he went back for the next guests. Organ music played softly in the background, and the people already seated spoke with a hush that nearly burst with anticipation. He'd been an usher or best man at more than a dozen weddings, but he'd never understood why people got so excited about them. As far as he was concerned, a wedding day was the last day of the rest of a man's life. Nothing to celebrate, to his mind.

Oh, sure, the bride and groom thought they were happy. Maybe they even *were* happy for a while. But soon enough, reality was going to set in. Dissatisfaction was going to kill that happiness. She wouldn't be satisfied with whatever he could give her. He wouldn't be satisfied to give up all his interests. They'd start to chip away at each other, until they stopped being the naive couple who thought marriage was the key to everlasting happiness. He'd seen it enough times to know it was inevitable. Hell, he'd lived with it, through his parents, long enough to be convinced that marriage was a one-way trip into purgatory, with one or both of the couple trying forever to make amends for being who they were, flaws and all.

Now, the music was changing, signaling the guests to quiet down and get ready. Along with another usher, Josh took a quick look around to make sure no stragglers needed to be seated, then closed the church doors. The rest of the ushers were already at the front of the church, lined up along the stairs leading to the altar, where Paul and his best man waited with the minister. Josh knocked on the door of a room to one side of the entrance, where the ladies waited with the bride and her father. Hope, of course, was in there, but he hadn't caught even a glimpse of her since she'd arrived in jeans, carrying a huge plastic garment bag and a tote bag. It was all very mysterious, with the muffled sound of women's voices occasionally coming through the door. He had to admit he felt a definite hum of anticipation at the thought of seeing Hope at any minute.

The minister's wife opened the anteroom door, and Josh caught a glimpse of several women in light-colored, filmy dresses, but not Hope. He gave a couple of quick tugs to his sleeves, then offered his arm to Mrs. Delacorte. Behind him, the other usher did the same for Elaine's mother. When the minister's wife nodded, Josh smiled at Mrs. Delacorte, then began walking her down the aisle to the front pew. He seated her next to her husband, then took his place on the stairs. From his vantage point, he could see Paul, the poor sucker, shaking like a leaf.

Looking out over the guests, Josh felt his anticipation mounting. When the music changed again, signaling the entrance of Elaine's attendants, his heart gave an unexpected little skip. He'd never felt anything like that at any other wedding. Maybe he'd caught Paul's case of nerves.

As she walked down the aisle, Hope looked straight into his eyes and smiled. His heart bucked against his ribs. Man, oh man, she was beautiful! When the ceremony was over and Paul and Elaine had begun walking back up the aisle, Josh offered his arm to Hope as they'd rehearsed. This time, the touch of her fingers through his sleeve sent a jolt of electric awareness right to his brain. He looked into her sparkling eyes and almost tripped on the last step.

It was, he told himself, the shock of her being so beautiful in that pale purple floaty dress, with her red-gold hair piled on her head in some kind of braid and that sweet smile on her soft lips. That, and the general wedding hysteria that could even make a sensible guy like him get romantic. Thank God it was only a temporary kind of insanity.

Two hours later, holding Hope close while the band played an old love song, Josh wondered when he'd come to his senses.

* * *

Hope felt herself drifting in Josh's encircling arms and struggled mentally to find her balance. Even before yesterday, she'd been telling herself it was neither fair nor realistic to compare Kyle and Josh. Unfortunately, it was also becoming impossible not to do so. Kyle had always danced smoothly, holding her just right, leading firmly. Josh danced as if he were making love, holding her a little too close, drawing her in rather than leading her. She felt engulfed by his masculinity, which seemed as overpowering in a tuxedo as in his work clothes. Every brush of his thigh against hers, every brush of her breasts against his chest, reminded her of his strength and her femininity.

As the final notes of the dreamy song faded, Josh stopped abruptly, startling Hope out of her reverie. She stepped back slightly and followed his smiling gaze down toward Roberta, her oldest niece. The girl stood staring up at Josh, adoration glowing in her eyes.

"I believe I promised this young lady another dance before she has to go home," he said with a wink for Hope.

Hope watched him hold Roberta at a discreet distance and guide her overeager steps in a simple, slow dance. Roberta was chattering away, and Josh was bent at what must have been an uncomfortable angle for his tall body, listening attentively. For a man who claimed no interest in children, she mused, he was wonderful with them. Earlier in the festivities, he'd lifted six-year-old Erica for a dance, making her giggle helplessly as he swooped and dipped with her. Then he'd let solemn little Carla lead him onto the floor for the twist. Several other children, offspring of cousins, had gravitated to Josh's side when they discovered his ability to find quarters behind their ears.

"He's a good guy," her brother-in-law murmured, coming up behind her. When she turned to smile at Tom, he held out his arms, and they joined the other dancers. "I'm glad you found out in time that Kyle was such a jerk."

Had Josh told Tom why Kyle had walked out on her? "What do you mean?"

"Well, hell, I saw him around Christmas last year with some blonde plastered all over him, and you were still living together. I saw them again a couple of weeks ago, and I was tempted to plant my fist in his face."

"It wouldn't be worth the bruised knuckles."

"Too right. I didn't say anything because I didn't want to upset you. Maybe I should have."

"I probably wouldn't have believed you," she assured him. "Or I would have made up an excuse for him. You know, that it was all one-sided, and that Kyle was probably trying to peel the blonde off without hurting her feelings. I wasn't ready to know what he was really like."

"I still feel bad," he answered. "But I'm glad you and Josh found each other. Gail and I were saying we can't remember the last time we saw you having so much fun with Kyle."

Hope smiled ruefully. "I don't think I ever did," she admitted. "Josh is a very good friend."

"Sure." He winked. "Like Gail and me. The best kind of friends." Before she could protest, Tom spun her around. Hope caught sight of Carla, clapping her hands in delight as she bounced on Gail's lap.

As the next song started, Hope's father tapped Tom's shoulder. She slid into her dad's arms and followed his old-fashioned intricate dance steps. Then he closed his arms around her in a familiar bear hug that made her feel like Daddy's "big-little" girl once again. She blinked rapidly to clear the tears that suddenly filled her eyes.

"I like that Kincaid boy, Hope. Bring him over again so we can get to know him better."

"We're just friends, Dad. He's only here to do us a favor."

Her father chuckled as he released her. "Like I said, Hope, I like that boy. Good thing I've got a few pennies put away. Looks like I'll be dancing at your wedding soon. Unless you two plan to elope?'' He winked broadly.

Hope shook her head. ''Friends, Dad. Honest. Josh is allergic to marriage.''

Her father waved his hand as if to dismiss that idea. ''Most men are until they meet the right woman.'' He patted her shoulder. ''Ah! There's your mother. She owes me another dance. Go find your young man, honey.''

''He's *not* my young man,'' she muttered to her father's retreating back. ''He's a friend. Just a friend.''

''Money in the bank or bats in your belfry?'' Josh asked from behind her. ''You're talking to yourself.''

She turned to face him, dismayed by the way her pulse suddenly skipped at the sight, the sound, the presence of him. ''That's because nobody listens to me,'' she told him.

He pulled her into his arms and began to dance. ''I'll listen,'' he murmured, leaning his chin against her ear.

''I know. The trouble is, you're the only one I don't have to convince.''

It really had seemed like a good idea at the time, Josh reminded himself as he caught sight of Hope walking out of her office with two men in obviously expensive suits. Hope herself looked like a million bucks. She wore a turquoise suit that skimmed her curves and showed just the right amount of leg to look classy while still making a man's temperature rise. The men wore crisp shirts and perfectly knotted ties. He looked like a bag man in his dirty jeans and shirt, with his heavy work boots. The two men wore shoes polished enough to bounce light beams into space. He wore a tool belt. They wore beepers and Rolex watches.

Feeling totally foolish about his errand now, he shifted the picnic basket he carried and weighed the possibility of escaping before Hope noticed him. If he moved fast enough, he could get the basket back to Gray's place and try this another time. He started to turn around. Too late—she was shaking hands with the two suits, then looking right at him. Her brows went up, but then her lips curved into a smile that lit her eyes and did something weird to his respiration. Probably all that sawdust he breathed all day.

She came toward him, the high heels she wore causing her hips to sway in an interesting way. "Hi! What are you doing here?"

Conscious of the receptionist's open curiosity, he hoisted the basket a little higher. "Let's go into your office." He followed her, enjoying the view of her trim figure from the back as much as he had from the front. When they were inside her office, he nudged the door shut with his elbow and brought the basket to her desk. "This is for you."

The way her forehead crinkled made him want to kiss it smooth. "A picnic? I wish you'd phoned. I'm meeting my friend Chantelle for dinner."

He shook his head. "Not exactly." He caught her wrist and tugged her toward the desk. "A good guess, but completely off base. Take a look." With his free hand, he lifted the lid of the basket.

Hope glanced at the basket, then back at him. "There's nothing—"

"Meow..." The voice from the basket stopped her.

"A cat?"

He grinned. "See for yourself."

There might as well have been a snake in that basket, the way she inched over to it. He stood back a bit, trusting to nature to take over. Sure enough, the second she peered into the basket, she made one of those funny female sounds, almost like a cat herself.

"Oh, Josh!" She looked into his eyes, and something in his chest seemed to do a somersault. "Oh, they're so sweet!"

"I was hoping you'd say that. Someone's always dumping cats at construction sites," he told her, which was the truth, but not about this particular litter. These cats had been born at Gray's vet clinic, and had been carefully tended. He wouldn't take the chance of giving Hope sick pets. Still, he could play to her sympathies. "The mama cat doesn't look much more than a kitten herself. I hate to take them to the Humane Society, but they need a home."

"Josh, I can't take them. I work all day."

"Yeah, well, what about when you have a kid to take care of? A cat and three kittens are a hell of a lot easier than a human baby, but they still need some attention. You can practice being a single mother."

The words just came out. Hope gasped and recoiled as if he'd hit her. To his disgust, he saw her eyes fill with tears before she could turn away and hide them by looking into the basket again. He called himself every kind of insensitive jerk.

"Hope, I—"

"I don't believe you did this!" she whispered. "You got me a basket full of *cats* so I can practice being a *mother?* Are you out of your mind?" He opened his mouth, but she shook her head. "Go away, Josh." He tried to speak again, but she waved him away. "Just go."

With his heart somewhere in his shoes, he reached out to flip the lid over the cat and her kittens, but Hope slapped his hand away. He looked at her. "What? Don't tell me you're going to take them anyway?"

"Yes, damn it! You said they need a home."

He felt as if he'd missed a step and landed too hard. "Hope, I... I'm sor—"

"Out!" she ordered.

This was one time when he really didn't want to cut his losses and go, but he had a feeling he'd only make things worse if he tried to say anything else when he already had one boot planted in his mouth. Still, he couldn't leave like this, with her hurt and angry and him with his unsaid apology and guilt. While her back was still turned toward him, he lifted his hand and touched the silky coil of red-gold hair at the back of her neck. Her shoulders stiffened under the suit jacket. He dropped his hand.

As he walked out of the KidsCan Togs offices, he felt hollow and raw. He felt worse about losing Hope as a friend than he'd ever felt about any of his former lovers walking away.

Hope blinked away her tears and gazed into the basket, transfixed by the blissfully purring little mother cat and her tiny babies. When she cautiously extended her hand and touched the cat's silky fur with her fingertips, the creature trilled and blinked up at her.

"Hope?" It was her secretary's voice. "Are you all right? Josh took off like the hounds of hell were nipping at his heels. Did you two have a spat?"

A spat? Lovers had spats. Hope frowned. "We had a slight disagreement." And she would probably never see him again.

"Oh! Look what he brought you! Aren't they darling?"

Hope had to smile despite the riot of feelings she was trying to sort out about Josh's cruelty and her angry reaction. "They are sweet. I've never had a pet before, except for a goldfish when I was about ten. Paul flushed it down the toilet."

Her secretary chuckled. "I don't think he'd thank you for reminding him of that now."

Hope chuckled also. "Not now that he's an old married businessman." She watched, fascinated, as the mother cat licked one of the kittens. It reminded her that she didn't know anything about the care and feeding of her new pets. "You have cats, don't you, Milly? What do I have to do for them?"

Milly reached into the basket and stroked the mother cat between her ears. "Lots of love and attention, good nutrition, regular doctor visits." The little cat purred loudly and rubbed her head against Milly's fingers, eyes blissfully closed. Milly smiled at Hope. "Essentially, you treat them like babies who never grow up and leave home."

Milly's words echoed Josh's enough to make Hope sigh. Her secretary patted her shoulder. "The vet I always take my cats to isn't far from here. If the boss lets us out a few minutes early," she said with a wink, "I'll lead you there and introduce you. Since they're strays, you want to make sure they're healthy and have all their shots."

"Shots? But they're so tiny." Suddenly, she felt very protective of the little family that was now dependent on her. "It won't hurt them, will it?"

"Don't worry, dear. Dr. Hendricks is very gentle." Her secretary patted her arm. "And you'll see how easy cats are."

A half hour later, her secretary's words were small consolation. Hope had a pile of pamphlets in her purse, samples of cat foods for nursing mothers, which she'd learned were called "queens," and a can of milk substitute with a doll-size bottle, just in case. Grayson Hendricks, D.V.M., a giant of a man with sad brown eyes, tumbling dark curls and a gentle manner, now held one of the kittens up, tail first. It squealed as if he were torturing it and extended tiny pink claws. Her heart contracted at the sound of its cry, and she had to clench her hands to keep from trying to rescue the poor little thing.

Maybe Josh hadn't been so insultingly wrong after all.

"Two little girls so far," Dr. Hendricks told her, setting the kitten back in the curve of its mother's body. The screams ceased instantly. The cat welcomed her baby with a couple of licks of her pink tongue. Repeating the procedure with the third kitten, who also shrieked and squirmed until it was back with the mother, Dr. Hendricks announced that it was a boy. Hope finally gave in to the urge to stroke the kittens, adding her reassurances to their mother's.

"Once you're in the computer, we'll send a reminder to bring them in for spaying and neutering, as well as booster shots. When the kittens are weaned, the mother should also be spayed." He smiled. "Unfortunately, it's impossible to tell a cat in heat to just say *no.*"

Hope felt herself blush, thinking about the man who had made that difficult for her, too.

"I see. Well." She cleared her throat. "Is there anything else I need to know?"

Dr. Hendricks smiled. "Just read the pamphlets. Everything should be spelled out for you, but if you have any questions, call. We have a twenty-four-hour answering service." She nodded and reached out to secure the latch on the basket lid. "Oh, and we'll need their names for our records."

"Names?" she echoed. "They were a bit of a surprise, so I haven't thought that far ahead yet," she admitted ruefully. One more thing her new charges had in common with children, she thought. "They don't have to go to kitty school, do they?"

He chuckled. "No. Their mother teaches them everything they need to know. Of course, when you go away for anything more than overnight, you'll have to either board them or get in a pet sitter to look after them."

Hope nodded, wishing she hadn't banished Josh, so she'd have the pleasure of wringing his neck. But being honest with herself, she had to admit she simply wished she hadn't been so quick to feel angry at him. No, not angry. Hurt. His implication that she was being thoughtless and perhaps a little selfish about wanting a child had hurt her. His criticism had hurt because she wanted his understanding, even his approval. Somehow, he'd become very important to her. And, damn him, he'd been right about how little thought she'd given to the practical side of raising a child by herself.

With a sigh, she thanked Dr. Hendricks, then carried her basket to the reception area to pay her bill. Once she arrived home, Hope deposited the feline family in a corner of a spare bedroom and set up the litter box Milly had provided, in a corner of the adjoining bathroom. She phoned Chantelle to apologize for running late and offered to meet her at their favorite Chinese restaurant soon. Then she opened a can of the foulest-smelling stuff she'd ever encountered and filled a small dish with the disgusting goop. When she brought the food upstairs, the mother cat hastily disengaged her nursing kittens. Ignoring their pathetic complaints, she attacked her dinner with enough gusto to remind Hope there was no accounting for taste. Unable to turn away from the kittens' cries, Hope lingered to stroke their downy coats until their mother returned.

Later that evening, after hugging Chantelle good-night, Hope drove home emotionally numb. She was so happy for her friend, and so envious, that somehow, the two canceled each other out, leaving her feeling empty. Upstairs in the spare room, the mother cat trilled a greeting and left the kittens to trot over and wind around Hope's ankles. Hope bent and stroked the pretty little tabby, smiling at her enthusiastic purring, then straightened and sighed.

She owed Josh an apology. He'd been absolutely right about her ignorance, and worse, her arrogance. In her desperation to have a child, she'd forgotten that *having* a baby was only a start. Now she knew she would have to rearrange her life to put another person first. And she would. As soon as she made her first appointment at the fertility clinic, she'd start altering her priorities so that KidsCan Togs came second. That would mean giving Paul more responsibilities, but that would probably be a good thing. Even if he wasn't quite ready yet, he'd grow into it. After all, she hadn't been born a CEO. She'd had to learn from her father. Josh had been right about that, too.

A flood of self-doubt washed over her as she lay in bed. She'd thought her decision to have a baby on her own was a brilliant solution, but there were so many things she hadn't begun to consider. She'd assumed she could do everything herself, but Chantelle's comments about Rob's excitement over being a father had shaken her. What if her own child was a boy? Who would be his role model? She didn't know anything about being a boy. Would it be enough for a little boy to have uncles?

Hope sat up and resolutely fluffed her pillow, then flopped back down. Well, so what if Josh had been right about some things. And so what if she had a lot to learn. Every woman who became a mother had to learn how. Besides, if that half-grown cat in the other room could be a natural mother, why, with all her advantages, couldn't she?

Chapter Ten

One thing about Grayson Hendricks, Josh thought as he watched his old friend pause in the doorway to the Boots 'n' Saddles Bar and Steak House—he was hard to miss, even in a crowd. And several of the young ladies at a nearby table sure hadn't missed Gray's entrance. They were wasting their time, but Josh wasn't going to be the one to tell them that the good-looking giant was still hung up over the woman who'd used him and tossed him away as if he were an old shoe.

Gray caught his eye and started toward the booth Josh was sprawled in. The young ladies followed him with their eyes, but Josh doubted his friend even noticed he was passing by a table full of interested females. Their regular waitress noticed Gray from behind the bar and signaled that she'd be bringing his usual beer momentarily.

"How's it going?" Josh asked.

"It's going," Gray answered. The waitress swooped past, leaving a frosty mug of beer in front of him. Gray lifted the mug and drank deeply. "Hot out there," he commented. "I would have been here sooner, but my last client took extra time." He gave Josh an odd look. "New cat owner. Four cats, in fact. Said they were a gift from a friend who found them at a construction site."

Josh couldn't believe Gray's words were making his face burn. "Oh, yeah?" He picked up his own beer mug and took a drink.

"Yeah. Hedging your bets by playing on her sympathies?"

His face grew hotter at the bull's-eye Gray had just scored. "Something like that."

"Well, thanks for recommending me. I can always use new clients."

Josh shrugged, unwilling to admit Hope had tossed him out of her office before he'd had the chance to mention Gray's services. "Your clinic is halfway between her office and her house, so it makes sense."

Gray nodded. "Nice lady. Good-looking, too." With one finger, Gray traced a deep groove in the surface of the table, then looked up. "No wedding ring. Is she seeing anyone?"

Josh stared at Gray, trying to see into his friend's head. He knew the kind of women who attracted Gray: wounded, fragile women who needed help putting themselves back together, not strong, secure women like Hope. Had Gray looked into Hope's turquoise eyes over a basketful of cats and decided it was time to try a normal relationship?

Finally, he shook his head. "Not that I know."

"Not even you?"

He met Gray's assessing look straight on. "Not even me. We're just good friends. Why?"

"Because I might be interested, and it's not like you to be *just* friends with a woman who could knock the sandals off a monk."

Josh set his mug down with a thump that nearly sloshed beer over the side. "Hope's not your type."

"Oh, no?" Gray sat up a little taller, and Josh belatedly remembered how much iron his old pal could pump. "Just what is my type?" Gray asked, his voice low and tight.

"You know. Victims." He ignored Gray's narrowed eyes. "Women who've been hurt and need healing." Josh shook his head. "That's not Hope. She's like tempered steel."

Gray snorted his disagreement. "Man, you call yourself a good friend? Are you blind? I could tell after two minutes that that lady is hurting. Sure, she looks strong, but there's real pain in those eyes. You watch her with those kittens sometime. I thought she was going to cry every time one of them squeaked. Their mother didn't seem half as concerned." Gray lifted his mug. "Maybe that's why all you two are is friends. She may be too raw to let you get close. I suppose you gave her your usual warning about picket fences and babies?"

Josh felt as if he'd taken a direct hit, but before he could do more than growl that Gray didn't know what he was talking about, their waitress appeared, pad in hand. They both ordered the sirloin-steak specials, but Josh felt as if his appetite had deserted him. He was still bothered by Gray's interest in Hope. On the one hand, it was about time Gray got over what Josh thought of as a narrow escape from a lifetime of trouble and started looking around for new women. Lord knew, there were plenty out there. All a guy like Gray had to do was stand still and look forlorn. Women loved that wounded-bear look. But on the other hand, why Hope?

Could Gray be right that Hope was more vulnerable than he'd thought? He had to admit his first impression of her, back in May when they'd met, was that she was sad. But she hadn't seemed particularly troubled for a while. In fact, it seemed to him that she was pretty happy these days. Even her secretary had said so. Hell, he'd figured she was over that jerk Kyle by now. She'd said herself that she hadn't been madly in love with the guy. But there was this whole bit about having a baby that maybe he hadn't tried hard enough to understand. Maybe the reason she'd gone ballistic over his suggestion she practice mothering the kittens before she had her own kid was that she was *hurt,* not angry. If that was the case, then he was as big a jerk as Kyle.

Gray cleared his throat, yanking him out of his thoughts. "Do you still want to borrow a bike for the hospital ride?"

"Nope!" He grinned at Gray's look of surprise. "I pick up my new Honda Goldwing tomorrow after work."

"All right!" Gray grinned back and offered him five. "Bet I bring in more pledge money than you do this time."

"We'll see." This was an annual challenge between them, all in a good cause: the hospital renovation fund. "How about, whoever gets the lower amount of pledges has to make up double the difference?" He felt pretty confident, since he'd beaten Gray every year for the past five in raising money for the hospital.

Gray lifted his mug. "You're on." They both drank, then lowered their mugs. "You bringing anyone this year?"

"Depends," Josh hedged. *Like, on whether Hope was ever going to speak to me again,* he added to himself. "I never could get Hope to ride on that old rattletrap bike I had back in high school. Maybe she'll feel safer on the Goldwing."

The look Gray shot him made him wonder if his friend had intended to ask Hope himself to go on the ride. The thought didn't sit well with Josh, but he didn't understand why. Hell, he and Hope were friends, and all fantasies aside, that was all they were likely to be. What business was it of his if Hope was attracted to Gray? No doubt about it, Gray would make a much better husband and father. He should be happy if two of his best friends found each other.

Stabbing his fork into the green salad their waitress set before him, Josh identified the emotion threatening to choke him, and it sure wasn't happiness. It was the old green monster.

* * *

For two days after she'd ordered Josh out of her office, out of her life, Hope felt as if guilt had become a ball and chain attached to her ankle. She couldn't seem to think, to perform, with her usual efficiency, because all that seemed to occupy her mind was Josh's stricken expression when she'd told him to go. The only thing that mitigated any of her guilt was the fact that she'd kept the cat and her kittens. Finally, she acknowledged what her conscience had been nagging her about for forty-eight hours: she had to apologize to Josh for losing her temper and thank him for giving her a very sweet, if impulsive, gift.

So Friday afternoon, she left the office early and drove home, resolved to speak to Josh before he left for his RV for the weekend. The mother cat, now named Tabitha, greeted her from the basket with her trilling meow, then disengaged herself from the kittens to wind around Hope's ankles until Hope picked her up. The kittens, Winkin, Blinkin and Nod, cried for their mother, but quieted as soon as Hope knelt and stroked their downy coats. Tabby purred like a well-tuned Ferrari, and the kittens were beginning to take after her. Hope had discovered almost immediately upon taking them home that even a few minutes of petting and cooing to them calmed her work-frazzled nerves. Now, after only two days as a cat owner, she couldn't imagine how she'd gotten along without them.

At four-thirty, Hope parked in front of Josh's town house. Ignoring the way her heartbeat tripped unevenly, she stood on his front porch, a big bunch of multicolored flowers clutched in one hand as a peace offering. His van was parked in the driveway, so she was sure she'd caught him before he left, but there was no answer when she rang the doorbell. He might be showering, she thought, then had to push away the enticing image of that lean, powerful male body glistening with suds and water.

After ringing the bell several more times, she decided she'd been foolishly impulsive to simply drop in on him without warning. Had she really subconsciously assumed he was waiting for her to come to him? That certainly wasn't Josh Kincaid's style. He could be inside at that very moment, with another, more willing woman, while she was standing with her flowers on his porch like a lovesick teenager. She should have phoned him, made her apologies and let it go at that.

Hope turned and started down the stairs at the same moment that a large white motorcycle rumbled into Josh's driveway. She froze in midstep, recognizing the rider despite the black-tinted face mask. The sound of the engine stopped, and Josh lifted black-gloved hands to remove the helmet. His grin made the blood rush to her cheeks.

"Let me guess," he called, his grin widening, before she could think of anything halfway sensible and coherent to say. "You were in the neighborhood and wanted to see where a brass-plated jackass lives."

She watched him dismount and walk toward her. The closer he came, the harder her heart thudded against her ribs. She had to swallow twice before she could speak. "No. I came to apologize for having a fit over the cats, and to thank you for them."

His grin faded and he shrugged one leather-clad shoulder. "No need. You were justified. I sorta stuck my feet in my mouth. What you do with your life is your business." Then he gave her a boyish smile. "I'm glad you like the cats."

Hope smiled back. "I love them." She thrust the flowers toward him, stopping him in his tracks. "These are for you. A peace offering."

Josh looked at the flowers, then met her eyes, his expression stunned. She had to stick them in his face before he actually took them from her. "No one ever gave me flowers before."

"Then we're even. No one ever gave me cats before."

Josh took a deep breath. "Are you busy tonight?" She shook her head. "Good. I'll take you to dinner to celebrate."

"Celebrate?"

He waved his hand at the gleaming motorcycle beside him. "My new toy." He beamed. "I just picked her up. Isn't she a beauty?"

She cast a skeptical glance over the huge machine in the driveway. It didn't look the slightest bit feminine, but Josh seemed to think it was female. She thought it looked like something out of the *Terminator* movies, all metal and chrome. "I never did ride on a motorcycle," she confessed, recalling easily how he'd teased her about refusing to ride on his noisy old bike in high school.

"So I'll be your first." He winked.

"Okay," she said slowly. "As long as you promise not to go too fast."

Josh laughed. "Speed limit. I promise. Do you have a jacket with you?" She shook her head. "It gets cool riding at night. I might have one somewhere that will fit you well enough. C'mon in." He moved past her and put his key into the door lock.

For a moment, she hesitated. It wasn't too late to run to her car and drive away before she allowed him to scare the daylights out of her on that monster machine. And she knew he would try, just to tease her about having to be in control. But in her heart, she knew she wanted to ride with him now, just as she had back in high school, when she'd been so afraid of the daring bad boy he'd seemed to be.

Besides, being his friend, she simply couldn't spoil his pleasure in his new toy.

Hope followed Josh into the town house. A short flight of carpeted stairs ran up from the entry hall, into what looked like a living room, and another ran down into darkness. Josh flicked on several lights in the upper level and invited her inside.

"I've got cold soft drinks in the fridge. Help yourself," he told her, waving toward a small galley kitchen. "It'll take me a minute to find the right jacket." He was already taking another set of stairs two at a time, heading, she guessed, for his bedroom closet. Hope wandered in the opposite direction, curious to see how Josh lived.

She looked around in mild surprise. No wonder Josh hadn't offered the typical male "excuse the mess" line. There wasn't any mess. The carelessly folded newspaper on a side table next to the large black leather sofa didn't count as mess. It was the only thing out of place in the entire living room—dining room space. The heavy leather chairs and mellow wooden tables reflected strongly masculine, simple taste. The mantel, a highly varnished slab of wood with the bark still on its edge, held an array of sports trophies. Several pieces of Inuit soapstone carvings perched on other shelves. A rough-bark basket filled with pine cones sat in the middle of the wooden trestle dining table. There was a wall unit with a television and VCR in the middle, flanked by stereo components, all very high-tech looking, and surrounded by shelves of CDs and books. The lamps strategically placed by the chairs and the sofa ends were serious reading lights, not artsy decorator ones. She hadn't known what to expect of Josh's home, but this room made sense. She wondered if the rest of the house looked as neat and functional, or if the entire upstairs had been turned into a giant laundry hamper. That, she decided, would have to remain Josh's secret.

"Try this," Josh said, coming into the room. Hooked over one finger, he held a white felt jacket with black leather sleeves.

Hope shrugged into the jacket, which engulfed her. She held up her arms, covered past her fingertips by the sleeves. Josh chuckled. "It's the smallest one I've got. Let's try some creative folding."

He stepped closer and began folding back the knitted cuffs of the sleeves. His subtle scent filled her head. The touch of his fingers on her bare hand sent a totally unexpected shock of awareness through her. Probably, she rationalized, it had literally been a shock, a static-electricity one. But the same thing happened when his strong, adroit fingers freed her other hand from the overlong sleeve. A simple touch and her nerves sparked like live wires. Unwilling to acknowledge the effect he had on her, Hope pulled her hands away and busied them in zipping the jacket closed, keeping her head down so she wouldn't accidentally meet his eyes.

Josh cleared his throat, which, of course, made her look up into his face. "Okay?" She nodded. "Let's go. There's a spare helmet for you."

Suspecting this was not the smartest choice she could have made, but not certain exactly why, Hope followed Josh outside. He helped her fit the helmet over her head, then had the audacity to take her hair, which she'd worn in a loose ponytail, and stuff it down the front of her jacket. His fingers brushed her chest just above her breasts, causing more of those disturbing sparks, but she clamped her lower lip between her teeth and refused to react. He might have overstepped himself a little by reaching into her jacket, she thought, but he was really only trying to do her a favor. Otherwise, she'd probably end up spending hours brushing the tangles out of her hair. She'd already made a fool of herself once this week by overreacting to one of his friendly gestures. She wouldn't ruin the truce between them by doing it again.

Josh showed her the footrests, then slid one leg over the seat of the motorcycle. Suddenly, it roared to life. He reached behind him to pat the remainder of the padded leather seat, which hardly looked generous enough to accommodate an extra person without crowding. Taking a deep breath, Hope placed one hand on Josh's broad shoulder and slid her leg over the big machine, thinking as she did so that it was a lot like trying to ride double on a knight's fully armored charger. She gripped both his shoulders to steady herself as he reached behind to fold down the armrests.

"Okay?" The clarity of his voice, coming though the walkie-talkie in her helmet, startled her. She managed to answer that she was, indeed, okay. "Hang on," he told her.

Hope thought she'd been hanging on, with her fingers clenched like talons on his leather-clad shoulders. But the instant she felt the machine move forward, she gave a tiny, involuntary shriek and wrapped both arms around his chest and plastered herself against his back. Eventually, Hope realized that Josh was, in fact, driving at a lawfully sedate pace, and that the big bike felt steadier than the surefooted trail horses they'd ridden on Victoria Day weekend. But by then, she'd gotten comfortable with the feel of his solid body and was afraid that if she released his waist to use the armrests, she'd unbalance him. And now that she was having fun, she'd hate to do something stupid to send them into a ditch.

How, Josh wondered, could the best thing he could imagine doing also be the worst thing he could imagine doing? When he'd found Hope on his doorstep, after fantasizing all the way home about how it would feel to ride with her clinging to him, he figured it was one of those gifts of timing. And now that he knew exactly how it felt to have her body pressing tightly to his, her long legs wrapped around his hips and thighs, even the wrong way around, he wanted to be anywhere but where he was. It was bliss, and it was torture. Why couldn't he have simply accepted her apology and suggested they order a pizza?

* * *

Sunday afternoon, Josh watched Hope mingle with his old friends and their wives—almost no bachelors left except him—and congratulated himself for being so smart. He'd already fended off three phone calls from women he'd dated in the past, who'd hinted strongly that they wouldn't say no to an invitation to this annual barbecue. But he was able to tell them honestly that he was taking a special friend. It didn't even bother him to think that, by giving them that impression, he'd made it damn near impossible to ask those three perfectly nice, extremely attractive women out again without a lot of explanation. He simply wanted to be with Hope.

On the other hand, her announcement that she intended to become a single mother still had his head spinning. It didn't help that everyone at the barbecue seemed to have kids. Every time she was introduced to someone with a baby, Hope got that same dreamy look on her face. Fortunately, he knew it didn't have anything to do with him. At least this year, when his friends hinted that he and Hope made a good couple, he didn't have to worry about her misinterpreting his intentions. They both knew exactly where they stood with each other.

It irritated him that everyone he knew expected him to get married just because most of his friends were. Was he supposed to follow them over the edge of a cliff like a lemming, and tie up his life the way they all had, just because they were pals? Sure brought to mind that old saying "Misery loves company." And in his mind, marriage led to misery. Hell, only a few minutes ago, someone had announced that one of the longest-married couples in the group had filed for divorce, so they'd be missing the barbecue. That was the couple everyone held up as a shining example, even though Art had given up his job coaching minor-league hockey for Jane, who hated hockey. Now, it was probably impossible for Art to get back his old job. If he wanted to be in hockey at all, he'd have to settle for coaching little kids on weekends. It just wasn't worth it.

"Oh, look!" Hope waved at someone across the lawn. "It's the vet I took the cat and kittens to. Do you know him?"

"Gray Hendricks? Sure," Josh answered cautiously. He didn't like the way Hope's eyes lit up at the sight of his old friend. After that little talk he and Gray had had about Hope, he really didn't like the way Gray moved just a little quicker through the crowd after spotting them. He also didn't relish the thought of what Hope's reaction would be if Gray spilled the beans about Josh getting the cat and kittens from his clinic the same day he'd given them to Hope.

Hell, if he was going to make a list of things he didn't like, the way Gray held Hope's hand a little too long sure qualified. And the way he said "Call me Gray" when she'd greeted him as "Doctor." He wasn't too crazy about the way Hope smiled right into his old pal's eyes, either. He was tempted to put his arm around Hope and play the possessive lover.

"How are the kittens?" Gray asked.

"They're wonderful," Hope answered, smiling up at Gray. "They have names now." Josh frowned. She hadn't told *him* that yet. "The girls are Winkin and Blinkin, and the boy is Nod." Hope wrinkled her nose. "I ran out of inspiration for the mother, so I named her Tabitha, Tabby for short."

Josh felt himself seeing green as Hope and Gray talked about kitten behavior. Hope sounded as proud as the parents showing off their kids' photos. It made him think Gray was right about Hope's pain and vulnerability. without knowing anything about her frustrated desire for a child. His mind made the short leap to the idea of Gray fathering Hope's child. The thought of Hope in his friend's arms hit him like a punch to the solar plexus. Giving in to his possessive impulse, he draped his arm over Hope's shoulders.

He felt her stiffen, and pulled her a little closer to his side until she relaxed and let her hip rest against his.

Gray met his eyes for a long moment, then gave a quick nod. "I saw the Goldwing out front," he said. "Classy machine." Then he smiled at Hope. "Has he talked you into doing the hospital ride with him?"

Josh smiled down at Hope. "Not yet," he answered for her.

Someone called Gray from across the yard. "Catch you later," he said, giving Hope a direct smile before moving away.

The instant Gray was out of hearing distance, Hope moved out from under his arm. "You're riding in the annual fund-raiser?"

"Yeah. Do you want to join me? It'll be fun. Good people, good cause."

She beamed. "I'd love to. I'll get everyone at the firm to sponsor us."

"Good. 'Cause Gray and I have a bet on as to who can raise more pledges."

"Say no more. Get me the pledge forms, and I'll get you the sponsors. The KidsCan people are great that way. And if you're nice to the boss, you'll probably get yourself a corporate sponsorship, too."

"Oh, I plan to be *very* nice to the boss," he told her. Could he help it if he was hoping she'd be feeling charitable to him, too?

When Josh parked the motorcycle in her driveway, Hope was happy to see her house. The timers had turned on strategically placed lights, giving the windows a welcoming glow punctuated by the bright lanterns lighting her front steps and porch. It had been a long, long day, after a long, busy week. She couldn't wait to get inside, get into a hot shower and fall into her bed. But first, she had to get off the bike, where she'd been plastered tightly to Josh's body for hours.

She braced her hands on his shoulders to lever herself up from the seat. Even through the thick leather of his jacket, she could feel the hardness of his shoulder muscles flexing under her fingers. That sensation momentarily distracted her from getting her feet under her. Feeling incredibly clumsy, she tripped and nearly fell over the driveway curb.

Josh's hand closed around her arm, holding her up. She couldn't see his face through the dark-tinted helmet visor, but she could feel his concern.

"I'm okay," she said quickly, grateful that the darkness hid her blush.

Still holding her arm, he swung his leg over the motorcycle and stood beside her with enviable grace. She let him unfasten her helmet, then waited for him to remove his own and hang them both on the handlebars.

"Would you like to come in for coffee? You still have to ride home." She held the door open in invitation.

"Coffee would be great," he answered, stepping inside. "Thanks."

"Coming right up," she said over her shoulder. At that moment, Tabitha came running to them, trilling and winding around her ankles. Hope bent to pet the cat, then clucked to her and headed into the kitchen. Josh followed. When Hope turned around to ask him if he'd like cookies with his coffee, she discovered he'd picked up the small mother cat and was cradling her in his arms. Tabby's purring rivaled the rumble of Josh's motorcycle. Hope smiled at the cat's pleasure. She knew all too well how nice Josh's arms could feel wrapped around an appreciative female body.

He leaned one hip against the counter, still cuddling Tabby. "Where are the kittens?"

She shrugged out of her leather jacket. "Upstairs, in a spare room. Give me a second to fill the coffeemaker, and I'll show you."

A minute later, with Tabby leading, and Josh following, Hope questioned the wisdom of bringing Josh upstairs. The lights were dim, and it was obviously just the two of them, with only a basket of cats for distraction. He could be very seductive without half trying.

When Josh ignored her to crouch beside the basket, she chided herself for being foolish. He'd given her his word that he would be her friend and not pounce on her. As he'd said before, he didn't make promises often, but when he did, he honored them. So she contented herself with sinking into a chair with a barely stifled yawn, and watching his big, strong hands as he stroked the kittens and let them claw and chew harmlessly on his fingers.

"I'm glad you like having them," he said without looking up. "Do you think you'll keep them all when they're weaned?"

"I hadn't thought about giving any of them away. It would be like breaking up a matched set." She saw his nod, then wondered why he'd asked. "Are you thinking of adopting one if I do?"

He half turned and smiled. "Nah. There are always kittens looking for homes if I decide I need another pet."

"Another pet? Do you have one now?"

"Used to have a dog. A big shepherd-Lab cross." Josh swiveled around and sat with his back against the wall near the basket, his knees drawn up. Tabby crawled into his lap and climbed up his chest to lick his chin, making them both chuckle. "Sometimes, I miss the old boy. He came to work with me most days, until he got too arthritic. The kids in the town house next door would take him out a couple of times a day after he had to stay home. Poor old Ziggy. He was a good pal."

When Josh let his guard down, Hope felt as if she were being given tiny gifts of his trust. It made her throat thicken with emotion. "How old was he?"

"Almost seventeen." Josh stroked Tabby, who trilled her thanks, then climbed delicately into her basket of kittens. "Damn near killed me to put him down. I kept wishing he'd go in his sleep and not force me to make that decision, but he kept hanging on. Gray was Ziggy's vet ever since he opened the clinic." Josh let out a long breath. "Man, the two of us got stinking drunk that night."

Hope swallowed past the lump in her throat. "Well, if you do think you'd like a kitten—"

"Nah. Too much responsibility for a Teflon kinda guy, right?" The grin he gave her was crooked and terribly winsome. But before she could protest that she didn't believe he was nearly as irresponsible as he claimed, his grin faded and he looked at her with a strange intensity in his eyes.

"Hope, I've been thinking. I know you're serious about wanting to have a baby on your own. I still don't *understand* it, but I guess it's your right to make that kind of decision. But as your friend, I gotta say, I really don't like the idea of you having some stranger's kid."

Hope opened her mouth to tell him that his likes and dislikes didn't factor into her decision, but he held up one hand to silence her.

"So here's my idea. You don't have to give me an answer right away. Just think about it. And, you know, consider it in the spirit it's meant, friend to friend. Right?"

Hope held her breath, afraid to follow where her own thoughts were straying.

"I won't be insulted if you say no, but hell, Hope, we're friends. I'm not the smartest or the best-looking guy in the western hemisphere, but I'm not too bad a specimen. So I was thinking that if I . . ." He looked away. Still staring at a spot on the far wall, he cleared his throat. "If I . . . You know . . ."

Hope couldn't move, couldn't release the breath trapped inside her, couldn't believe what Josh seemed to be saying.

"Damn it, Hope! I want to help you have your kid."

Chapter Eleven

Josh stole a glance at Hope. She looked as though she'd been frozen solid. *Blown it this time, Kincaid,* he thought. *There goes one beautiful friendship.*

Finally, he couldn't stand her silence. "Hope?"

She turned her head slightly and blinked a couple of times as if coming out of a trance. "Did you say what I thought you said?"

"That I'm volunteering to father your baby? Yeah, that's about what I said."

Her breath whooshed out of her. "Josh, I don't know what to say. I'm stunned, I guess. You, of all men... I'm stunned, but I'm touched. It's so sweet of you, to offer. But—"

"No strings, I swear. I know you want a kid. You know I don't. I'm the last guy in the world who wants to create my own personal dynasty. All I'm offering is a contribution of the necessary genetic material so you don't have to take chances on some stranger's genes."

Hope leaned forward, her eyes wide. "You're really serious about this?" Her voice came out hushed. He tried to ignore how sexy it sounded.

"Damn right I'm serious."

"Why?"

That was the one question he was hoping she wouldn't ask. He didn't know the answer himself. He didn't understand her aching need for a child, but he wanted her to be happy.

He shrugged. "Because we're friends, and friends look out for each other. Hell, if you were looking at used cars, I wouldn't let you buy a clunker."

Her soft lips curved into a smile. "I guess that makes some sense, but a baby isn't a used car. What about legal considerations? An anonymous donor never has contact with the child, but you and I—"

"Have your lawyer draw up a contract that gives you all the rights. I can be a designated uncle or something. The only thing I don't want to do is give up our friendship."

She shook her head. "No, I don't want to give that up, either. Josh, this is crazy."

His grin felt a little crooked. "Hey, there's no insanity in my family, except for this. I can get you a clean bill of health from my doctor." To his relief, she smiled. But then, her smile turned into a frown, and he suspected she was going to refuse him. "I know this is coming out of left field. You don't have to give me an answer right now. Think about it, okay?

"Yes, I'll . . . I will. I'm just . . ."

"Yeah, I know. Stunned."

She nodded. He watched her for a long, silent moment. She'd leaned back in her chair, eyes closed, as if she was trying to absorb what he'd said. He was still a little stunned himself that he'd gone and done what he'd been thinking about since the first time she'd mentioned having a baby on her own. Other women he'd known had talked about having his baby, and all he'd felt was panic. So why did he feel this primal urge to father Hope's child? It had to be the fact that she wanted a baby for herself, no strings attached to the father.

Finally, she sat up and looked at him. "It's an intriguing proposition, Josh. But—" she looked away and her cheeks turned pink "—I'd feel funny about asking you to go into one of those little rooms with the porno movies and magazines, to get you in the mood to...you know... With a jar?"

He felt his jaw drop. A *jar?* What the hell was she talking about? As if she'd read his mind, she said, "That's the way it's done at a clinic."

"What's wrong with the way nature intended it?"

She glared at him. "I knew you had to have an ulterior motive! It's like that whole *When Harry Met Sally* thing, about how men can't be friends with women they don't secretly want to have sex with."

Her accusation stung. "I don't have an ulterior motive. I can live the rest of my life very well without getting into your pants. But this jar thing... And I don't even want to guess what they'll do to you. Pretty cold and clinical. That's a hell of a way to start a new life if you don't have to."

Hope got out of her chair and started pacing. With a sinking feeling in his gut, he watched her, certain that this time she was going to turn him down flat. Finally, she halted and sank down to the carpet, her expression troubled.

"So what you're suggesting," she said, looking past his left shoulder, "is that we don't go to a clinic or a doctor? That we try to do it—" her cheeks turned bright pink "—ourselves?"

"Exactly."

"Oh." She moved her gaze to a point past his right shoulder. "I see. Well, that will take even more thinking about, and some getting used to. I mean, I'm still trying to deal with you offering to father a baby for me. I never thought beyond artificial insemination. I'm not sure how to think about making l— I mean, having se— Well, doing it naturally. With you."

"It's not like I'm Quasimodo, is it?" he teased gently, knowing damn well she wasn't repulsed by him. Far from it, no matter how hard she tried to hide it. He never would have offered if he thought otherwise.

"Oh, no! Not at all! It's just that I don't want this to change anything between us. Our friendship, that is." Finally, she met his eyes. "It would have to be clearly understood that it was strictly sex for the sake of getting me pregnant. We'd have to be businesslike about it, right? So, no obligations to each other, besides our friendship. I mean, I don't want a permanent relationship, and neither do you. Right? So we'd have to be very, very careful."

Careful not to enjoy it too much? he thought, but didn't dare say out loud. This couldn't be easy for her. Not as it was for a guy. He was asking her to consider short-term sex without love, without a relationship. The only women he knew—not personally, of course—who could say yes easily to that usually got paid by the hour.

"Right." He flashed her a smile he hoped looked reassuring. "I think we can handle it without screwing up our friendship." His words played back, and he felt heat rise to his cheeks. Luckily, she didn't seem to notice.

A frown creased her forehead. "Josh, I'm too tired to think now. I need a couple of days."

"I figure you've got about three weeks to decide, if you want to try the next time you're ready."

Still frowning, she nodded. "I'll think about it and let you know soon." She stood up slowly. "The coffee must be ready." Without another word, she walked out of the room.

Josh pushed himself up from the floor and followed Hope to the kitchen. Funny thing, he thought, but they'd just coolly discussed having a sexual relationship without even touching once. So why, if this was going to be a strictly friendly, strictly business kind of deal, did he feel as if he'd spent a couple of hours of heavy foreplay, so ready to make love to Hope that his nerve endings sizzled?

This was a question a Teflon kind of guy didn't want to deal with.

Hope closed the door behind Josh, then leaned against it as if all the strength had dissolved from her bones. Josh wanted to father her baby!

The moment that he'd offered, she'd realized that she'd been subconsciously hoping he would all along. Had he guessed what she hadn't seen for herself until the words were hovering between them? He must have. Why else would he have made the offer?

Why else, indeed, except that he wanted to get her into his bed?

How did she feel about that? Even though she was alone in the house, Hope's face burned at the thought of making love...no, of having sex with Josh. She didn't dare reveal the simmering desire she'd felt for him since she'd first tasted his kiss. That would make their liaison much too personal. He'd probably feel that she was trying subliminally to trap him. And she'd only end up feeling foolish. Or getting hurt, if revealing her desire ruined their friendship. It would have to remain her guilty secret.

But without that desire, there was no way she could ever decide to accept his offer.

Monday evening, Josh heard the phone as he was opening his door after working overtime. By the time he reached for the receiver, the answering machine had clicked on.

"Josh, it's Hope." His heart gave a leap at the sound of her voice. "Call me when you—"

"Hey, I'm here. Just walked in. What's up?"

"Oh! Hi. I, um, I've been thinking about your offer." The uncertainty in her tone made his heart sink. "In fact, that's all I've been able to think about."

He'd been having the same problem. He'd nearly electro-cuted himself that afternoon, because his mind had been on making love to Hope, not on the wires he'd been working with.

"So, have you made your decision?"

"I think so." There was a long pause. He braced himself for the letdown, surprised by how much he cared about her wanting him to try to father her baby. "I have an appoint-ment with my lawyer tomorrow. How soon can you get to your doctor?"

Hope hung up the phone with fingers that were freezing cold, despite the warm weather outside. What had she just done? She wanted a baby so very much, but was this the right thing to do? Before Josh had made his offer, she hadn't thought beyond test tubes and petri dishes. Now, she was planning to have sex with her closest male friend in or-der to try having that baby that meant so much to her.

Enough to sacrifice Josh's friendship, if they couldn't deal with each other after being intimate? No, she didn't think so. Rubbing her forehead with her fingers, Hope conceded that she honestly didn't know the answer to that question. There were probably going to be a lot more ques-tions she wouldn't have answers to. Questions like, What if it didn't work out?

And what if it did?

If only she could meet someone exactly like Josh, but someone she could safely fall in love with, someone who wanted a committed relationship. Then she could give up this solitary baby chase and gladly let nature take its course.

Tuesday evening was always a quiet time at Josh's favor-ite Chinese restaurant. He sat in a red vinyl padded booth, sipping a light beer and waiting for Hope. Two weeks ago, after her phone call, he'd gone to his doctor. Today, he'd called her to tell her he'd picked up his results, and they'd agreed to meet for dinner in a neutral place. Between calls, whenever he'd seen her, she'd been so jumpy that he was sure she would call it off. He didn't care if she changed her mind about trying to have a baby to raise by herself. All he cared about was that she not take any of the chances of going to a clinic and using some unknown donor.

The restaurant door opened, and Hope breezed inside. She looked cool and classy in a dress that floated around her long legs and showed off her small waist. Her face seemed to light up when she spotted him, and she moved a little faster toward his booth. Lord, she was beautiful! But should he even be noticing that if they were going to do this clinical-sex thing? He didn't think he could stop being aware of her. She wasn't just physically beautiful. It was something about *her,* not only her looks. Whatever it was, it was the reason he cared about her as a friend. He sure hoped they didn't spoil that with sex.

"Hi! Sorry I'm late, but I had to wait for my lawyer to drop off the letter of agreement." Hope's cheeks turned pink as she sank onto the bench opposite him. She slid the manila envelope across the table to him. "I think it took her a while to get her mind around the concept."

"Yeah. My doctor had a little trouble with the idea, too. But he came through." Josh slid his own envelope across to Hope.

A waiter approached. Hope ordered a diet cola. "Maybe we should order dinner first," Josh suggested, "so we don't get interrupted once we start with these."

"Fine with me." She picked up a menu, then looked up. "You know this place better than I do. What do you recommend?"

Her question caught him off guard. He'd expected her to take charge of her own meal instead of asking for his advice. It was a totally chauvinistic, politically incorrect feeling, but he liked the fact that she'd done it. "You like spicy or sweet?"

"Both."

He'd meant food, but his libido seemed to have other ideas when Hope answered in that soft, husky voice of hers. Shifting to get a little more comfortable in his suddenly too-tight jeans, he signaled the waiter. After placing their order, he lifted the sealed envelope she'd given him. "Shall we?"

Hope nodded, her face going pink again, but she didn't open his envelope. Acutely aware of her gaze, Josh slid his finger under the flap of the envelope and withdrew the papers. Neatly typed in triplicate. One copy for Hope, one for him and one for the lawyer's files.

"You've read this?" he asked. She nodded, still toying with his envelope, not opening it yet. "And it's what you want?" She nodded again. "So give me a pen. I'll sign."

She fished a pen out of her purse. "Read it anyway, please, Josh. There might be something that you don't agree with. We can initial any changes, then sign the copies. The waiter can witness for us."

Anonymous but official. He understood she didn't want anyone she knew to find out. But for some stupid reason, it bugged him that an unknown waiter in a Chinese restaurant was going to witness their signatures to something so important—at least, important to Hope.

He skimmed, not really caring what the agreement said. Total custody was Hope's. He had no obligations. No responsibilities. No rights. No money was changing hands. He was in good health, with no known genetic disorders. The number of attempts before success or failure would be mutually decided. The child would bear Hope's last name. His name wouldn't appear on the birth certificate or any other official papers.

When he reached the end of the letter, he saw that Hope had already signed on her line.

"One thing I don't like," he said. "This part about the birth certificate. What are you going to put, 'father unknown'?"

"Well, yes, I guess..."

He shook his head. "The kid should know who his or her father is eventually. The timing can be your decision, but I don't think it's fair to keep the kid in the dark about half his background. And it's not fair to you for the kid to think he was the result of some anonymous quickie."

Now, Hope's face turned red. "No, I guess not. That sounds fair, as long as I have control over when to tell him or her. Change the wording, and we can initial it."

He crossed out the offending line and printed in the new terms. Her fingers brushed his when he passed the pen to her, and she jerked her hand away as if she'd gotten a shock. He wasn't sure he understood her skittishness, but he resisted the urge to cover her hand with his.

"One more thing," he said. Her eyebrows rose. "We're still going to be friends, right? Which means I'm going to see you and the kid from time to time, right?" Hope nodded, her eyes wary. "I'm not looking for any custody rights here, but I think we should agree up front that I'm some kind of honorary uncle."

"I have no problem with that," she answered, holding out her pen again. "Honorary uncle is fine."

He squeezed in the words making him an uncle, then initialed them and passed the pen to Hope. As she wrote her initials beside his, he thought about the two changes he'd made. Why did he care whether this hypothetical kid knew he was his—or her—real father? And why did he care whether or not he had any official status in the kid's life? Damned if he knew, unless he'd been bitten by that primal bug that made men want kids almost as much as women did. Scary thought, that one.

Hope gave him back the pen. He called the waiter over and explained that he needed a witness to his own signature. The waiter nodded. After they'd both signed the three copies, Josh mentally doubled the man's tip and passed two copies of the papers back to Hope. The last one, he slipped into the envelope with his name and address typed on it.

She gave him a weak little smile. "I guess now it's my turn to read all about my baby's father."

"Probably should have done that first," he muttered. "I might have lied about insanity in my family."

She laughed softly. "I doubt it. Don't take this the wrong way, Josh, but you're one of the most stable people I know, despite your efforts to convince me otherwise."

He snorted and looked away, watching her slim fingers slipping open the envelope. He couldn't meet her eyes at that moment. He felt like an impostor, and he didn't want her to see through him.

Hope read more slowly, more carefully, than he had. "We're both positive blood types," she commented. "That's good. There won't be the negative Rh factor to worry about." He shrugged. It wasn't something he knew anything about, but if she said it was good, he was happy.

She read in silence for a while longer, then set down the papers and smiled. "Don't let it go to your head, but you're apparently perfect." He gave a snort of disbelief. The waiter set a bowl of hot-and-sour soup between them. Hope slid the papers back into the envelope and tucked it into her purse.

"I'm starving," she announced. She ladled some soup into his bowl, then served herself. He was about to wonder how she could be so cool about dinner after what they'd just done, when he noticed that her hands shook slightly. "I had back-to-back meetings all day, and didn't get a chance for lunch. Mmm. Smells wonderful."

The soup was good, as usual, but Josh couldn't care less. The whole meal was great, and now that they'd stopped discussing getting Hope pregnant, he almost enjoyed himself. But there was something wrong, and he simply couldn't pin it down, couldn't say what, exactly, was bothering him.

Hope barely tasted her food. Her stomach felt tangled. Her hands shook too much to control her chopsticks. The magnitude of the agreement they'd signed kept stunning her a little more every time she thought about it. What had seemed simple when she'd signed her name in front of her lawyer now seemed complicated. Monumentally compli-cated. And more than a little scary.

What would it be like to have sex with Josh? She could imagine making love with him. That would be wonderful, but totally out of the question. *Making love* with Josh would ruin their friendship. He'd bolt at the first hint of any attachment on her part, other than her fondness for him as a friend. That would be awful. She would rather have this baby on her own, as she'd originally planned, than lose Josh in the process. The only way to preserve their friendship, therefore, was for her to keep Josh's two roles strictly sep-arate, in her mind and in her life. It was a decision she would simply have to have the strength to live with.

He walked her out to her car when they finished their meal. His gleaming motorcycle stood farther down in the parking area. "So, now what?" he asked as she fumbled with her door lock. "Am I right about this weekend?"

Her voice wouldn't work the first time she tried to an-swer, and she knew her face was flaming in the parking-lot lights. "Probably," she finally managed to whisper. "I'm taking my temperature every morning, so I'll know when I'm . . . ready."

"Okay. So call me." He gave her a jaunty grin. "I can be ready any time."

"That's . . . good, I guess. Thank you."

"Hey, that's what friends are for, babe. Drive safely."

Before she could read his intentions, he'd bent and brushed a quick kiss on her cheek. For some silly reason, that simple gesture brought tears to her eyes. Not wanting him to see, she ducked her head and got into her car.

Josh sauntered toward the Honda, threw one leg over the saddle with easy grace and started his engine. She flashed her lights to tell him she was fine, then backed out of her parking space and headed home, still in a state of minor shock at what she was about to do.

Why, Josh wanted to know, was someone ringing a fire alarm next to his bed? No, it was the damn phone. At half-past eight on a Saturday. He was asleep, damn it, and he intended to stay that way! Eyes shut, he grabbed for the receiver and shoved it somewhere near his face. Who the hell called a working man at this hour on his day off?

"This better be good," he growled, hoping it wasn't going to be one of those disaster stories about a site he had to get his butt to ASAP. He hated those calls.

"Oh! Josh! I'm sorry!" Hope's voice sounded very small in his ear. "I didn't think about waking you."

The fog cleared from his head. "Hope. You okay?"

"I... I'm fine. I... I wanted to tell you I'm...*ready....*"

He cleared his throat. "Now?"

"Now ." Her voice sounded even smaller.

"Okay. Give me a few minutes to shower, and I'll be right over." He hung up the phone, then realized he hadn't said goodbye. By the time he picked up the receiver, all he could hear was the dial tone.

Getting into a hot shower was automatic. He could do that in his sleep. He could even tell himself this was just another day, another shower, like any other day. But when he rubbed his hand over his face, he decided he'd better shave rather than risk scraping Hope's soft skin raw. Then his libido took over, and he felt his nerves start to hum in anticipation. The circumstances weren't his first choice, but his body had been primed for Hope from the first time he'd seen her again after all those years. By the time he'd climbed into clean clothes and stumbled down the steps to get his bike out of the garage, his hands were shaking.

Hope opened the door before he had a chance to ring the bell. She wore that thick white terry robe, and her hair was down around her shoulders like a red-gold cape. Her feet were bare, and her long fingers held the top of the robe together at her throat as if she were trying to fend off an attack. Her eyes looked huge because her face was so pale. He sure hoped she wasn't afraid of this.

He'd do everything he could to make it good for her. This kid of hers was going to be conceived in the right mood, or he was going to die trying.

Josh looked so cool, so confident, Hope thought, watching him step past her into the front hall. She prayed he wouldn't notice that she was shaking like a leaf in an earthquake. There was, theoretically, nothing to be nervous about, she kept telling herself. It wasn't as if she was about to have sex with a stranger. She was going to try to make a baby with her very good friend, a beautiful baby that would grow up loved and happy.

"I… We can go right upstairs if you want," she told him, helpless to make her voice sound normal.

"Sure. This is your deal. You call the shots." He smiled and lightly touched her shoulder. "Lead on."

Clutching her robe around her, Hope started up the stairs. Not quite an hour ago, it had seemed so sensible to shower after phoning Josh and to greet him in her robe, naked and ready. Now, she felt naked and very, very *un*ready.

Still, the music she'd selected carefully was playing on her portable CD player. The blinds and curtains were closed, so the sunlight filtered into the room like gold mist. When she'd heard his motorcycle rumble up the driveway, she'd unplugged the bedroom phone and made sure the answering machine was on. Then she closed the door where Tabby and her kittens were to keep the friendly little cat from interrupting. She'd even gotten waffle mix ready the night before so she could make them breakfast when they were...finished. The coffeemaker was set to go on in ten minutes, which should give them more than enough time to do what they had to do, while it was brewing. Certainly, making love with Kyle had never taken longer than that, and this was just going to be sex.

Steeling herself, Hope stepped to the side of the bed and turned toward Josh. He stood in the doorway, an odd look on his face, his strong hands poised at his belt buckle. Hope thought back to the kisses they'd shared at the Wilsons' cabin, to the way she had responded to him. And to the way that stolen moment had replayed itself too many times in her dreams. Releasing the lapels of her robe and sinking onto the edge of the bed, she warned herself not to lose control and respond that way now. If she did, Josh might get the wrong idea about her feelings. Or rather, he might get the right idea, which was totally inappropriate.

Josh winked at her and pried his boots off, setting them and his thick gray socks outside the doorway. Then he stepped toward her, his fingers tugging his simple white T-shirt out of his jeans waistband. The sight of his bare chest made her swallow. When his fingers began to work at the brass buckle of his belt, however, she lowered her gaze to his bare feet. They were, she thought, beautiful feet. She hoped their...no, *her*...baby had such beautiful feet.

She heard the scratch of his zipper, and then his jeans and a pair of black briefs covered his feet. Not knowing where to look now, Hope closed her eyes and prayed Josh would simply take over. Surely, he knew what he was doing in this department. He wouldn't need her help. She didn't have to participate for this to work.

The first touch of his hand on her cheek made her stifle a tiny yelp of surprise. Keeping her eyes firmly shut, she covered his hand with hers, trying to tell him without words that she was in his hands. Then she felt his touch, as light as a breeze, running down her arms and over her thighs. Even through the thickness of the robe, his fingers left a trail of sensations that only made her tremble more. When he fumbled with the tie belt of the robe, she realized he'd knelt at her feet. A little disoriented, she blinked her eyes open and found him watching her. His smile was like the sight of a life preserver in a storm.

Josh parted the lapels of her robe with infinitesimal patience, baring her shoulders slowly, leaving the rest of her covered. Then he touched her skin, only at her shoulders, making her nerves tingle.

"You really are exquisite," he murmured. A moment later, he leaned in and captured her lips with his.

Hope wanted to lose herself in his kisses, but she was afraid of what he might read in her response. She pulled back enough to break the contact.

"It's okay, Josh," she whispered, dismayed at how husky her voice sounded. "You don't have to pretend this is a normal situation."

There was a brief silence. Then he said, "Oh. You want me to just get down to business?" Unable to meet his eyes, she nodded. "Okay. Let's get this off and get horizontal."

Their hands tangled a couple of times, but she finally pushed her robe off and lay down. She heard Josh's breath catch, but didn't dare open her eyes when she knew he was looking at her. A moment later, she felt the bed shift near her feet and realized he was climbing in at the bottom. The searing brush of his fingertips along her insteps and her calves confirmed her conclusion. His touches rose up her legs to circle her knees and trace electric patterns on her thighs. Then his lips pressed against first one knee, then the other. That wasn't so bad, she thought, until she felt his mouth brush her belly. The tiny stinging gesture nearly made her levitate off the bed.

"Josh! What are you doing?" she gasped, clenching her fists to keep her hands off him.

"I'm getting you in the mood," he murmured, his mouth still much too close to her midsection for her comfort.

"I'm already in the mood," she told him brusquely. "My temperature is right, and my mind is made up. I don't need you to do all this other stuff."

"Oh, yeah?"

"Yes."

His fingers slid like raw silk over her bare breasts, sending hot streaks from her suddenly awakened nipples to the center of her body.

"Stuff like this?"

"Right. I don't need you to do that."

"Ah. I see."

She knew that if she opened her eyes, she'd find him smiling at her. She could hear it in his tone. But she didn't dare open her eyes. "I'm ready. Honestly."

The first gentle touch of his fingers between her legs startled a cry from her. Suddenly, her body was quaking inside. She wanted nothing more than to feel him caress her as a lover would, and she knew, with desperate certainty, that if she let him know how she felt, he would be gone before she could blink. So she held herself still while he touched and stroked with agonizing tenderness. She could feel him, hard and ready, where his body pressed against her side.

Finally, hoping he would stop torturing her with caresses that made her feel as if every nerve in her body was on fire, she parted her legs and reached blindly for him. His back felt smooth and hot under her fingers as she tried to pull him down over her. His body resisted like a coiled spring as his fingers probed and stroked maddeningly. Her body refused to resist the magical heat of his touch, no matter how she tried to pretend otherwise. The tension made her quiver like a leaf in a storm.

"Josh, please!" she managed to gasp. "I don't need you to do that."

"Yes, you do, sweetheart. You aren't ready for me. I don't want to hurt you."

His shaft nudged her thigh, smooth and hard, and she almost whimpered with the need to feel him inside her. "You won't hurt me. I know you won't."

"Shh. Let me do this right," he whispered. His hand swept over her belly and up to her breasts, lingering to tease her nipples into hard beads.

In a panic to hide her body's response to him, Hope brushed his hand away. "No. That isn't necessary," she said desperately. "I'd really like to do this and get it over with."

In the silence that followed, Josh moved a little away; from her. After a long while, he said, "It doesn't work like that, Hope. We need a little finesse here. I'm not a machine."

She blinked away tears of frustration. "I know that! But we already agreed that it won't be lovemaking."

After a long silence, he shifted his weight away from her. "Well, maybe our minds agreed," he muttered, "but my body seems to be taking exception to this arrangement."

Finally, she dared to look at his face, but she couldn't read his expression. "What are you saying?"

"See for yourself."

He was half-reclining, leaning back on his elbow. She risked a quick glance down his muscular chest, then a longer look, following the thin line of dark curls past his deeply indented belly button, down to where his manhood lay like a sleeping kitten.

Chapter Twelve

"Is there anything I can do?" Hope asked in a very soft voice.

Josh yanked the lace-covered blanket over his lower body. "No," he grunted, but he really wanted to yell, *Haven't you done enough already?*

"I can wait awhile if that will help," she offered in that same soft voice.

That just made him feel worse. "No, it won't. I guess I'm not in the mood now." But he had been. He'd been more than ready, and then, *phzzt!*

"I thought guys were always in the mood when a woman throws her naked body at them."

"Apparently not." *Was,* he wanted to tell her. *Should be.* Something was definitely wrong, and it sure as hell wasn't anything to do with the naked body lying beside him. God, what was wrong with him? He'd been dreaming of this opportunity, fantasizing every detail in the unlikely event that he should get so lucky as to find himself in this particular position, with this particular woman.

"I understand this happens sometimes."

"Not to me it doesn't," he snapped. He could feel her draw back, as if he'd hurt her, but he couldn't look her in the eye. He simply didn't understand why, when he wanted her so badly that he ached, his body had failed him.

"Josh, I'm sorry." She moved away from him. He raised his gaze only enough to see her slender frame slip into the heavy robe. "I guess I'm not the kind of woman who turns you on, but thanks for trying."

That made him sit up. Hope sat on the edge of the bed, looking totally dejected. "Whoa! This isn't about you. I'm the one with the problem."

Or was he? Everything had been in perfect working condition until Hope had started rushing him. All that talk about *sex* and getting it over with had killed his mood. She'd insisted she was ready, when he knew damn well she wasn't. Maybe that was the key. Josh replayed the moments in his mind. Hope had definitely responded to him at first. But she seemed to be fighting it at the same time that she was trying to hurry him along. That didn't make sense.

She turned her head only enough so he could see the curve of her cheek. "I don't understand what went wrong, but I can't help feeling guilty," she murmured. "I hope I haven't done too much damage to your ego."

"My ego is fine," he muttered. "There's nothing for you to feel guilty about," he told her because he hated seeing how sad she looked. But maybe she was right, and it was her fault in a way. How was he supposed to make love to a woman who resisted getting turned on? He didn't have a clue why she'd fought against her own body, but he knew he couldn't make love to her like that. Somehow, he was going to have to figure out how to convince her to enjoy the process.

"Maybe," he said, feeling his way through the idea, "it's because we're friends. I mean, a lot of sex is a mind thing, too. Maybe my mind is having trouble shifting gears."

She hugged the robe around her and frowned down at him. "What do you mean? That because we're friends, you can't get...you know...attracted to me anymore?" Her cheeks got pink again. "I mean, I couldn't help noticing at the cabin, when we were, um, kissing.... You were, um, attracted then, weren't you?"

Now that was an understatement. "Yeah. But that was before we decided to be plain old good friends."

She sank down on the edge of the mattress, her back toward him. "But even after that, when I had cramps, you...you responded." He grunted. "And you started out ready now. So it must be something I did wrong."

He reached out and stroked the silky hair streaming down her back. "No, baby. You didn't do anything wrong."

"But I'm the one who insisted on being friends."

Josh closed his hand around her slender arm. "Yeah, but if you'd been a lover, not a friend, there's no way I would have volunteered to help you have a baby. Remember? I wouldn't do this for a girlfriend. Only for a *friend* friend."

Hope laughed softly. "That doesn't make any sense, but I think I understand." She turned to smile at him, but it looked like a very sad smile. "Well, thanks anyway. I'm sorry it didn't turn out the way we thought. I hope this doesn't mess up our friendship after all."

It occurred to him that she was ready to give up. That meant she had two choices. Give up her dream of having a baby, or go to a sperm bank and take horrible chances. Neither choice worked for him. Which meant he had only once choice himself. Figure out some way to get back to the blazing, blinding physical reaction he'd had to her the first time they'd kissed. Well, when the going got tough, the tough got going.

"We're not quitting," he told her. Her jaw dropped. "I'm serious. I know what went wrong. This is just a minor setback. But from now on, we do it my way." Whatever that was. He'd think of something.

"But—"

"Look, if we miss this month's window of opportunity, is that so bad? From what I hear, stress isn't good for getting pregnant anyway. So you shouldn't be trying so hard."

She appeared to think for a moment, then nodded. He did some thinking, too, and came up with a brilliant idea.

"Here's what I think went wrong. We tried to be too clinical. I'm not the kind of guy who wants sex any way I can get it. Never really have been, if you don't count how I was as a horny teenager. Just because I don't want to get tied down doesn't mean I seriously want sex with any woman who offers. Hell, I haven't had a one-night stand since I lost my virginity."

She shifted so that their eyes met. "But what are you saying about us?"

"I think we should go out, like a couple. Hell, we do anyway. But I think we should stop worrying about our friendship and pretend to be lovers." He was, he thought modestly, a genius.

Hope's eyes went wide. "Pretend to be lovers?"

"Yeah. You know, dates. Holding hands. Kisses. I bring you flowers. You cook me dinner. And then, when the timing's right, I'll bet everything works the way it's supposed to. What do you think?"

She was silent a long moment before she said, "I thought it was women who needed the illusion of romance, not men."

He gave a short laugh. "Hey, so I'm one of those sensitive nineties guys. What do you say? You with me on this? Because I know it will work."

Again, she was silent, but she'd turned away so he couldn't see her face. Finally, she sighed. "What if it changes our friendship?" she asked in a very small voice.

"Friendships aren't like rocks, Hope. They're supposed to change."

She faced him again, her forehead puckered in a frown. "I need to think about this some more. Would you like some breakfast?"

"Sounds good." He reached out and tugged at a coil of her silky hair. "And after, let's take the bike out to the Kootenays for the weekend. The weather's supposed to be great. Leave extra food for the cat, pack light and we'll pick up something to barbecue on the way. The RV's all set up, and there are two bunks. I'll teach you how to fly-fish tomorrow morning. And no sex," he added with a wink, "unless it comes up naturally."

Several hours later, Hope smiled at the flourish with which Josh opened his rented RV door. "Ta-dah!" he crowed with a grin, then waved her up the steps. "Come into my parlor," he said, following her inside, "as well as my kitchen, dining room, bedroom and bath. Nothing if not efficient."

Hope looked around. Josh was right. The RV made very good use of the small space. The kitchen was a marvel of built-ins and scaled-down models, and the rest of the area had been fitted like a boat, with benches and tables that folded down or bolted up out of the way. At the very back of the RV, half-hidden behind heavy curtains, she saw the two bunks, one above the other, and despite her efforts at control, felt her face grow warm. Oh, Lord, would she ever live down even the most innocuous reminder of this morning's disaster?

Josh set the groceries they'd bought nearby down on the counter. "You can bring in your stuff from the bike," he told her, bending to load things into the small refrigerator. "Take your pick of the bunks."

Face on fire again, Hope hurried out to the bike and drew her overnight bag from one of the deep carriers flanking the back wheel. She'd taken Josh at his word and packed only the essentials for a two-day stay in the boondocks: jeans, underwear, warm tops, thermal pyjamas, heavy socks. No makeup, because she didn't have to impress Josh or the trout. No perfume, which, he'd warned her, would attract bugs. He'd promised her the use of his generic shampoo and a hair dryer, and, after a barbecue, a stress-free evening of reading or playing Scrabble. She might as well be spending the weekend with a girlfriend, she thought as she went back into the RV.

Except that the possibility of sex with Josh just might, as he'd put it, come up naturally.

She doubted it, though. It was pretty clear that whatever spark there had been between them had been extinguished by their friendship. Under ordinary circumstances, she mused as she stored her bag under the lower bunk, that would have been a good thing. But as she'd lain there that morning, shaking with nerves, she'd realized that *she* still felt that spark, even though, ironically enough, now Josh didn't. It was going to be an interesting weekend, she thought, bracing herself to join Josh in the small space of the RV. But not, as he'd claimed, stress free.

Somehow, probably due more to Josh's good nature than to her lame efforts, the conversation flowed between them as they set up his hibachi, grilled their hamburgers and shared the prepared salads they'd bought. The sun still hovered, low and pale gold, when they'd finished cleaning up. Josh suggested they grab their jackets and a flashlight and take a walk. Eager to be outside the small RV for as long as possible, Hope agreed.

"Looks like the Wilsons' place is empty," Josh commented as they strode through the meadow toward the river.

''Mmm. Mrs. Wilson says she's tired of the trek out here at her age, but Mr. Wilson hates the thought of selling it. They're thinking of renting it out.'' And she was thinking about the hot, breathless kisses she'd shared with Josh in the Wilsons' cabin.

Josh grabbed her hand to help her over a fallen log. She could have stepped over it herself quite easily, but she liked the way his hand felt around hers. Somehow, she couldn't find an excuse to pull away, so they continued toward the river hand in hand. As she walked, she became increasingly aware of the warm, hard texture of his palm against hers. Her nipples puckered and tingled at the memory of his hands on her breasts.

She needed a distraction. ''Do people fish at night?'' she asked as they picked their way over the stones at the river's edge.

He picked up a pebble and tossed it impressively far across the water. ''Nah. Against the law, except for smelts. The fish have to sleep sometime. They're early risers.''

''How early?''

He grinned at her. ''Early enough to catch the little bugs who wake up with the sun.''

''I was afraid you'd say that.'' Because that meant they'd have to go to sleep soon, and the prospect of sleeping so close to Josh after the morning's disaster made her quake with nerves.

He placed his hand on her shoulder. She tried to ignore the tingling his simple touch sent along her overly sensitive nerves, from her shoulder to her fingers to the back of her neck.

''No fear. The birds won't let you sleep past five-thirty, anyway.''

''Oh, well, that's okay, then,'' she said dryly.

Josh laughed. ''Let's go. I want to check my gear so we don't waste any time in the morning.''

She turned with him, and they started the walk back to the RV. Its lights glowed a welcome in the falling twilight, but she deliberately moved her feet as slowly as she could. "What kind of bait do you use? Not worms, I hope."

"No bait. Lures. Each one a work of art designed to seduce some beautiful trout into biting."

The image did nothing for her, except the part about seduction, and then she wasn't thinking about fish. She was thinking about those moments in the Wilsons' cabin, when she'd lost herself in Josh's arms and taken his kisses as hungrily as a starving lioness. And those moments that morning, when his touch had made her ache with suppressed hunger. Just the thought sent waves of desire washing over her, filling her with a wild heat that made her shudder.

Josh caught hold of the hand he'd dropped while they'd stood at the water's edge. They walked the rest of the way back to the RV, hands linked warmly, not speaking. Hope felt edgy as she walked beside Josh, not knowing what to expect from him. Not knowing what she wanted to do. And knowing that they soon would be sharing temptingly close quarters.

Somehow, despite the narrow confines of the RV, Hope managed not to touch Josh as they cleaned up the kitchen. She stalled in the compact washroom as long as she could, but with no makeup on and her hair loose, there wasn't much to do. Stepping out into the hallway, Hope found herself face-to-face with Josh. Gratefully, she noted he wore gray sweats hacked off above his knees and a shapeless blue T-shirt. His dark brows rose at the sight of her bright red thermal pyjamas, but he wisely said nothing as he climbed the ladder into the upper bunk.

Trying to control the trembling inside her, she slipped under the heavy quilt on the lower bunk. Suddenly, it was dark in the little RV, and Hope was all too aware of the sound of Josh shifting positions in the bed above her. She imagined she could smell his warm skin. Memories of his kisses mingled with the caresses on her bare body that she'd tried so hard to ignore that morning. Now, she ached for his touch, for him to put out the fires he'd started and left smoldering. The time was probably still right for her to get pregnant. What if, she wondered, she climbed into his bunk now?

"Hope?" His voice came softly through the dark silence, but it startled her nevertheless.

"Yes?" Was he going to ask her to join him?

"See you in the morning."

Josh stood over the hibachi and watched Hope, perched on a log nearby. She'd been quiet all morning, except when she'd fallen headfirst into the shallows when her first—and only—strike of the morning had fought back harder than she'd expected. At least he'd caught her rod before the trout had slipped away. It would be some consolation to serve her catch, along with his, for lunch.

"The fish are ready," he announced, coming outside. "If you bring out the salads and drinks, we can eat out here."

She got up, dusted off her cute little seat and went into the RV. A minute after he'd turned the fish over and the potatoes were ready to come out of the coals, Hope came out with a stack of plates, salad containers and his red-checked vinyl tablecloth. He pretended to tend the fish, but his attention kept straying to the sight of her slender body, moving gracefully in faded jeans and a baggy turquoise T-shirt. She still hadn't given him her answer to his proposition, but he was beginning to think she'd decided to say no. Why else, he reasoned, would she be so withdrawn?

Hope held out two plates for the fish and potatoes. Back at the tablecloth, spread on a level patch of grass, they sat opposite each other. Unable to think of anything to say, Josh dug into his food and stole the occasional glance at Hope.

"Mmm! I hope this is my fish," she said finally.

"It is. Why?"

She grinned. "Then revenge is very sweet."

He grinned back. "Never knew you had a vengeful side."

"You never dumped me in a river."

"After hearing the things you called that poor fish, I don't think I'd try, either."

She dangled a delicate morsel of fish above her lips, winked at him and popped the bite into her mouth. "Good decision."

He watched her swallow, then dab her lips with her napkin. Her expression when she met his eyes again had lost all of the earlier playfulness, and his heart sank.

"Speaking of decisions," she said. "I've been thinking all day about your suggestion. The logic is totally backward, Josh. It can't help but change our friendship completely if we pretend to be lovers, and I like our friendship the way it is." She gave him a soft smile that faded too soon, then looked down at her plate.

He couldn't form the words to let her off the hook.

She looked at him again. "I've also been thinking about the sperm-bank option, and I'm no longer comfortable with it. So this is what I've decided. We'll try it your way, but if I don't get pregnant within six months, I'm going to stop trying."

He couldn't have heard that right. "What?"

She shrugged. "It won't be fair to tie up your social life indefinitely and treat you like some hostage stud, servicing me at my beck and call. What if you meet someone special? How are you going to tell her you can't date her until you're finished fathering a child for your friend?" Hope shook her head. "I can't let you do that."

His brain was still scrambling to catch up to her when she picked up her finished plate and stood up. All he could do was gape at her.

"So, if you're done with your lunch, I guess we should clean up and get ready to go home. We can write in the changes to the agreement and initial them like last time."

She was in the RV before he could get to his feet. By the time he got inside, she was biting into an apple. He grabbed the apple out of her hand and took a bite before tossing it into the sink. Hope swallowed, her eyes wide.

"Josh? Are you…angry? You have a strange look in your eyes."

He slid his hands through the silky hair spilling over her shoulders, then cupped the back of her head, holding her right where he wanted her. Slowly, he moved closer until his feet bracketed hers and her body was a breath away from his.

"Angry?" He smiled. "Nah. Just getting a head start on the changes to that agreement."

And finally, he did what he'd been aching to do since the last time he'd kissed her. He lowered his head until her startled expression went out of focus, then covered her mouth with his and showed her that, when Josh Kincaid made a commitment, he gave it everything he had.

He could taste her surprise. It took a little coaxing, a few teasing kisses, before her lips softened. Even then, he kept kissing her lightly, playfully, fighting the urge to plunder her sweet mouth. *Patience,* he told himself over and over, like a mantra. And finally, his patience paid off.

Hope made a soft little sound and wrapped her arms around his shoulders. Her lips parted for his tongue at the same time that her body flowed fully against his. The blood sang in his veins, roaring in his ears and surging its way to his loins. It was like simultaneously being struck by lightning and drowning.

He slid his hands down to cup her small bottom. Her tiny gasp sent shock waves through him. His fingers dug into her firm flesh as he lifted her more firmly to him, letting her feel how hard he was. She made another one of those soft little sounds and moved her hips restlessly against his. It would be so simple to guide her to the lower bunk, to ease her down and make love to her.

That was, after all, what she wanted. What he'd agreed to do. Signed on the dotted lines. But it wasn't, he realized with a shock, what he wanted to do.

If they made love now, she might get pregnant. Then they'd be back at square one: friends. Even if she didn't get pregnant this time, she might not go along with the pretence of being lovers. All night and most of the day, those possibilities had tormented him, until he'd come to a conclusion that didn't make a lick of sense but was more true than anything else he knew: he didn't want to go back to being Hope's good buddy. He wanted to be her lover for real.

And as he took her mouth in one more kiss, his brain still worked well enough to warn him that if he gave her the slightest hint that he was serious about being her lover, she'd tear up their agreement and their friendship before he could blink. Sometimes, he warned himself, self-control was a good thing. It was time to stop, before he got carried away—and carried Hope away to the back of the RV.

"Josh?" she said softly when he lifted his head. Her face pressed against his neck, and her lips grazed his skin like the brush of a live wire. "Are we going to try again now?" Every feathery touch of her lips set another match to his already flimsy resolve. "I think the timing is still good."

Somehow, he managed to stop himself from simply letting nature take over the way his body was urging him to do. Hope's timing might be good, but his was way off.

"Not yet," he told her, tangling his fingers in her silky hair as he rubbed her slender back. "I never ever take a woman to bed on a first date."

She lifted her head from his shoulder. Her eyes, when she looked up at him, were heavy with arousal, which wasn't making this any easier for him. If anything, her dreamy expression was definitely making things harder.

"But this isn't a date," she argued with a little pout to her full lips that he couldn't recall seeing before. It was a very seductive little expression that could scuttle his plans if he didn't stay on his guard.

He grinned, pretending to ignore the invitation of her mouth so close to his. "Right. And we have an agreement to amend, so we can't start dating until we get back and sign it."

"Oh," she said softly. Her gaze drifted down to his mouth. Josh groaned. Her eyes lifted to his again. "You're turning into a control freak, Josh Kincaid," she murmured. Then she smiled and moved closer until her lips were practically touching his. "Sometimes, maybe it's better to let serendipity take over," she murmured against his mouth.

Damn! he thought as he gave in just a little to temptation and brought his mouth down on hers. She made a sweet, soft mew in her throat that sounded very much like surrender to pleasure. His pulse went into overdrive. If she'd been like this yesterday morning, he sure wouldn't have had trouble performing.

Her breasts pressed against his chest. He could feel her nipples through their shirts. Her hips moved against his in a subtle invitation that sent all his blood pooling in his loins, so that he knew he would ache if they stopped. But he also knew that if they didn't stop now, he'd ache in other ways if he couldn't keep seeing her.

Somehow, he found the strength to break the kiss. "I don't want to risk another, uh, you know, failure," he muttered, giving her trim little bottom one last, appreciative squeeze. "I'm only testing the equipment before we start the experiment."

He let her step back, then caught her elbows when she looked about to collapse.

"Oh," she said, her eyes looking a little dazed. "Well."
She cleared her throat. "Well. Everything seems to be in
working order."

"Yes, ma'am, it does." He winked, then released her elbows, even though he was still more than half-tempted to
drag her back to that lower bunk that smelled faintly of her
sweet skin. But that would lead him right back to the di-
lemma he was trying to avoid. He couldn't afford to give her
a chance to make any more decisions. He was learning that
the best way to deal with Hope's tendency to control situa-
tions was to keep her off balance. So he stepped to the tiny
sink and said, "I'll wash, you dry."

For most of the ride home, Hope barely saw the beautiful scenery fly past. She sat clinging to Josh's strong torso,
contemplating ways to convince a jury that killing him
would be a totally justified homicide. How could he have
done that to her? Kiss her practically senseless, then make
some stupid joke about his "equipment" and wash the
dishes as if nothing had happened? As if she couldn't tell he
was more than ready to finish what they'd so disastrously
started yesterday morning?

He'd made her *melt!* He'd made her hunger and yearn
and burn and all those things she didn't want to feel for a
man ever again. It was too complicated to feel those things,
especially for a man she couldn't ever have a relationship
with. There'd be no happily-ever-after with Mr. Teflon, and
it wasn't fair of him to make her want it to be. That was why
she wanted to have a baby by herself. She understood that
her child would eventually grow up, and grow away from
her. That was the nature of the parent-child relationship.
She could deal with that. She *couldn't* deal with the idea that
a man would grow away. Especially a man who hadn't exactly grown up first. Like Kyle. Or Josh.

The bike hit a bump. Hope clutched Josh tighter, then
cursed herself for automatically seeking stability from him.

She was lucky she didn't slide off the bike like a fried egg from her favorite Teflon pan.

"You okay?" His voice came through the speaker in her helmet.

"Fine," she said into the microphone near her mouth, and loosened her hold.

But she wasn't fine. She was tingling with frustration, and it wasn't all physical. The idea of pretending to be lovers with Josh had taken hold in her mind, a frighteningly strong hold. Fortunately for her, she knew him well enough by now not to tell him how much she liked the idea. If he thought for a second that she might be serious, he'd probably leave more skid marks than Kyle in making his escape. The more he believed he had to convince her to change her mind, the less worried about his precious freedom he'd be. And the longer she could enjoy the company of a man who was becoming much, much too dear and much, much too important to her.

Chapter Thirteen

Three Saturdays later, around dusk, while Hope was stuffing the last of the torn gift wrappings into a green garbage bag, the door chimes rang. Wondering if any of the guests at Chantelle's baby shower had left something behind, she opened the door. Josh, in his motorcycling leathers, grinned at her. To her dismay, her heart flipped and started racing at the sight of him.

"Hi. I thought you were building a cabin," she said as he walked past her into the house.

"I was. Still am." He shrugged out of his black leather jacket. "I finally figured out I'll never finish the thing myself, so I hired a local crew to do the carpentry. I'll do most of the electrical myself, but it's nowhere near ready yet." He dropped his jacket on a chair and caught her hand in his. Astonished, she watched him lift her hand to his lips and place a warm, slow kiss in the center of her palm. "Besides, I only have about a week to get back in the mood, so I don't want to waste any time."

Hope swallowed. She tried to tug loose her hand, but he held it gently yet firmly, and continued to press tiny kisses over her knuckles. "We've been out together three nights this week," she argued weakly. "It seemed to me you were very close to being in the mood, as you put it, every time. I don't want you to give up your personal life for me, Josh. I know you want to build that cabin yourself—"

"No, I want to *have* it built, so I can use it. But I made some changes to the plans, and it's way too big now for me to do, even with a couple of buddies."

She finally succeeded in reclaiming her hand, which tingled from the play of his soft lips and slight stubble on her skin. "There's tons of food left over. Come into the kitchen and talk to me while I clean up. Would you like coffee? There's still plenty in the urn."

"Sure."

Hope poured mugs of coffee from the rented urn, then brought Josh a plate and fork. "Help yourself to any of it. I'll send you home with a care package if you want. Everyone brought something sinful to the shower, and of course, they're all on diets, so no one ate anything." Josh gave a snort of disapproval, shook his head and carved a slice of the chocolate mousse cake. She started scraping the rented plates and loading them into their packing crates. "Tell me about the changes to the cabin."

"It's more of a cottage now," he said around a mouthful of cake. "Being crammed into that RV convinced me I want some room to move around in, maybe have some company come up without being on top of me. So now there are four bedrooms, instead of one, and three baths, plus a mud room off the kitchen."

It sounded like a family house, she thought, but worried that if she said so, he'd spook at the implication that he was establishing something resembling roots. He guarded his image of the freewheeling bachelor so carefully, even though it didn't seem to have much basis in reality. Except, of course, that he was a bachelor.

"Are you expanding outward or upward?"

"Both. The second story will have a big master bedroom with a private bathroom." He took a bite of the chocolate-pecan pie Gail brought and rolled his eyes. "Mmm! That's too good! Two smaller bedrooms upstairs will share a bath. And the fourth bedroom is on the first floor, sort of a combination den and guest room, behind the living room. The third bath is wedged between them."

"I can see now why you can't do the whole thing yourself." She took a sip of her coffee, eyed the pecan pie, then thought better of it. "If I promise not to throw your fishing rod in the river again, can I be a guest?"

Josh grinned. "Any time. How'd the shower go?"

Hope sighed and set down the last of the rented plates. "It was great. There were twenty of us, and Chantelle got some wonderful gifts. Everyone knew how much she and Rob have wanted a baby and how long they've been hoping, so it was a very special occasion." She smiled and sat across the table from him, suddenly tired. "Lots of happy tears."

His grin faded to a frown. "Are you all right?" Unable to meet his eyes now, Hope stared down at her entwined fingers and nodded. "You don't look all right."

Hope shrugged. "I'm very happy for her, Josh," she said, lifting her gaze to his. Her throat felt tight. "But I can't help being envious, which I hate. And I hate feeling sorry for myself."

"No need, sweetheart. I'm planning to do my damnedest to give you that baby you want."

His determined expression made her laugh; but the tightness in her throat turned her laugh into a sad little hiccup. "As you keep telling me, there are some things we can't control. No matter what I do, it may not be possible. I keep trying to remember that whenever I get too optimistic."

"Well, don't get too pessimistic. From what I hear, negative thoughts can scare those eggs out of hatching, or whatever they do in there." He gave her a sweetly naughty smile she barely managed to return.

"I know. That's what I'm afraid of. I keep having this dream," she found herself confessing, "that I'm in a nursery surrounded by babies. There's someone who holds up the babies for their parents, and I keep reaching out for one, but everyone else gets to take a baby home except me. And these voices keep telling me it's hopeless."

Josh was out of his chair before Hope could blink. He drew her to her feet and wrapped her in his arms. Stiff with surprise, it took her a moment to allow herself to relax against him. He pulled the pins out of her hair and shook it down, then stroked her head and her back, silently, soothingly. Finally, she wrapped her arms around him and clung, deeply touched by his support.

"You done in here?" he asked gruffly, still holding her.

"Except for the food."

"Leave it for now. You need a break. Let's go visit the cats."

He released her slowly, then took her hand and led her up the stairs to the room she one day hoped would be a nursery. Tabby trilled and came trotting to them as soon as Josh turned on the light. The kittens meowed, then one by one, clawed their way up out of the basket and tumbled onto the carpet. Even before she'd joined them on the floor, Hope was smiling. Once again, Josh had been right about what she needed.

Josh sprawled on the floor beside her. Tabby rubbed her head against his hand, demanding attention. The kittens tottered toward him. Hope scooped Nod up into her hands and nuzzled him while Winkin and Blinkin tried to climb up Josh's rib cage. Finally, he lifted them both onto his chest.

"Time for a bigger basket," he commented.

Hope shook her head. "No. They're ready to see the world, or at least, the house. I'll close off most of the rooms and make sure there's nothing they can get hurt on. And Tabby will take care of most of their training." She smiled as Blinkin, with an indignant squeak, tumbled backward off Josh's chest. "Kids have to grow up sometime."

Josh moved the kittens away, then rolled onto his side and propped himself up on his elbow, his gaze direct. "Yours, too. I mean, you aren't so fixated on having a baby that you forgot they grow up?"

Hope set Nod down with his sisters, then placed her hand on Josh's shoulder. "That's part of the joy of having children," she told him. "To me, at least. Watching them grow into individuals. Helping them learn. Praying they don't make too many mistakes, and cheering their triumphs. That's the way my parents raised us, and that's why I want to have my own children. Or child. Not because I'm lonely or vain."

Josh reached out and pulled her down beside him. He pressed a kiss onto the top of her head. "Your parents are good people," he murmured. "And you're very, very special. A kid would be lucky to have you for a mom." He drew her higher up in his arms and kissed her nose. "I'll do everything in my power to make it happen," he added, his voice low and intimate.

And then his mouth covered hers. Each time she thought she was getting used to kissing him, she discovered that he could bring her higher, faster. Like a banked fire, she felt herself grow warm as his kisses stirred her. Desire flowed like molten honey in her veins. He fitted her body to his as they lay on their sides, and she instantly felt his arousal. His want, his need, fueled hers, stealing her breath. His hands roamed her back, pressing her closer. She clutched at his hair, unwilling to let him break this intoxicating kiss just yet.

But eventually, inevitably, he ended the kiss. Shaken by her responses to him, by her desire for *him,* she lay against him and tried to get her breathing under control.

"Another week?" he asked softly.

She nodded into his shoulder. "About that," she answered, wondering how she was going to stand the wait. But she didn't dare say a word about her feelings. Keep it clinical, she told herself, despite Josh's assertion that they needed to act more romantic. If they acted any more romantic, she was going to end up with a broken heart.

"I'm taking my temperature every morning, and keeping a record. I guess I'll call, the way I did last time, when I'm ready."

He stroked her cheek, his roughened fingertips incredibly gentle. "I don't think we're going to have to worry about any equipment failures this time."

For their next "date" Hope had planned a simple dinner—barbecued chicken, salad, corn on the cob—but her stomach was so tied in knots by the time Josh took the chicken off the grill that she only picked at her food. He didn't seem to notice her nerves. She tried to concentrate on what he was saying about finishing his cabin, but his presence was much too distracting.

Working together the way they had so many times before, they cleared the table and loaded her dishwasher. Already, Josh seemed at home in her kitchen, putting things away in their right places. Even after four years, Kyle had left piles of dishes, condiments and serving pieces on the counter, claiming he didn't have a clue where they went. At the moment, Hope mused, she would have preferred that Josh not be quite so comfortable in her life, but she didn't want to examine the reasons why.

Josh shut the refrigerator door. "Hey, let's get out of here. How about a movie? Anything you want to see?"

He picked up the newspaper and opened it to the cinema listings. Hope went to peer over his shoulder. She pointed to a couple of films she'd like to see, trying not to notice how good he smelled or how solid and warm his arm felt when she brushed against it. Josh certainly didn't seem to be having trouble ignoring her proximity, even though all week, whenever they'd been together, he'd touched her as often as possible. It was so frustrating, she was tempted to throw herself at him, except she was afraid that would cause another "equipment failure."

After eliminating the most violent and the most mushy of the possibilities, they settled on a comedy. Within minutes, they were in her car and on the way to the movie theater. Josh bought popcorn and soft drinks, and their hands kept brushing every time she reached into the bag he held between them. Finally, she gave up on the popcorn and kept her hands in her lap.

The comedy turned out to be more romantic than Hope had expected, about an unlikely pairing of opposites who professed to be no more than business rivals until they fell into bed and into love. Not wanting Josh to suspect her of ulterior motives for suggesting it, she squashed herself into the far side of her seat so their shoulders wouldn't keep touching. Nevertheless, his presence dominated her awareness, barely allowing her to follow the movie. She cringed farther away from him whenever anyone on-screen was kissing, but she couldn't hide from the memories of Josh's kisses.

Josh walked with Hope to her front door. He knew he should simply kiss her good-night and remind her to call him when her temperature went up. He knew she was nervous. Well, that damn movie had made him nervous. Much too close to home for his comfort. The last thing he wanted was to find out by accident that he'd fallen in love. No, make that the second-last thing. The very last thing he wanted to find out was that Hope didn't want him. His only smart course of action was to keep this arrangement strictly on Hope's terms, which meant staying friends. Only friends. Which also meant leaving now. This very minute. Before he did something he'd regret.

So when Hope opened her door, he bent and kissed her cheek and said, ''Invite me in, Hope.''

Breathless, Hope stared into Josh's eyes, dark like midnight now, and saw the need that wasn't supposed to be there. Not his need, but her own, reflected in the mirror of his earnest eyes. His steady gaze held hers while her resolve, her reasons, her control, melted away like ice under a hot sun. Her keys fell from her suddenly nerveless fingers. She didn't look down at the floor where they lay. She couldn't look away from Josh.

As if in a dream, she reached up and touched his cheek. The heat of his skin seared her fingertips. Before she could pull her hand away, Josh captured it and pressed her palm against his face. His lips grazed her wrist, sending her pulse racing.

''Say yes,'' he murmured hoarsely, then closed his eyes and drew in a long, deep breath.

She gasped softly and let her heart answer for her. At the sound of her whispered ''Yes,'' he let his breath out and opened his eyes.

Without another word, Josh led her into the house. She was vaguely aware of him kicking her keys out of the way of the door, of him releasing her hand long enough to remove her jacket, as well as his own. When he took her hand again, she followed him toward the stairs, but it felt more as if she were floating than walking. She'd been trying to imagine this moment since before their first attempt at sex, believing she could somehow control the situation, control her feelings, control her needs. Now she understood she couldn't control any of those things, and didn't even want to try. As she followed Josh down the hall to her bedroom, she realized that they had completely reversed their roles. She was willing to let her feelings take over, while Josh was now the one in control.

She stood beside the bed while he pulled the pins out of the twist in her hair. When her hair fell free, she tipped her head back and smiled dreamily up at Josh. As his head bent toward her and his lips brushed hers, his hands went to the front of her cotton knit sweater. His fingers fumbled with the tiny buttons. His lips brushing across hers couldn't distract her from noticing that his hands trembled. Hope smiled under his kiss as she realized that she'd given up control but not power. Until that moment, she hadn't cared about the power to make a man tremble. But then, until that moment, she hadn't begun making love with Josh Kincaid.

Hope brushed his hands away and opened the top few buttons of her sweater. Then she lifted it from the hem, and, closing her eyes, pulled it off over her head. As she tossed the sweater somewhere, she heard Josh's sharp intake of breath. Before she could open her eyes, she felt his fingers trace the upper edges of the simple bra she wore, and it was her turn to gasp at the sensations that splintered over her skin.

His hands cupped her shoulders, and his mouth took hers in a long, slow kiss that stirred the banked fires deep inside her. She let herself melt under his kiss, holding on to his shoulders for support, noticing in the back of her mind that he still wore his shirt. Eventually, she slid her hands to his front and opened the buttons halfway down. Then Josh lifted his mouth from hers long enough to whisper an impatient curse and tear open the rest of his buttons as he yanked his shirttails out of his jeans. With a groan, he slid his arms around her and pulled her close to his chest. Seconds later, he'd unhooked her bra and was sliding it out from between them. Her bare skin met his, and she felt her nipples bead against him, sending tingling messages of arousal to the center of her body.

Josh continued to kiss her. She let him tease her lips with his tongue, let the want and the need build, until finally, she parted her lips for him. He groaned and made love to her mouth with his lips and his tongue until her knees threatened to buckle. They'd kissed like this before, yet not like this, not with this white-hot hunger raging inside her. Oh, she wanted more!

Hope felt Josh ease her onto the bed, but she refused to let him break the kiss. She savored the dark sweetness of his mouth, only vaguely aware of him unfastening her denim skirt and sliding it down. When she felt the rasp of his jeans on her bare legs, she tried to undo his belt, but her fingers wouldn't cooperate. She could feel his smile against her lips as he pulled his belt out of the loops and unfastened the metal button at the waist of his jeans. But when she reached for the tab on his zipper, he captured her hand and took his mouth from hers.

"Not yet," he said gruffly.

"We aren't even," she argued, nuzzling his neck.

"Right," he agreed. "I'm way, way ahead of you, and this is one race I don't want to finish first."

"Oh!"

"You just lie back and let me get you caught up," he murmured, drawing her hand up over her head.

Hope opened her mouth to tell Josh this was supposed to be her project. The least he could do was let her participate. But the electrifying touch of his warm, wet mouth closing over one breast sent all her protests up in smoke. The coil of need that stretched from her nipples to her core seemed to tighten with every stroke of his tongue. She heard her own gasps and sighs of pleasure as if they came from far away. She heard his answering moan as he transferred his mouth to her other breast, and realized he was enjoying her pleasure.

Josh ran his free hand over her torso, the callused warmth of his caresses sending tiny sparks over her skin. This time, when he drew her other hand above her head and clasped both her wrists together, she didn't think of protesting. Instead, she arched toward his mouth, offering herself to him. Her last coherent thought, as he hooked his fingers into the edge of her panties and started to tug them down, was that she'd been an idiot to think she could simply have sex with this man, as if she'd been a breeding animal and he a prize stud.

Once she was totally naked, Josh teased her with the softest possible strokes of his fingertips. He trailed hot, wet kisses across her collarbones and down between her breasts, down to her belly button. His fingers drew patterns on her breasts, her ribs, her belly, her thighs and hips, straying ever closer to the part of her that yearned to be joined with him. Those teasing touches made her more aware of the restless heat, the liquid softening, deep inside her, where she wanted, needed, him to touch her.

And then he feathered the curls at the apex of her thighs. Hope drew in her breath and arched to his hand. With a low moan, Josh took one nipple into the heat of his mouth, and his fingers slid between her thighs. Hope cried out at his first intimate touch, stunned by the sensations that rioted through her body.

"Josh!" she heard herself nearly sob, "make love to me!"

He lifted his head and smiled down at her. "I am, sweetheart. I am."

"You know what I mean!"

"Yeah. I also know I'm not going to last long, and I want you to enjoy this, too. Trust me, Hope." His smile turned to a wicked grin. "I know what I'm doing."

"I know what you're doing, too. You're making me crazy. I'm not supposed to enjoy this. I'm only supposed to get pregnant."

He shook his head. "Used to be, folks thought a woman couldn't get pregnant unless she was satisfied, too." His fingers stroked her, causing shockwaves of sensation that stole her breath. ''Now, maybe that's not true,'' he went on, ''but I kinda like that theory. So like it or not, sweetheart, you're just gonna have to enjoy this.''

His mouth on hers cut off any possible protest, but Hope was already beyond words, beyond thought. No other man had ever been so generous to her; no other man had ever made her feel so safe to relinquish her need to be in control. At that exact moment, Hope knew she was completely, irrevocably in love with Josh Kincaid.

And then his caressing hand brought her to a shattering peak of sensation that turned her thoughts to smoke on the wind.

Chapter Fourteen

Hope felt herself drifting back to reality. She opened her eyes to find Josh smiling down at her, looking almost as satisfied as she felt. She was still too breathless to speak, too stunned to know what to say. All she could do was sigh and smile back. Then the truth brought her the rest of the way down to reality with a painful thud. She felt her smile fade.

I'm in love with him, she thought, *but if I tell him, I'll lose the best friend I've ever had.*

"Hold that thought," Josh said, still grinning.

Her head knew he referred to her obvious arousal, but her heart heard his words as a reminder to guard her feelings very carefully. She watched him swing his legs over the side of the bed, heard the scratch of his zipper, then turned away as he stood to remove his jeans. *I'm not supposed to be making love. I'm supposed to be pretending,* she warned herself. A moment later, she heard Josh say her name softly.

Without turning to face him, she answered, "What?"

"Are you sure you want to go through with this?"

Surprised by his question, by the uncertainty in his voice, she turned. The raw male beauty that met her eyes made her breath catch in her throat. Josh stood beside the bed, tall, lean, powerfully muscled and powerfully aroused. He was the primal male, ready to mate. She was the primal female, ready to be his mate and bear his child. But her feelings went so far beyond primal lust, beyond the friendship that was her only link to Josh. Her heart felt like a caged bird, trapped, unable to fly where her instincts cried out for her to go.

She had to keep her love for him a secret, but she felt that she would die if she couldn't share it with him.

Unable to speak for fear she'd start to cry, Hope raised her arms to him. With a sigh that betrayed his relief, he sank down beside her and took her into his arms. For a long moment, she simply clung to him, absorbing his warmth and strength. He held her close and stroked her hair, undemanding even though his hard shaft pressed against her belly.

And then she realized that the rhythm of his breathing had changed, and that his caressing hands had pushed aside her hair to stroke patterns on her back and bottom. Electric patterns that caused her nerves to fire and made her shift restlessly against him. Hope flexed into those arousing caresses and wondered if his fingers were trailing real sparks on her skin or only sensual sparks.

His hands were gentle but firm when he cupped her head and eased her back until he could cover her mouth with his. This time, she didn't wait for him to seek entrance, but opened her lips and welcomed the sleek heat of his tongue. When she met him stroke for stroke with her own tongue, his groan echoed deep inside her.

Hope began her own tactile exploration of his body, skimming her fingertips over his warm, smooth skin. She traced the hard contours of muscle, the ridges of bone, the silk of fine hair. When she stroked lightly over the posterior she'd admired in tight, worn jeans, Josh gasped and pressed his body harder to hers. She rocked her hips in answer, reveling in the hardness trapped between their bodies.

Josh lifted his head and gazed into her eyes. She answered his unspoken question, this time with a smile that turned to a gasp of surprise when he pushed her onto her back and took a nipple into his hot, wet mouth. This time, her heart gave her body permission to respond. Arousal pulsed deep inside her, wringing a softly desperate groan from her. Oh, how she wanted this man! How she needed this man! How she needed to tell him she loved him wordlessly, in the timeless language of man and woman.

Her body arched into his touch when he ran his hand from shoulder to hip, then stroked maddening circles on her belly, teasing her with promises of more. Her fingers tangled in his hair, but she couldn't decide whether to hold his head to her breast so he could continue his delicious caresses there or yank at his hair to beg him to stop tantalizing her with his hand. Finally, he slid his fingers up her inner thigh and gently parted her, slickly probing, stroking, fueling the fire within her.

Impatiently, Hope reached for Josh, drawing him to her, wrapping her legs around his hips. She felt him pressing into her gently, as if he were afraid to hurt or startle her, and she tightened her legs, urging him farther. He resisted, and joined their bodies slowly. His powerful arms, braced on both sides of her, shook with tension, even after he was deep inside her. His tenderness made her want to cry. His stubbornness made her want to scream. She settled for a low moan that caught in her throat and a blatant arching of her hips to tell him his caution wasn't necessary.

"Ah, Hope! Take it easy!" he whispered hoarsely. "I haven't gone bareback since I was sixteen. It's more than a little intense."

She looked up at him in surprise. Tension had turned his handsome face into a mask of concentration, making her realize that he was very close to the edge.

"Josh, don't hold back," she whispered. "Don't hold back."

With a groan that reverberated right through her, he began to move his hips. When he surged into her again, Hope had to shut her eyes against the rush of sensations building like a tidal wave, threatening to carry her away. Without warning, she rose on a swirling wash of heat and tension and lights sparkling behind her shut eyelids. Clinging to Josh, she cried out and let herself shatter. For a moment, there was nothing in the universe except the explosion of pleasure and the man in her arms.

Josh held himself above her while she struggled to breathe, then thrust again. Within seconds, Hope was riding another cresting, breaking wave of sensation, helplessly clinging to Josh, the only solid thing in her world. Once again, he let her float back to awareness, then began a slow, measured rhythm that quickly became a wild dance between them. In disbelief, Hope felt her body gather for another climax, then let herself go. A moment later, Josh groaned and surged powerfully into her, then collapsed.

For a long while, Hope lay under his warm weight, too sated to care that she was being pleasantly squashed. The sound of their breathing, especially Josh's harshly drawn breaths, filled the room, reminding her that she'd forgotten to set the stage with music this time. Then she smiled ruefully at the memory of how her efforts to set the stage and control the situation had turned Josh off the first time. Much better, she conceded, his way.

Finally, Josh stirred, then eased himself off her. Before she could miss his warmth, he drew her against his side and wrapped his arms around her. Contentedly, she sighed and slipped her free arm across his chest.

"You okay?" he asked, pressing a kiss to her forehead.

"Mmm" was all she was able to say.

"Well, next time will be better. Promise."

Hope lifted her head so quickly that she connected with Josh's chin. "*Better?* I don't think I can deal with anything better."

His low laugh rumbled through her. "We'll see."

She doubted that very much. "Josh, I never..." Feeling heat rise in her cheeks, she stopped.

Now it was his turn to lift his head. "Never?"

She avoided his eyes. "Not like that."

To her surprise, he pressed another tender kiss to her forehead. "That old boyfriend of yours was a loser in more ways than one," he murmured.

She snuggled against him. "I don't want to talk about Kyle."

Josh tightened his arms around her. "Neither do I," he told her. "So why don't we just lie here and talk about whatever comes up?"

It took a moment for her to catch his meaning. Then she sputtered with laughter until he kissed her quiet.

In the morning, Hope awoke before Josh. With her thermometer clamped between her lips, she lay beside him and watched him sleep. He was sprawled on his stomach, the light blanket bunched around his waist, his face turned away. Remembering their lovemaking the night before, a bittersweet ache washed over her. She had to blink away tears before she could read her temperature.

Reluctant to waken him, Hope eased herself out of bed and went into the bathroom. When she came out a few minutes later, Josh lay on his back, cradling his head on one bent arm, watching her walk naked toward him. He smiled slowly, appreciatively, and she nearly cried again with relief that their night of passion hadn't sent him running in fear for his freedom ... yet.

"How's your temperature this morning?" he asked, his voice still gravelly from sleep.

"Up a little," she told him, meaning her body was getting ready.

His smile turned into a shamelessly wicked grin. "So am I," he drawled, "more than a little." And then he lifted the covers and beckoned her to come to him.

Hope slid into his arms and met him kiss for kiss, touch for touch, until she was awash in sensations and emotions, and her voice broke when she cried his name. In the aftermath, as they lay tangled together, she held her breath. Would he read too much into her passionate cry? Would she guess her true feelings? And if he did, how long before he walked out of her life?

But to her profound relief, Josh didn't say anything at all about their lovemaking. Instead, he invited her to shower with him, which led to a breathless coupling under the spray of hot water. Later, when she was drying her hair, he kissed her and told her to be ready for dinner and dancing that evening. He would pick her up after visiting his parents for lunch. Feeling very much as if she were inching along a path that could turn into the edge of a cliff under her feet at any moment, Hope watched him ride his motorcycle down the street.

If only she could control her simmering urge to confess her love, she wouldn't have to give up her friend. If only...

Josh stood up when his mother bustled into the kitchen. He met her with a hug and kiss, then stood back to take a look at her. Was it his imagination, or was her hair a little more gray, her face a little more lined than the last time he'd seen her, only a few weeks ago?

"Hi, honey," she said to him. "Sorry to keep you waiting, but I just got back from the grocery store. Lunch should be ready any minute."

"No hurry, Mom. I came for the company, not the food."

His father came into the kitchen, a folded newspaper tucked under one arm. As usual, they shook hands in greeting. His father offered him a beer.

"Too early for me," he answered. "Cola or juice is fine."

"I'll get it for you," his mother said.

"Beer for me," his father told her.

Suddenly, the same conversation, the same ritual that had been going on all his life, irritated Josh. Why, he wondered, couldn't his father open the refrigerator door and get a drink for himself?

"That's okay, Mom. I can get it. What are you drinking?" He caught her look of surprise and felt guilty for all the times he'd let her wait on him the way his father obviously expected.

"Whatever you're having, honey," she told him.

Josh took two cans of cola and a bottle of light beer out of the refrigerator. He passed the bottle to his father, then poured one of the cans of cola into a glass, which he gave to his mother. Then, realizing that if he were with Hope, he would be doing his share without thinking twice, he took plates out of the cupboard. His father sat at his customary place at the head of the table, and opened his paper. Josh set cutlery and napkins at each place.

"Thanks, honey," his mother said.

When he turned to smile at her, he was shocked by how exhausted she looked. "You look tired, Mom," he commented.

She glanced at his father, who didn't so much as rustle his paper, and shrugged. "I am tired. I've been doing some private nursing, part-time, on top of my full-time load at the hospital."

"Why?"

Again, his mother looked at his father, a longer look this time. When he didn't react to the silence, she sighed. "Your father is between jobs again."

Josh sat down hard in a kitchen chair and stared at his mother. She gazed back, her expression neutral, but he felt his fury rising. Fury at his father for being so selfish, and at himself for being so damn blind.

"This is the way it's always been, isn't it, Mom?"

She gave a sad little laugh. "Yes, this is the way it's always been."

Josh stared at his father, who said nothing, did nothing behind his newspaper to indicate he'd heard their conversation. There was no way he couldn't have heard, Josh knew. The kitchen was small, and his father's hearing was excellent. But when he thought about it, he realized that his father had always ignored anything his mother said about finances, about employment, about responsibility.

"Henry," his mother called, opening the oven, "can you put a hot pad on the table?"

"Sorry, Ruth, I have no idea where you keep them," his father said, then casually turned his paper around to read the next page.

Something inside Josh snapped. He grabbed the paper out of his father's hands and glared down at him. "You've lived here for sixteen years, damn it! How come I know where the hot pads are and you don't?" Hell, after being in Hope's kitchen only a couple of times, he knew where she kept her basic stuff. Did his father think he was living in a hotel, with maid service?

Throwing the newspaper onto the floor, Josh turned on his heel and went to the drawer where his mother had always kept the hot pads. He pulled one out, slammed the drawer shut and smacked the hot pad onto the table. Without a word, his mother set the steaming casserole dish down, but her eyebrows seemed to be a lot higher on her forehead than a moment before. Josh looked away from her and glared again at his father.

"I'd like my paper back," his father said mildly, as if nothing unusual had happened.

"Yeah, well, I'd like to know why my mother has to work two jobs while you're reading the paper. I don't suppose you went to the grocery store with her? Or helped her make lunch?"

His father now looked genuinely surprised. "Of course not. Your mother is perfectly capable of handling the mundane chores."

With a sigh Josh recognized as resignation, his mother sat at her usual place at the table. Josh braced his hands on the table and leaned toward his father.

"So are you," Josh retorted through clenched teeth. His chest felt tight. His head felt as if it would explode.

His mother put her hand on his. "Leave it, honey."

"No, damn it, Mom! I won't leave it. Dad, I want to know. Why does Mom have to support you and wait on you? Why can't you stay in a job for more than a couple of years?"

"I'm an idea man, Josh. An imagination man. You know that." To his amazement, his father took up the serving spoon and helped himself to a large portion of the casserole. "You've always understood. We used to talk about it even when you were a little boy. I'm a creative type of person, while your mother is a practical sort of person. I can't concentrate on ideas if I have to worry about the day-to-day details of life. That's your mother's specialty." His father pronounced the last words as if he were heaping praise on his wife of thirty-five years.

Josh sank back in his chair. "Yeah, we used to talk about how creative you are. Or rather, you used to tell me how marriage and dull work were going to stifle your creativity."

With his mouth full of food, his father grunted agreement.

Josh looked at his mother, who was spooning some of the casserole onto his plate. She shrugged. "Eat your lunch before it gets cold. I made those cookies you like for dessert."

A new wave of guilt hit him. Two jobs, all the household chores, and his mother took the time to make his favorite cookies! And she was absolutely right. This was the way it had always been in his parents' house. But she was wrong about something else.

"I guess I've changed, Mom. I don't like what I'm seeing, and I'm feeling guilty for assuming Dad was the one who was making all the sacrifices. Sorry, Mom. I hate to tell you, but you've got a selfish jackass for a son."

The smile she gave him then nearly broke his heart. "Who is she?"

The question came out of left field. "Who is who?"

"The woman who's behind your changes. She must be someone very special."

He felt his face sting and knew he must be redder than a fire engine. "She's just a friend. Not what you're thinking."

"Ah." His mother took a bite of her portion of the casserole, her expression amused and disbelieving.

"Seriously. She's a very good friend, that's all. The kind of friend who makes you think about things and question assumptions."

"Watch yourself, Josh," his father said sharply, stabbing the air with his fork. "A woman like that will turn your head, and the next thing you know, you're giving up your dreams and your neck is in a yoke, like a dumb ox."

Josh snorted. "Right, Dad. I'm *living* my dream. I've got my own business, and I've got enough money set aside to invest and to play. What are your dreams, the ones you gave up for Mom and me?"

His father smiled at him as if he were a dim-witted child. "My dreams are long gone, son. I could have made something of myself if I'd had the chance. But I've tried to make the best of the hand life dealt me."

Josh dropped his fork, his food untasted. "Give me a break, Dad. You made the best of the hand life dealt you by taking advantage of Mom. And I believed you. All this time, I believed that any kind of commitment would cramp my style or suck the life out of me. What a putz I was!''

Before his father could interrupt, he shook his head. ''I've been turning down Bob Eberhardt's offer to go into partnership because I was worried that I wouldn't be able to pull up stakes when I wanted to.'' He snorted again. ''The stupid thing is, I don't want to pull up stakes.'' Hope had shown him that. ''Why should I? I enjoy what I'm doing, I'm successful and it's satisfying work. But you were my dad, the great guy who took me fishing and did the fun stuff with me, and you taught me that responsibility would destroy my freedom.''

His father lifted his eyebrows, then went on eating.

''I used to look at Mom and think you were right. She was cranky, impatient, a nag. She didn't understand a man's dreams.'' He gave his mother an apologetic smile. ''I never understood what *she* gave up.'' Not until he'd met Hope, and started thinking about motherhood. And fatherhood.

It was his father's turn to snort disagreement. ''Ruth never gave anything up. She had exactly what she wanted. A husband, a child, a house in the suburbs.''

''Right. Some husband, always quitting his job and forcing her to work overtime. Some son, who was the reason she had to get married in the first place.'' His mother's soft gasp caught his attention. ''Sorry, Mom. I figured that out years ago. I just never stopped to think how lucky I was that you did. I always believed Dad's side. Now I'm seeing the truth, and I feel pretty damn stupid and pretty damn guilty.''

His father, finished with his lunch, pushed his chair back from the table. ''If you'll excuse me, there's a game on TV. Come join me if you have time. We haven't watched a game together in ages.'' He walked out of the kitchen, stopping to retrieve his crumpled newspaper but leaving his dirty plate on the table.

His mother touched his arm. He turned to look at her. "Thank you, honey. And whoever she is, thank her." He opened his mouth to protest, but his mother shook her head. "I don't think I've ever told you how proud I am of you. I love you, my son."

Her words caused a lump in his throat that made speaking impossible, even if he'd had anything coherent to say. Instead, he caught her hand in his, leaned over and kissed her cheek.

"Mom, I've got money in stocks and certificates I'd be glad to cash in. I don't like you working so hard. Let me help with the mortgage and the cars, okay? Call it repayment on school and a million other things I didn't know you did for me until I had to do them myself."

His mother smiled and ruffled his hair. "Not necessary, honey. But if you'd like to do something for me, bring over that young lady of yours. She sounds like somebody I'd like to meet."

His face burned. "I told you, Mom. She's—"

"I know. Just a friend." She patted his hand, but the look on her face told him she still didn't believe him. He was beginning to wonder if he could believe himself, but that was venturing into uncharted territory. Emotional territory Hope herself had warned him not to trespass on.

Hope entered the tavern with some trepidation. She'd never been keen enough on country and western music to take large doses of it, and she'd never been in a restaurant that featured it. But when Josh had phoned to tell her they were joining his friend—and Tabby's family vet—Grayson Hendricks and a date there, she couldn't very well spoil his fun. So she'd changed out of the sophisticated little black dress and sexy high heels she'd been wearing in anticipation of his promise of dinner and dancing. Now, she wore a slim denim skirt and embroidered vest over a cream silk blouse, and sensibly low-heeled shoes.

In retrospect, given their arrangement, she'd decided it was better not to dress seductively. Josh whistled anyway, playfully, when she'd opened her door. Her heart had pounded as she'd fought the impulse to throw her arms around him and declare her love. Even if they were behaving like honeymooners in bed, she would have to remember that they were friends in reality. To preserve that friendship, she'd have to find the strength to keep at bay the feelings that, for her, only for her, were no longer an act.

"There's Gray," Josh said as they stood in the entry and scanned the big room full of noisy, casually dressed people.

He caught her hand in his and started leading her toward a booth in the far corner of the dining room. They hadn't gone more than a few steps when a tall, gorgeous brunette whose jeans and Western shirt appeared painted onto her incredible figure, grabbed Josh's free arm. She seemed oblivious to Hope being attached to the other side of him. Briefly, Hope considered peeling the other woman's hands off Josh's arm, the way she might remove a leech from a swimmer. But any reaction on her part might alert Josh to her feelings for him. He would have to get out of this predicament himself. Assuming, she thought a little miserably, that he wanted to. After all, she reasoned, this other woman's attentions were a reminder that he really was free.

"Where have you been, lover?" the woman demanded with a sexy pout. Her voice was low and husky. Rather phony, Hope decided. "I haven't heard from you in ages. I've missed you."

"I've been around," Josh answered. Hope couldn't tell if it was the dim lighting or if his face had turned dark red. "Busy. I heard you've been busy, too."

The brunette's eyebrows went up, and then she smiled. For a moment, Hope thought the woman would lick her chops the way Tabby did over a particularly tasty morsel. "Never too busy for you, Kincaid. You should know that." Now, finally, the brunette's gaze flicked toward Hope. Then her smile for Josh widened, and she trailed possessive, red-clawed fingers down his shirtfront. "Call me when you get bored." Hope felt Josh's hand tighten around hers. With a farewell pat to his chest, the brunette disappeared into the crowd.

Josh swore under his breath. "Sorry," he muttered. "Someone I used to know." He started again toward Grayson.

"Rather well, so it would seem," Hope replied a little more tartly than she'd intended.

Josh stopped walking. He put both his hands on her shoulders and looked into her upturned face. "She's a cat, Hope. I took her out a couple of times, but she was more trouble than I wanted to handle. I don't like to repeat my mistakes."

His intensity surprised and touched her. "You don't owe me any explanations, Josh. Especially not for anything you did before we started this, um, arrangement. Your life is your business."

"I don't want you to think I'm going to take her up on her offer. I wouldn't anyway, but definitely not while we have this, um, arrangement." His smile teased her. "Okay?"

She smiled, trying to convey that she believed him and that she wasn't the tiniest bit jealous of his past life or his future life. Nevertheless, after three other women stopped Josh on their way to their table, Hope had to confess that she'd been bitten by the green-eyed monster. Seeing other women touching his arm, his shoulder, his chest, his face as if they had a right to, made her feel as if someone were twisting her heart. She'd never felt this way when Kyle had run into women he knew and had kissed or hugged them. But then, she'd already acknowledged to herself that she'd never loved Kyle the way she loved Josh.

Gray stood up when they reached the booth. He shook Josh's hand and smiled at Hope. "Good to see you again," he said, then nodded toward the corner of the booth. To

Hope's surprise, a tiny woman she hadn't seen past Gray's big form sat there, a nervous smile on her face. "Patty, this is Josh Kincaid and Hope Delacorte. This is Patty Waring."

Hope said hello. Patty nodded, looking tense and shy. While the three of them talked easily, Patty sat quietly, her gaze riveted to Gray's face. They seemed so mismatched that Hope wondered if Gray's healing instincts extended to humans, as well as to his animal patients.

Josh confirmed her guess the first time they danced, but not until he'd broken her heart a little. He held her close for a slow, sad song about unrequited love, and kissed her temple. Between the song and her own secret feelings, the gentle touch of his lips nearly made her cry. She had to bite her lip to keep from telling him she wanted to call off their arrangement before she could be hurt any more.

"Gray's doing it again," he murmured. "He keeps taking in strays. I'll bet dollars to doughnuts that Patty was battered, and Gray thinks he can make her better."

"I think that's admirable. What's wrong with it?" Hope countered, grateful for the distraction from her own misery.

"He's done it before, and they always break his heart. A couple went back to the creeps who were beating them. A couple others were so well rehabilitated that they found other guys. Tina was the one who really shafted him. She bounced in and out of his life for eight years. One day, he says they're getting married. She left him standing at the altar. Turns out she was into drugs in a big way, in trouble with everyone from the cops to the dealers. The big lug thought he could help her, right up until the night she died in his arms."

Hope felt tears sting her eyes. "Oh, Josh, that's so sad."

Josh snorted. "You know that expression, 'Nice guys finish last'? That's Gray. Always has this compulsion to heal broken critters. Just once, I'd like to see him with a woman who isn't a needy case." He spun her around as the song ended. "Too bad you don't have any more sisters at home," he said with a grin.

As they made their way back to the table through the crowd, Josh wrapped his arm around her shoulders and pulled her close.

They paused to let several servers with heavy trays pass them. "I thought Gray might be interested in you," he confided, much to her surprise.

"I doubt that," she told him. "I'm hardly a wounded critter. Besides, under the circumstances—" which were that she might soon be carrying Josh's child "—*I'm* really not interested."

They started moving again between noisy tables, bombarded by surrounding conversations, so Hope knew it was only her imagination, fueled by wishful thinking, that she thought she heard Josh say, "Good."

Chapter Fifteen

Josh collapsed onto Hope, his body shuddering like a train wreck. His heart pounded like a blown piston, and his breath sounded like an asthmatic bellows. His loins felt as if he'd been wrung out like a living sponge, pouring himself into Hope. When her hands slid over his skin, his nerves fired almost painfully.

He'd never felt so good in his life.

He knew he must be crushing her, but for a moment, he was totally paralyzed by his release. He wanted to lie there forever, bonded to her by heat and sweat and mutual pleasure. He wanted to stay inside her body, where she was hot and tight and pulsing from her own release. Plural, he reminded himself with a grin of pure male pride. Call him petty, but he'd felt pretty damn good when she'd admitted that no one else—especially not that jerk Kyle—had ever done that for her. It made this crazy thing they were doing seem a little less impersonal, a little more special.

Not that he'd admit that no other woman had ever been quite so responsive to him. He sure hadn't expected it from Hope. She'd taken him by surprise last night, especially after the way she'd fought against her own pleasure the first time they'd gotten into bed together. What a difference a month and a little romance made!

"Josh? Are you awake?" Hope asked, her voice sounding a little strained.

He grunted with the effort to communicate with his muscles, and slowly eased away from her. The instant he flopped onto his back, he realized something was missing: Hope, in his arms. Without letting himself think about the implications, he scooped her close to his side. When she made a little purring sound and put her hand over his heart, he felt something he'd never before experienced after making love. It took him a moment to figure it out. When he did, he was stunned. Contentment. He felt happy. Not simply satisfied the way she was, but mindlessly, bonelessly *happy* because Hope was lying next to him.

Well, he'd better stop feeling so damn happy, he warned himself. Hope had made it perfectly clear that this was a limited-time arrangement, and that as soon as she was pregnant, they would be back to "friends only" again. He didn't want to want anything more. He sure as hell didn't want to make a fool of himself by believing in their pretend romance.

A day late! The words kept circling Hope's mind as she checked her calendar for the hundredth time in twenty-four hours. Josh had warned her over the past two weeks that she might not get pregnant right away. She knew he was right. She'd known that from the start. She'd also known that his assertion that she could be fertile at any time was a lame excuse to make love to her almost every night. She didn't care. Love made her greedy for him.

But now she was a whole day late. She stood in her kitchen and placed her hands on her flat stomach. Even now, she could be pregnant. She could be carrying Josh's baby.

No, *her* baby, she mentally corrected herself. But how could she believe that when she was so in love with him that she ached? *Josh's baby.* The words stubbornly echoed in her mind and in her heart. She couldn't have the man himself, but she would have his precious gift of a child.

The peal of her phone startled her. When she answered, the sound of Josh's voice, low and intimate in her ear, set her pulse racing. At times like this, it seemed virtually impossible not to believe in their pretend romance. She always had to be careful not to blurt out how she really felt about him. Somehow, she would have to keep her love for Josh a secret, even as she carried his baby and nurtured his child.

"So, how are we doing?" he asked. He was phoning from his RV. She could hear the sounds of sawing and hammering in the background. Feeling guilty that he'd stayed away from the construction of his cabin on her behalf, she'd sent him to the Kootenays when she knew her period was due. There was no way, she'd assured him, that she could be fertile now. She was either pregnant or she wasn't.

"A whole day late."

He didn't say anything for a while. When he finally spoke, he sounded strange. "Well, that's great. I'll keep my fingers crossed for you."

The rest of their conversation seemed strained. When Hope hung up after Josh said one of the crew was calling him, she wanted to cry. What had happened to the easy-flowing conversations they'd always had? Obviously, her news had changed things between them. Was she going to lose his friendship after all?

An hour later, while she was reading and watching the news, she felt the first warning cramp. Two hours later, she was curled up in bed with her heating pad, while Tabby paced anxiously along her side. Her cramps gripped her with their usual full force, while hot, bitter tears slid down her face.

When Josh phoned the next evening, Sunday, to tell her he was back from the Kootenays, she burst into tears at the sound of his voice. Less than a half hour later, smelling of sunshine and sawdust, Josh was holding her in his arms and rocking her tenderly.

"It's okay, sweetheart," he murmured. "I don't mind trying again."

Nodding against his solid chest, Hope once again fought the need to confess her love. *I love you* trembled on her lips. Those three little words would cost her the chance to have Josh's baby and his friendship. She knew it was selfish, but she wanted both.

Josh followed Hope into her house, his ears still ringing from the kids' shrieks at little Carla's fourth birthday party. After the way Hope had been avoiding him for the past two weeks, since she found out she wasn't pregnant, he'd jumped at the invitation to the party. Hell, he would have crawled over broken glass to see her. He'd missed making love with her, but more than that, he'd missed just plain being with her.

He watched her walk into the kitchen, enjoying the way her denim shorts hugged her bottom and showed off her long legs. Her top left a tantalizing sliver of bare skin peeking above her waist. To keep his mind off that tempting sight, and what he'd like to do if he could sneak a moment alone with her, he'd spent most of the afternoon playing with the kids.

"Coffee, wine or beer?" she offered, opening the refrigerator.

"Beer is fine, thanks."

"I noticed you didn't have any at the party." She handed him a bottle of beer—his favorite brand, he noticed, but not what she usually kept—and poured a glass of white wine for herself.

He took the bottle and twisted off the cap. "It didn't seem like the right thing to do, with kids crawling all over me."

She smiled. "It's still nice out. Why don't we go out to the deck for a while," she suggested, already heading toward the back door.

Was it his imagination, or did she seem nervous? Over the past months, as her secretary had commented, Hope had definitely mellowed. But in the two weeks since he'd seen her last—when she'd had those wicked cramps again—she'd sounded jumpy and distracted over the phone. Could she be losing interest in him? Or was she feeling discouraged over not being pregnant? Whatever was bothering her, he hoped it wasn't anything to do with them. Not after the decisions he'd made recently.

The air was warm. Dusk was engulfing the details of Hope's backyard in shadows. They were alone together, sitting on deck chairs he'd deliberately moved close together. This might be the right time to tell Hope some of the things that he'd been thinking about.

"Josh," she said softly, "I'm sorry I was so standoffish the last couple of weeks. I guess I was more upset than I thought I'd be when I found out I wasn't pregnant."

"It's okay, Hope. I understand." And he did. He'd been torn between his own disappointment and relief. The need for Hope to have his baby raged like a hunger deep inside him. But selfishly, he wanted nature to hold off a while, so he could have Hope to himself a little longer.

She ran her finger over the rim of her glass, not looking at him now. "I, um, I almost decided not to keep trying." His heart sank at her words. "It's so hard to watch the window of opportunity shrinking and try to deal with the disappointment." He reached out and touched her arm. She gave him a quick, shy smile. "Almost, but not quite," she said so quietly that he had to lean toward her to hear.

When his brain processed what his ears heard, his heart had to dodge the sudden rush of butterflies. "Does that mean ... ?"

She nodded. "Mmm. Tonight would be a very good time to try again." An anxious look replaced her smile when she met his eyes this time. "If you're still willing."

A number of flip answers ran through his mind, but what he ended up saying, in total seriousness, was, "You know I am."

Again, she gave him that shy smile, and tipped her glass toward him before taking a sip. He waited for her to lower her glass, then took it from her fingers. Clasping her hand in his, he drew her to her feet and brushed a quick kiss over her lips. Much as he wanted to carry her off to her bed and bury himself deep in her hot, sweet body, he felt some instinct warning him to go slowly tonight. Hope seemed so shy, so distant, it was almost like starting over.

He took his time leading her upstairs, took his time kissing her, giving her a chance to change her mind. But she responded as if she meant to continue, not with the eagerness he'd come to expect, but with that shyness that made him want to take care of her even as he wanted to possess her. Her mouth yielded under his, so sweet, so hot and wet. By the time he had slid his hands up under her maddeningly short top, he was trembling with the effort to go slowly when his body was bellowing for hers.

He took his time undressing her, allowing himself the torture of touching and tasting the soft skin his trembling hands uncovered. Every tiny sound of pleasure she made was like another jolt of electricity in his already supercharged body. Eventually, he eased her back onto the bed. She lay looking up at him, so beautiful, so sweet, so unselfconsciously sexy, that he gave in to impulse and ripped off his clothes like a madman. Somehow, by the time he was lying beside her, pulling her into his arms, he'd gotten his wild impulses under control again. He had to make this good for Hope before he satisfied himself.

His patience paid off when her kisses grew heated. She wrapped her arms tightly around him, and he knew her strangely shy mood had evaporated. Wishing he could kiss her everywhere at once, he reluctantly gave up her mouth to taste the silky skin of her neck and shoulders. Her nipples beaded hard under his tongue. Her sweetness hit him like a sugar rush. Her soft cries and restless shifting against him nearly undid his control.

The need to possess her, to brand her, rolled through him like a tidal wave. He wanted this woman the way he'd never wanted any other. It was a mindless, primal craving that ripped away his facade of civilization, stripped away his defenses. Wanting Hope made him more vulnerable than he'd ever felt. Possessing her made him feel as if he could lift the world on his shoulders and stop speeding bullets with his hands. The paradox was exhilarating and frightening. He didn't know how to think about his feelings. Didn't know what to think about them.

"Oh, Josh," she whispered, moving restlessly under his kisses and caresses, "this feels so good!"

Her words turned his brain to mush, dissolving all his thoughts, all his fears, leaving only the exhilaration.

He trailed his kisses lower, seeking the female heart of her, the female heat of her. Past downy soft curls, he sought and found her. He felt her resistance and stroked her thighs and belly and breasts until she relaxed. Cupping her firm little bottom in his hands, he lifted her to his mouth and gave her all the pleasure he knew how to give. The taste of her, the hot slickness of her response, was like champagne in his veins, intoxicating, addictive.

When her body went rigid, then bucked beneath him, when he heard the soft mewling cries she made, he felt a surge of pride and awe rushing through him. Pride in his power to make her respond with such abandon, and awe that her woman's body had seemingly limitless capacity for the pleasure he was offering. Awe that she was his, for now, and a desperate sadness at the knowledge that "for now" might not be as long as he wanted her to be his. He didn't dare give that feeling a name, but it hovered and teased him anyway because he knew damn well what it was.

Desperation drove him to cover her, to possess her. He surged into the hot, tight slickness of her body and swallowed her surprised gasp with a kiss. Hard and fast, he thrust into her, unable to control the hunger that raged in his blood. With another soft cry, she wrapped her arms and legs around him, sending his need into a madness. Again and again, her body convulsed around him, her cries fueled his desire, until his own climax tore him apart.

When the fragments of his consciousness fell back into place, Josh pressed his face into Hope's neck and wondered what the hell had come over him. He'd had wild sex, but nothing, nothing like that had ever happened to him before. He couldn't decide whether to be smug, scared or ashamed at his wildness.

Hope's sigh brought him the rest of the way back to reality. He must be crushing her. God, what a thoughtless jerk! He'd always prided himself on being smooth, sensitive, expert. But here he was acting like an animal.

"Sorry," he muttered, easing off of her. He flopped onto his back and tried to catch his breath. When Hope didn't move, didn't even seem to be breathing, he grew alarmed. Sitting up, he looked down into her face, into her closed eyes. Carefully, he touched her shoulder. "Hope? Are you okay?"

Her eyes fluttered open, and she stared up at him, unfocused. Then she smiled, a slow, sweet smile that stole what little breath he had left. Her hand came up to stroke his chest, trailing sparks of sensations on his overcharged skin.

"I'm way past okay," she murmured. "Somewhere in the range of spectacular."

He wondered if his ego could get any bigger. "Just aiming to please, ma'am," he drawled to cover his almost overwhelming impulse to get up and howl at the moon.

"Well, you have excellent aim," she said softly. Then her smile faded, and she let her hand drop from his chest. "Although I doubt all that was necessary for getting me pregnant."

Was the shyness back? Was she somehow uneasy about her response to the way he'd made love to her? He suddenly felt he was walking on eggshells.

"Remember my philosophy," he told her, keeping his tone light. "It doesn't seem fair that I get all the pleasure and you get all the work, now, does it?"

Her smile came back. "No, I guess not. And I'm not complaining."

He rolled back down and gathered her into his arms. "Good. Because I'd ignore any complaints anyway."

"Why am I not surprised?" she muttered against his chest.

For a long while, they didn't say anything more. Josh let himself savor the gentle pressure of her body against his. He stroked her silky hair and trailed his fingers along her arm, enjoying the contrast between the roughness of his hands and the satiny softness of her skin. Finally, she stirred against him.

"Josh?"

"Hmm?"

"I hope you didn't really mind going to Carla's party. Tom and Gail said she has quite a crush on 'Uncle' Josh."

"Nah. I had fun," he said truthfully. "She's a cute kid."

"But you were practically swarmed by all the kids."

Swarmed by the kids was an understatement, he thought. He'd been pressed into holding infant siblings of the guests more times than he could count. He'd rolled and tumbled and tossed toddlers until his muscles had protested, and lost several rounds of Chutes and Ladders, without trying to, to the older kids. "It was fun, Hope. Honest. I've told you, I like kids."

"Other people's kids."

"Well, sure. I don't have any of my own." *Yet.* "I was thinking, though, about if what we're doing works, you know, and you do get pregnant." She'd been playing with the hair on his chest. Now her fingers went still. He realized he'd have to find the right words to say what he meant, and only what he meant. "I was talking to Bob the other day, and we got on the subject of owning instead of renting. So I thought, if you do have a baby, I'd look around for a house, something like this one, so you and the baby would be more comfortable visiting. Since I'm going to be your baby's 'Uncle Josh,' too. Right?"

"Mmm-hmm."

"I thought a handyman's special with a big yard and plenty of guest room would be a good idea."

"I see."

"I think I'll get a dog, too. Kids and dogs are a kinda natural combination, but I don't have enough room at my town house." Uneasy at her stillness, he asked, "What do you think?"

She was quiet for a while before saying, "I already have four cats. A dog is something you should get for yourself, Josh. The same with a house. I think you have to make those decisions based on your own needs, not on the occasional needs of a hypothetical child."

Ouch! "Well, that's what I'm doing," he countered. "It makes more sense financially to own, instead of renting. I can do most of the fixing up myself, with Bob's help, so I'd be raising the value of my investment instead of pouring rent money down the drain. And I miss my old dog, Ziggy."

"I thought you valued your freedom over property equity, and didn't want any kind of relationship that would tie you down."

Double ouch! "Yeah, well, I'm getting to that age where some freedom is kinda overrated. I guess you had me pegged right all along. For a guy who thinks of himself as a free spirit, my life's pretty rooted here." And he wanted Hope to be a part of that life.

"Well, that's good," she said softly. "It made me sad to see you overrate the notion of freedom and underrate yourself."

He could have taken the opening she'd given him, and told her he'd do anything to make her happy. But he could feel the distance in her voice, and sensed this wouldn't be the best time to bare his soul. No problem, he tried to convince himself. They still had five months left to their agreement. Five months of sharing things together. Five months of making love. Hell, he could control his impatience and let nature take its course for five little months. After all, he'd waited all his life for her. He could afford to take the time to get this right.

Monday, shortly before Hope planned to leave her office, Milly buzzed her that Josh had come by to see her. Hope's heart gave a leap that sent her pulse racing. She set down the computer printouts of inventory movement she'd been reading, appalled to see that her hands were shaking. Part of her longed to throw herself into Josh's arms and confess that she loved him and that she wanted to share his life, the house he wanted to buy, the dog he wanted to get for their baby.

The sensible part of her, protecting the vulnerable part of her, outvoted her heart. She'd have to be blind not to see he was having a change of mind, or heart, about not being actively involved if they had a child together. She'd seen his thoughtful looks when he'd been playing with the kids at

Carla's birthday party. She'd seen his awe and pleasure when moms had asked him to hold their tiny ones. It had cut like a knife to see how natural he was with children, when she'd forced him to sign away his rights to any child they might have.

But his change of heart was only about a child. He still wasn't ready or willing to love her, except as a friend. He'd talked about getting a house for his child, but not for his family. She wasn't willing to tear three people—Josh, their baby and herself—apart to satisfy her need for a child. She'd thought long and hard about the situation yesterday, and made her resolution after the last time they'd made love, early this morning.

Josh's knock was brisk, and he followed it by half a second. His handsome face wore a smile that lit her office like the sun coming out. When he swung her door shut behind him, his muscular form seemed to dwarf her space, probably because she was sitting looking up at him. Her knees felt too weak to support her, however, so she stayed seated. She tried to smile a greeting, but her face felt tight.

"Hi. I thought we could change our routine a little. I've got a butterflied chicken breast ready to barbecue at my place, and I thought we could stay there tonight. I've still got some videos you haven't seen." He grinned. "Real action things, lots of adrenaline, to get you in the right mood." He winked, apparently not aware that her answering smile was far from genuine.

"I'm sorry, Josh. I don't think that would be a good idea." Her voice came out as if a giant fist had closed around her throat. "My temperature's back down, and I think we need some time apart."

The color and light drained from Josh's face. "Time apart? Why? Are you feeling crowded?"

She seized the excuse, even though it wasn't what she was feeling at all. She wished he were crowding her. What she really felt was impending abandonment, impending hurt.

"A little, yes. After all, we're still only supposed to be friends, and we seem to spend almost all our free time together. Exclusively together."

He crossed his arms in front of his broad chest. "So you're saying you want time to see other people? You met someone else?"

"No!" This wasn't going right. "No, I haven't met someone else. I would never continue our... arrangement... if I'd met someone else. You must know me better than that. But I need some time to myself. This waiting isn't easy. And I don't feel right when we go on as lovers in between my fertile times."

"Because we're just supposed to be friends." He bit the words off. She nodded. "Friends support each other, Hope. And share the good times and the bad. I'm involved in this, whether you want me to be or not, and I intend to stay involved."

His quiet declaration scared her. He did mean to have a bigger role in her baby than simply sire. The house. The dog. It was all a preliminary to fighting their agreement. Her lawyer had warned her that Josh could be successful in getting joint custody, despite their arrangement. Even if he tried, it would tear her apart. And she knew she couldn't ever keep him from his child, even if he didn't want her. She could bear the pain herself, but she couldn't bear hurting him.

She stood and faced him, bracing herself, forcing herself to be strong. "I'll let you know in about three weeks if we were successful this time."

Josh flinched as if she'd struck him. Hope felt the blood drain from her head, and took a deep breath to steady herself.

"If we're not, I don't think I want to continue trying. I think you were right all along, that I'm being selfish and foolish. It was an emotional decision, not a logical one. If I'm pregnant now, I'll be thrilled. But if I'm not, I'm going to take your advice and wait for the right man, at the right time.''

His cheeks darkened and his eyes flashed. ''Fine. You do that. You treat your *friend* like a stud for hire, not a human being, just so you can get what you think you want, and then you change your mind.'' He shook his head. ''If I don't hear from you in exactly three weeks, I'm coming to you, Hope. I'm not going to let you shut me out like this, damn it.''

He turned, wrenched open the door and strode out of the office before Hope could react to his threat.

She sank into her chair and covered her face with her still-trembling hands. Oh, God! She'd tried so hard not to hurt him, but she had. Badly enough to prompt him to threaten the very action she'd hoped to forestall. She knew for certain that, if she were pregnant now, he would fight her for rights to their child. And she knew she wouldn't— *couldn't*—fight him back. If she had their baby, she would swallow her own pain at losing Josh and let him share in their child's life.

This time, her heart won out over logic and vulnerability, because she loved Josh too much to hurt him further. The next three weeks were going to be the longest of her life.

Josh made it home seconds before his stomach rebelled. Afterward, he slumped against the bathroom wall, feeling as if he'd been dragged behind a truck. How could Hope do this to him? How could she use him like this? Other women had come on to him because they thought he was good-looking and would be wild in bed. But not Hope. They'd been *friends*.

In disgust, he peeled off his clothes and stepped into the shower, not caring that it was too cold at first. He needed to scrub off the lousy feeling of losing something very precious. When the shower started to run cold again, he wrenched off the water and grabbed a towel. In his bedroom, he pulled on clean jeans. Not bothering with a shirt, he went into the kitchen. Not for dinner. With a bitter laugh, he dropped the chicken he'd planned for a romantic dinner into the freezer. No, his choices were Scotch, neat, or beer.

The thought of Scotch hitting his empty stomach made it growl in protest. He grabbed a beer and twisted off the cap. Beer would take longer than Scotch to get him stinking drunk, but it would do. And stinking drunk was what he planned to get, before he could let himself think about what Hope had just done to him. To them.

Pacing, Josh drained half his beer, then stopped short as if he'd been slugged. Well, maybe he had. Slugged by the truth. Why, he asked himself, did this whole thing have him on the spin cycle, when he'd known all along that his deal with Hope had been a limited one? Why had he instigated the pretense of being real lovers? Why did he want to be with her whether they made love or not?

He stopped pacing. Why was it so important for him to help Hope have a baby? *His* baby, instead of some anonymous donor's baby? And why was *he* the one thinking about houses with big yards and a dog for that baby to play with? Why the hell, for that matter, did he turn his plans for a rustic fishing cabin into a family cottage?

"Oh, Kincaid, you jerk," he muttered, "you're in love."

For a few moments, he felt justified about his blindness. It was the first time he'd ever been in love, so how was he supposed to know how it felt? He was a guy. Guys didn't know those things automatically, the way women did.

But now that he knew, what was he going to do about it?

He had to tell Hope how he felt. He had to make her understand that he'd been all over her like green on a lawn because he loved her. She might not be in love with him, but she'd understand what his problem was. And maybe she'd give him another chance. Maybe she'd give herself a chance to fall in love with him. For a while, he'd almost thought she had, but at the time, he'd been worried that it might get in the way of their friendship if he mentioned it. No matter how tactful a guy tried to be, he could really screw things up by just up and asking a woman friend if she happened to be in love with him. Especially a woman friend he was trying to help have a baby.

Josh flung himself down onto the sofa. Well, damn it, if he had to choose one or the other, he wanted Hope for his lover, not his friend. He was just going to have to figure out some way to convince her.

By Saturday morning, Hope felt as though she'd been shredded. Her patience had become so thin, she'd been snapping at everyone all week. Her secretary, the long-suffering Milly, finally told her to go away until she was better fit for human companionship. She'd stubbornly insisted that she was fine, stupidly tried to get her work done, belligerently refused to acknowledge how much she'd come to depend on Josh's company. How much she loved him.

There had been one silver lining to her personal storm of the past four days. She'd given Paul more responsibility, which made her whole family happy. If she really was pregnant this time—this last time—she knew now that she could gear down at work and not have to worry that the firm was going to fail without her constant attention.

If she was pregnant... She wrapped her arms around her middle and paced her living room. Tabby and the kittens raced along beside her, but for once, their antics failed to amuse her. How was she going to make it through the next two weeks until she could take a pregnancy test and know for sure? And if she was... If she was, she was going to have to tell Josh, and assure him of his right to be more than a nameless sire.

The chime of her doorbell halted her pacing. Tabby halted, too, and the kittens tumbled into their mother and each other with indignant squeaks, finally making her smile a little. She glanced at her watch. Ten a.m. Her pulse gave a little jump at the thought that Josh could be there. She longed to see him, to touch him. But no, he wouldn't come back after the way she'd treated him Monday. She'd hurt him, even though he'd tried not to show it. He'd covered his hurt with anger, but she'd seen through it. He'd said three weeks, and he'd meant it. Three weeks to find out if he was going to be a father. Judging by the tone of his voice and the expression in his eyes, he certainly wanted nothing to do with her in the interim. Or after, probably.

Hope opened the door to find a young man wearing bike shorts and a T-shirt, with a cell phone at his waist, his bike on the walk in front of the house. He handed her a white padded envelope. Her name and address were printed on the envelope in bold black letters, but there was no sender's name or address. The courier held out a pen and receipt form, which she signed, then wished her a good day and took off whistling.

Closing the door behind her, Hope turned the envelope over several times, searching for clues. Whatever was inside was very light and thin, she deduced. "Might as well open it," she told Tabby, who winked in agreement.

Hope tore the envelope open and peered inside. Something flat and red. No note. She reached inside and drew out a red cloth heart about the size of her hand. On the back were several strips of Velcro. Before she could do more than stare at the heart lying on her palm, the door chimes rang again.

Chapter Sixteen

With the felt heart balanced on one hand, Hope opened the door. The sight of Josh on her doorstep sent her own heart slamming into her ribs. Staring at him, she felt herself grow light-headed.

He smiled into her eyes. Hope stared up into his. Then she saw his hands go to the front of his chambray shirt. Wide-eyed, she watched him rip the shirt open to reveal a red T-shirt underneath. A red T-shirt with a roughly heart-shaped piece missing over the left side of his chest.

"I believe you have something of mine," he said, nodding at her hand. Then he stepped toward her.

Hope stepped backward, giving him room to come into the house. "The heart?"

"Mmm-hmm. You notice the back of it?" She nodded. "Velcro." He grinned. "The stuff that sticks."

"I don't understand."

His grin faded. "Can't blame you for that." He let out a deep breath. "Okay, you have my heart. It has Velcro, which means it will stick to you. Not Teflon, which will slide off."

"Oh."

He shook his head, then lifted his hands to her shoulders. "Hope, I don't think I'm doing a very good job of this. What I'm saying is, I want to marry you."

Shock stole her breath and short-circuited her brain. "You what?"

"For a bright woman, you can be very dense sometimes," he chided softly. "I said, I want to marry you."

"Oh!" She searched his face for some sign that he was teasing her. His expression was gravely serious. "But I don't even know if I'm pregnant, and I never expected you to feel obligated to marry me if—"

"Damn it, Hope!" His hands slid down to her upper arms, and he drew her close to his chest. She held herself stiffly, but the familiar feel and scent and warmth of him melted her resistance. With a sigh, she leaned against him and felt his heart thudding under her cheek. "That's better," he said, his lips on her hair. "Now, listen very carefully. I don't care if you're pregnant or not. Not now, anyway. I want to marry you."

"Why?" she asked into his chest.

"Because I love you, damn it!" he growled. His heart thudded faster. "I love you," he repeated gently.

Stunned, she tipped her head back to look up at him. "You do?" she asked quietly.

He nodded. "I know you don't feel the same about me right now, but I kinda hoped—"

"But I do!" she blurted. "Oh, Josh! I do love you!"

"You do?" It was his turn to sound surprised.

She nodded. "I was afraid you'd guess, and take off the way you said you do when your dates start looking at rings and babies. Remember?"

He swore. "And I was too dumb to know how I felt. I guess you thought I was taking advantage of our arrangement."

"No. I thought you'd decided to claim your right to be involved as a father, even if you didn't want me except as a friend."

His eyes registered dismay. "I wouldn't do that to you."

She smiled. "I wouldn't have made you do it. I couldn't keep you from your own child just because I could only be your friend."

"Friend, lover, wife, mother of my children. The whole enchilada." He pulled her close again. "I'm going into partnership with Bob. We're going to work out the details in the next couple of weeks."

For a long, wonder-filled moment, Hope stood leaning against Josh, simply breathing in the scent of him and filling her senses with the feel of him. He loved her. He wanted to marry her. He wanted to commit himself to her, to his work. It was so much more than she'd dared hope for, she couldn't quite believe it was real.

Josh released her slightly. She felt his hips shift and realized he was fumbling in his back jeans pocket. "Almost forgot." He nudged her arm. "This is for you, until we can get something better. I want to do this right."

This turned out to be a small black-velvet jeweler's box. His fingers shook against her trembling palm as he gave her the box. Hope stepped back and struggled with the uncooperative case. When she finally found the side that opened, she gasped at the ring inside. A ruby heart, framed by tiny diamonds, winked at her from the black velvet.

She looked up at Josh, tears blurring her vision. "I can't imagine anything more precious than your heart," she whispered around the lump in her throat.

With a groan, he pulled her close for a long, deep kiss that made her knees weak. Lifting his head, he murmured, "Let's get married soon."

She smiled up at him, suddenly feeling playful. "My father suggested we elope."

Josh gave a snort of disbelief. "That sly devil! No, we won't elope. If I'm going to do this, I want witnesses. I want a celebration. How soon can we do that?"

Hope thought for a moment. "We could probably get a garden wedding together by sometime in August. Nothing elaborate like Paul and Elaine had, though." Josh gave a shudder that made her laugh. "Right. Something simple. After I reel my mother in from the stratosphere, she'll know exactly what to do."

Suddenly, Josh released her, only to scoop her up in his arms. "Right now, *I* know exactly what to do." He started toward the stairs. "I'm going to start practicing to be a Velcro husband."

Epilogue

Josh cradled the blue bundle in his right arm, and the pink one in his left, and dutifully grinned at his father's camera lens for one more family portrait. Hope sat beside him on the sofa, warm, sweet smelling and still exhausted from delivering Ashleigh and Michael on their first anniversary, two weeks ago. Just as the flash went off, Michael lifted his tiny fist as if in a gesture of triumph. Josh caught Hope's eye and laughed softly.

"Michael's got his own way of doing things already," he said, earning a general laugh from the family gathering welcoming his children.

"So does Ashleigh," Hope countered, smiling. "Lady-like." She held out her arms, and he carefully passed the pink bundle to her. He was still a little nervous about handling the babies, because they were so incredibly tiny, but he was getting used to it. And since they'd managed to make those babies all by themselves, his ego was the size of the Goodyear Blimp.

"How about a shot of all the ladies in the family?" his dad suggested. "Then we'll get one of the ladies to take a shot of all the men."

Josh moved away to make room for his sisters-in-law, Gail and Elaine, plus Gail's three daughters, his mother-in-law, his mother and Gail's mother. His brother-in-law, Tom, held his youngest, Tom, Jr., who was gleefully drooling and high-fiving Uncle Paul. With a private grin and a soft pat on Michael's padded bottom, Josh realized that if anyone had predicted a little over a year ago that he'd be part of such an extended family, he'd have offered to sell them the Brooklyn Bridge, too.

The flash went off twice, his father claiming an extra shot for luck, then the men and women and girls and boys changed places. His mother took several different photos, mainly because Tom, Jr., was moving like a gerbil in a wheel.

With Hope beside him again, Josh looked up to see a sudden breaking of ranks as the women went into the kitchen of the house he now owned with Hope. He heard their chatter and laughter and the sounds of plates and cutlery, and smiled again at his beautiful wife. Hope smiled back with such joy that he felt humbled.

"Now, you be careful not to carry so much, Ruth," his father warned. "Let me get that," he added, taking the tray of coffee mugs from her.

Josh met his mother's eyes and winked. She winked back. His father hadn't said a word about their heated discussion of the past year, but he'd gone out and found a decent job, and stuck with it long enough to earn a promotion and a raise, no mean feat for a man in his late fifties. His mother no longer looked so tired, now that she was able to cut her hours to part-time nursing and spend more time on her hobbies. And damned if the two of them didn't sometimes act as if they were on their second honeymoon, although

Josh doubted that his father had gotten as far evolved as washing dishes.

The front door swung open, and Grayson Hendricks let himself in with a sheepish grin at Hope. "Josh said I could bring over your menagerie today." He set down the two cat carriers and bent to release T-Rex from his leash. The cats sang their complaints while Gray was opening the doors of the carriers. When they were freed, the three youngsters streaked for the upstairs, away from the noise. But Tabby trotted toward Hope, trilling. The grandmothers made immediate disapproving noises when the little cat climbed up to sniff each of the babies. Hope merely patted the cat, who curled up in her lap and purred loudly. Josh looked at the disgruntled grandmothers and shrugged.

"Come admire my kids and have some cake and coffee," he told Gray. "Hey, Rex, come meet your new owners."

Their dog, a young shepherd, picked his way through the family, stopping to greet each person with a sniff and wag of his thick tail, as if he were the host. When Rex reached his knee, Josh patted the dog's wide head and let him take a good sniff at Michael. Rex grinned up at him, then lay down with his chin on Josh's boot, prompting several more photo ops from the grandfathers.

While Gray was handing two small boxes to Hope, one pink, one blue, the front door opened again and the Eberhardts with Bob, Jr., and Chantelle, her husband Rob and their son, Peter, walked in together. The house seemed full, overflowing with people he was committed to, connected to, but it didn't seem to be crowding him the way he used to believe.

On the contrary, he thought as he pressed a kiss to Hope's temple. It felt pretty damn good to be a man love sticks to.

* * * * *

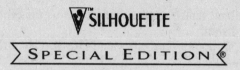

A BRIDE FOR JOHN
Trisha Alexander

Three Brides and a Baby

Patrick Taylor wanted his dad John to find himself a wife. Missy Broome thought her mum Shelley would be perfect for the job. Could two enterprising eight-year-olds make a match between their reluctant parents?

THE BLACK SHEEP'S BRIDE
Christine Flynn

The Whitaker Brides

Gentle Annie Kendall never expected to fall for a black sheep like Jett Whitaker. But her world wasn't the only one turned upside down as Jett began to wonder if he could make Annie the next Whitaker bride.

FULL-TIME FATHER
Susan Mallery

Erin Ridgeway had just given Parker Hamilton the biggest news of his life—he was the father of the five-year-old niece she had been raising. Suddenly, being a full-time father and husband started to sound very appealing to Parker...

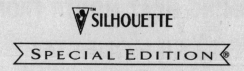

SILHOUETTE

SPECIAL EDITION ®

COMING NEXT MONTH

JUST A FAMILY MAN
Carolyn Seabaugh

Single mum Kate Prescott wasn't interested in a fling, and that seemed to be the only thing town bad boy Frank Vincenti could offer. But even rebels had to put down roots eventually, and Frank was about to surprise Kate with a very interesting offer.

A HOME FOR HANNAH
Pat Warren

Reunion

Hannah Richards admitted she found Joel Merrick attractive—but this self-made woman had long ago given up on winning at the game of love. But Joel was already working on ways to show her that she'd finally found what she was looking for.

THE COWBOY AND HIS BABY
Sherryl Woods

That's My Baby!/And Baby Makes Three

Forgetting Melissa Horton had never been easy for Cody Adams. And now that he'd discovered she was the mother of his baby, he had even more reason to reconcile with his one true love...

COMING NEXT MONTH FROM

 **SILHOUETTE**®

Intrigue
Danger, deception and desire

THE IMPOSTOR Cassie Miles
MANHATTAN HEAT Alice Orr
STRANGER IN PARADISE Amanda Stevens
PRINCE OF TIME Rebecca York

Desire
*Provocative, sensual love stories for the
woman of today*

DON'T FENCE ME IN Kathleen Korbel
BABY FEVER Susan Crosby
COWBOY DREAMING Shawna Delacorte
BRIDE OF A THOUSAND DAYS Barbara McMahon
A GIFT FOR BABY Raye Morgan
EMMETT Diana Palmer

Sensation
*A thrilling mix of passion, adventure
and drama*

DANGEROUS Lee Magner
SURVIVE THE NIGHT Marilyn Pappano
ANOTHER MAN'S WIFE Dallas Schulze
THE LITTLEST COWBOY Maggie Shayne

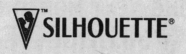

▼™ SILHOUETTE®

Treat yourself to...

Wanted: Mother

*Silhouette's annual tribute to motherhood takes
a new twist in '97 as three sexy single men
prepare for fatherhood and saying "I Do!"*

Written by three captivating authors:

Annette Broadrick
Ginna Gray
Raye Morgan

Available: February 1997   Price: £4.99

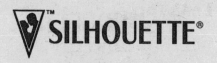
™ SILHOUETTE®

Who needs mistletoe when Santa's Little Helpers are around...

SANTA'S LITTLE HELPERS

We know you'll love this year's seasonal collection featuring three brand-new festive romances from some of Silhouette's best loved authors - including Janet Dailey

And look out for the adorable baby on the front cover!

THE HEALING TOUCH	by Janet Dailey
TWELFTH NIGHT	by Jennifer Greene
COMFORT AND JOY	by Patrica Gardner Evans

Available: December 1996   Price £4.99

Available from WH Smith, John Menzies, Volume One, Forbuoys, Martins, Woolworths, Tesco, Asda, Safeway and other paperback stockists.

Look for

from

They're strong.
They're sexy.
They're fathers?

Three handsome heroes are in for the surprise of their lives
when they find passionate romance...and unexpected fatherhood.
Watch for these heartwarming stories celebrating love—and
parenthood—written by three delightful writers.

January 1997
GAVIN'S CHILD by Caroline Cross

February 1997
BABY FEVER by Susan Crosby

March 1997
YOU'RE WHAT! by Anne Eames

Only from Silhouette Desire

▼™SILHOUETTE

Intrigue™

Angels should have wings and flowing robes - not tight black jeans and leather jackets. They should be chubby cherubs or wizened old specters - not virile and muscular and sinfully sexy.

But then again, these AVENGING ANGELS aren't your average angels!

Enter the Denver Branch of Avenging Angels and meet some of the sexiest angels this side of heaven.

Sam - THE RENEGADE by Margaret St. George
January 1997

Dashiell - THE IMPOSTOR by Cassie Miles
February 1997

and the littlest angel-to-be
Ariel - THE CHARMER by Leona Karr
March 1997

Kiel - THE SOULMATE by Carly Bishop
April 1997

They may have a problem with earthly time - but these angels have no problem with earthly pleasures!

MILLS & BOON®

Weddings ♣ Glamour ♣ Family ♣ Heartbreak

Since the turn of the century, the elegant and fashionable
DeWilde stores have helped brides around the world
realise the fantasy of their 'special day'.

*For weddings, romance and glamour,
enter the world of*

Weddings By DeWilde

**—a fantastic line up of 12 new stories from popular
Mills & Boon authors**

FEBRUARY 1997

Bk. 9 FAMILY SECRETS - Margaret St. George
Bk. 10 WILDE MAN - Daphne Clair

*Available from WH Smith, John Menzies, Volume One, Forbuoys,
Martins, Woolworths, Tesco, Asda, Safeway and other paperback stockists.*

DANGEROUS LOVE
Catherine Lanigan

Richard Bartlow was a man people noticed. He was ruthless when he needed to be and sincere when he wanted. He was sexy, ambitious and charming. And he was dangerous.

All the females in Richard Bartlow's life—his wife, naive heiress Mary Grace Whittaker; the other woman, ad agency executive Alicia Carrel; and his mistress, New Age massage therapist Michelle Windsong—serve calculated purposes in his climb to success. Destined never to meet, the women are brought together with far-reaching consequences when Richard plots a final act of deceit to save himself from possible imprisonment and begin a new life.

"Lanigan succeeds in spinning a highly suspenseful, romantic tale."
—Publisher's Weekly

"As a storyteller, Catherine Lanigan is in a class by herself: unequalled and simply fabulous."
—Affaire de Coeur

MIRA®

AGAINST THE RULES
Linda Howard

The tables had been turned...

At seventeen, Cathryn Ashe had fought Rule
Jackson and lost. Then she left home, drawn
to the anonymity of the city. Now Cathryn
was back on the ranch again, sure of herself
and her new-found independence, and ready
to challenge Rule like never before. And she
would win—because now she was his boss
and she held all the cards.

But Rule had raised the stakes, and if she lost
this time the penalty would be high. This time
Rule would take more than her innocence—he
would take her pride, her future and her
heart—the heart that had always been his for the
taking.

"You can't read just one Linda Howard!"
—bestselling author Catherine Coulter

"Howard's writing is compelling"
—Publishers Weekly

MIRA®

LOVE GAME
Mallory Rush

A once-in-a-lifetime love affair—that's what beautiful widow Chris Nicholson and dangerously attractive Major Greg Reynolds agree to.

After years of loneliness, Chris has given up on her fantasies of the perfect husband—but she needs the memories of one incredible love affair to warm her in the years ahead. Then she can settle down with a man who will make a good father for her little girl.

The last thing in the world Greg wants is commitment—or a family. He does, however, desire, need and fantasise about Chris. But once is never enough…

"Love Game is everything a romance should be—enthralling, passionate and outrageously sensual."
  —Meryl Sawyer, author of A Kiss in the Dark

MIRA®

'Happy' Greetings!

Would you like to win a year's supply of Silhouette® books? Well you can and they're free! Simply complete the competition below and send it to us by 31st July 1997. The first five correct entries picked after the closing date will each win a year's subscription to the Silhouette series of their choice. What could be easier?

ACSPPMTHYHARSI

_ _ _ _ _ _ _ _ _ _ _ _ _ _

TPHEEYPSARA

_ _ _ _ _ _ _ _ _ _ _

RAHIHPYBDYTAP

_ _ _ _ _ _ _ _ _ _ _ _ _

NHMYRTSPAAPNERUY

_ _ _ _ _ _ _ _ _ _ _ _ _ _ _ _

DYVLTEPYAANINSEPAH

_ _ _ _ _ _ _ _ _ _ _ _ _ _ _ _ _ _

YAYPNAHPEREW

_ _ _ _ _ _ _ _ _ _ _ _

DMHPYAHRYOSETPA

_ _ _ _ _ _ _ _ _ _ _ _ _ _ _

VRHYPNARSAEYNPIA

_ _ _ _ _ _ _ _ _ _ _ _ _ _ _ _

Please turn over for details of how to enter ☞

How to enter...

There are eight jumbled up greetings overleaf, most of which you will probably hear at some point throughout the year. Each of the greetings is a 'happy' one, i.e. the word 'happy' is somewhere within it. All you have to do is identify each greeting and write your answers in the spaces provided. Good luck!

When you have unravelled each greeting don't forget to fill in your name and address in the space provided and tick the Silhouette® series you would like to receive if you are a winner. Then simply pop this page into an envelope (you don't even need a stamp) and post it today. Hurry—competition ends 31st July 1997.

Silhouette 'Happy' Greetings Competition
FREEPOST, Croydon, Surrey, CR9 3WZ

Please tick the series you would like to receive if you are a winner

Desire™ ❏ Sensation™ ❏ Intrigue™ ❏ Special Edition™ ❏

Are you a Reader Service Subscriber?   Yes ❏   No ❏

Ms/Mrs/Miss/Mr _____

(BLOCK CAPS PLEASE)

Address _____

_____

_____ Postcode _____

(I am over 18 years of age)

One application per household. Competition open to residents of the UK and Ireland only.
You may be mailed with other offers from other reputable companies as a result of this application. If you would prefer not to receive such offers, please tick box. ❏

C7A

mps *MAILING PREFERENCE SERVICE*   **DMA**